Also by Amelia Grey

A Gentleman SAYS "I DO"

AMELIA GREY

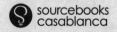

sourcebooks
casablanca

Published by Sourcebooks Casablanca, an imprint of Sourcebooks
P.O. Box 4410, Naperville, Illinois 60567-4410
(630) 961-3900
sourcebooks.com

Originally published in 2012 in the United States of America by
Sourcebooks Casablanca, an imprint of Sourcebooks.

Printed and bound in Canada.
MBP 10 9 8 7 6 5 4 3 2 1

One

Anger can be an expensive luxury.
—Italian Proverb

IVERSON BRENTWOOD WAS OUT FOR BLOOD.

It hadn't taken him long to locate the address of the person he was looking for. His body tense, he lifted the collar of his greatcoat and stepped down from the comfort of his dry, warm carriage and into the chilling spring rain. Settling his hat lower on his forehead, with keen purpose, his boots splashing the puddles, he walked toward the front door of the elegant house in Mayfair. Banks of cold fog drifted in from the Thames and swirled in the dreary late afternoon air. The one bright spot was a lone light that shone from a front-room window of the place he sought.

Droplets of water fell from the brim of his hat as he stepped under the overhang of the stoop. Unclenching his tight fist, Iverson lifted the heavy door knocker and rapped it quickly a couple of times. The clang seemed to rattle the windowpanes in the house and reverberate down the quiet street. He waited impatiently in the fading light of day as the seconds ticked by, and then rapidly struck the brass plate a few more times.

It was hell being a twin, or so Iverson had thought until he arrived in London and found out hell was actually realizing the man he always thought was his father wasn't. The easiest thing for him and his brother to do would have been to sail back to Baltimore on the first ship. Instead, he and Matson had decided to keep with their original plan and move to London, and prove to their older brother and the gossip-mongers that they weren't going to hide from anything. And the questioning glances and whispers about their parentage had settled down, until today.

A tall, buxom woman wearing servants' attire jerked open the door. Her thin, graying brows scrunched together in an irritated line across her forehead, as did her lips on her flat, pinched face. She looked him up and down with peculiar, deep-set brown eyes and then sniffed with annoyance.

"Ye didn't have to hit the knocker so hard. I'm slow, not deaf, ye know."

Iverson had never been taken to task by a servant and was momentarily surprised by the woman's insolent manner. He was in no mood to be hauled over the coals by a peevish maid. But before he could gather his wits and put her in her place, she snapped her large hands to her ample hips, glared at him once again, and said, "What can I do for ye?"

The woman clearly wanted him to know she had better things to do with her time than bother with him. Her surly attitude made him even angrier with her employer. It shouldn't surprise him that the scoundrel he was after had such a disrespectful servant in his employ. Iverson should have expected it.

Refusing to let go of his temper until he faced his intended prey, Iverson held his offensive retort in check and remained in what he considered a civil attitude. "I'm Mr. Iverson Brentwood here to see Sir Phillip Crisp."

The servant rolled her eyes beneath puffy lids and lifted her rounded chin as if to dismiss him. "I'm afraid that's not possible."

"And why isn't that possible?" he asked, his ire growing stronger.

"He isn't here." She extended her hand, palm up, and added, "I'll be happy to take your card and give it to him when he—"

"That won't be necessary," Iverson answered, assuming this woman's brusque attitude was merely a ruse to keep people away from Sir Phillip. Iverson wasn't going to be duped that easily and certainly not by a churlish servant who didn't know her place. He swept off his dripping hat and laid it in her outstretched hand. "I'll stay until the man returns." He then stepped past her and entered the well-appointed, dimly lit vestibule, unbuttoning his damp greatcoat as he went.

Sharp disapproval flashed across her face. "What are ye doing? Ye can't just come in here without an invitation."

Iverson had no quarrel with the woman, but he was tired of her disagreeable manner. He gritted his teeth, scowled, and said, "On the contrary, madam, I can, and I just did." He draped his wet coat across her extended arm. "I intend to see Sir Phillip before I leave this house today."

"But I don't know when he's returning," she barked, clearly outraged.

Her shrill voice grated on Iverson's ears, but if he had to endure the noise of the banshee in order to get to Sir Phillip, so be it. Anger burned in his chest, and he would not be put off so easily.

"That won't be a problem," Iverson said, peeling his

well-fitted leather gloves from his hands and plopping them on top of his hat. "I'll wait. No doubt he'll be here by supper time, or for sure bedtime."

"Excuse me, sir."

At the sound of the softly spoken feminine voice, Iverson turned and saw one of the loveliest ladies he'd ever beheld. She was tall, graceful, and beautiful. Thick and shiny chestnut-colored hair was attractively arranged on top of her head, leaving nothing to distract from the lovely shape of her face, the slender column of her neck, or her gently rounded shoulders. She was dressed in a modest, pale-lilac gown that suited her ivory coloring perfectly. The high waist of her frock fit snugly under the fullness of her breasts, causing Iverson to take a second glance. There was a distinctly wholesome quality about her that immediately caught his eye, and Iverson was instantly drawn to her.

His hot anger toward Sir Phillip Crisp started cooling.

She stopped a short distance from him, but he saw no fear in her delicate features—in fact, just the opposite was true. She seemed confident, very much in command of herself and unruffled by the situation she was confronting. With deliberate concentration, he watched her and couldn't help but wonder about her connection to Sir Phillip: daughter, sister, mistress, or wife?

She looked suspiciously at him and said, "I must ask who you are and why you are frightening Mrs. Wardyworth."

There was a slight tilt to her head and lift to her shoulders that immediately let him know she was challenging him. Her bright green eyes blazed with more questions than she had asked. The firm set to her gorgeous lips insisted he state his case without delay or face her judgment.

Iverson knew the polite thing was to introduce himself, but for the life of him, the only thing that came to mind was to say, "Frightening her?" He glanced around to the peevish servant smugly watching him. "No man, woman, or beast could frighten her. I doubt Napoleon's army in their heyday could have terrified this ill-mannered harpy."

"Did ye hear what he called me, missy?"

Keeping her imperious demeanor, the young lady turned to the woman and calmly said, "Yes, Mrs. Wardyworth, I heard."

"The bugaboo insisted on coming inside. Brushed right past me as if I weren't standing right in the doorway, he did."

Iverson couldn't believe his ears. Had the servant called him a bugaboo right in front of her mistress?

"I understand. I'll handle this now. Why don't you have Nancy make you a cup of tea?"

Mrs. Wardyworth sniffed again. "I think I'll do that. Would ye like for her to make a cup for ye, too?"

"That would be lovely."

Mrs. Wardyworth smiled sweetly at the lady and then looked down at Iverson's coat, hat, and gloves in her hands as if she didn't have the faintest idea what to do with them.

"Let me take those from you," the young woman said and lifted the damp things from the servant and laid them on a nearby table.

"Thank you, missy," she said. "You always know exactly what to do."

Mrs. Wardyworth glowered at Iverson as she turned and lumbered down the corridor. He had never seen a servant be so openly rife with impudence to a guest and not be thoroughly chastised by her employer.

Iverson grunted a laugh that rumbled softly in his throat as he slowly shook his head. He looked at the poised lady before him and said, "I've heard of pampering the help, but I don't believe I've ever witnessed it in such dramatic fashion until just now."

Her eyes narrowed, and she looked at him intently. "Then you are by far a richer man for having seen how a few kind words can brighten a person's day and lift their spirits."

Iverson was near speechless again. Not only was the servant surly, now he was being chastised by this unflappable, overly self-confident lady. What kind of household did Sir Phillip have?

"Is that so?" Iverson quipped, not wanting to be scolded by such a delectable-looking female. "Then please tell me why my pockets don't feel any heavier."

A hint of a smile twitched at one corner of her mouth. "I wasn't referring to money, and you well know it. Now, tell me, what can I do for you, Mr.—?" Her light-green gaze slowly swept down his face to settle on his lips.

A flash of awareness tightened his chest and quickened his lower body as she looked at his mouth, letting her attention linger there for much longer than necessary. "Brentwood," he said and swallowed hard. He wasn't sure he liked being attracted to her. "Mr. Iverson Brentwood."

Her gaze flew back up to his eyes in a brief moment of panic, and he would have sworn he saw her swallow hard, too. No doubt she had read or at least heard about the rubbish that blasted poet, Sir Phillip, had written about Iverson and his twin brother's arrival in London. And if that had been all the man had written, Iverson might have been inclined to overlook it or even laugh it off, as Matson had suggested they do, but there was no way he could let pass the slur it cast on his mother.

That had Iverson fighting mad. His mother was no longer alive to defend herself, and he wouldn't let anyone besmirch her memory and get away with it.

Iverson had a feeling Sir Phillip would be as easy to control as Lord Waldo. Shortly after Iverson arrived in London, the Duke of Rockcliffe's youngest brother had the gall to ask him why he and his brother looked so much like Sir Randolph Gibson, given he wasn't their father. The answer Iverson gave him was a quick punch that left him with a black eye for a few days. Lord Waldo had never mentioned the subject again, and neither had anyone else. That one unplanned cuff had put a stop to much of the churning gossip, until today, with the publication of the parody *A Tale of Three Gentlemen*.

It wasn't that Iverson had enjoyed or wanted to hit Lord Waldo. In fact, it was distasteful to him. It was a gut reaction. Only later did Iverson realize if he had let Lord Waldo get away with asking such a personal question, others would follow suit, and before long his family would have been the laughingstock of London. Once again, his honor dictated he quell anyone else's tendency to ask probing questions or write unforgiving humor about his parentage.

Iverson was determined to put the rumors, gossip, and ill-mannered remarks back in the closet where they belonged by scaring the devil out of Sir Phillip. Everyone had to know there would be a price to pay for making comments or writing about something that was none of their concern.

"I see you recognize my name," he said, his simmering anger at Sir Phillip rising again.

"It would be difficult not to."

"No doubt because you read Sir Phillip's claptrap in *The Daily Herald* today?"

Her delicately arched brows raised a fraction. Her shoulders lifted ever so slightly before she pinned him with an intense stare. "Mr. Brentwood, I heard your name shortly after you arrived in London last fall, as did anyone who stepped inside a ladies' parlor, a gentlemen's club, or the gaming hells near the wharf. Surely I don't have to tell you that by now the name Brentwood has been whispered in every taproom and manor house in London."

Iverson's breath caught in his throat. She was absolutely stunning when her feathers were ruffled, and he had obviously done that by denigrating Sir Phillip's writings. He'd never met a young lady who was so bold. He didn't mind that she hadn't pulled her punch or shied away from the cold, hard truth, but instead threw an insult right back into his face. She certainly had backbone and wasn't afraid to let him know it. That made her extremely attractive to him. He had never cared for the timid, retiring wallflower. He didn't know that he'd ever met anyone—let alone a lady—who had the nerve or fire to take him on and give him such a face-to-face dressing down.

He chuckled to cover his admiration for her courage and his slight discomfort at the veracity of her words. He gave her a perfunctory nod. "Gossip does travel fast and long, especially when it's salacious."

Assuming she had gotten the better of him, at least for the time being, she relaxed her shoulders. Another hint of a smile played around the corners of her attractive mouth and Iverson found it very inviting. In fact, much to his immediate distraction, there wasn't much about her he didn't find greatly appealing.

"Quite frankly, Mr. Brentwood, I didn't know there was any other kind."

Her admission reminded him that the poet was often in the gossip columns, too. In just the few months Iverson had been in London, he'd known of Sir Phillip's name being linked to a married actress, a widowed countess, and a madame by the name of Shipwith.

"Tell me, who are you?" he asked.

Pride shone in her sparkling eyes, and her feminine chin lifted another notch. "Miss Catalina Crisp. I am Sir Phillip's daughter, and his only child."

Iverson didn't know why, but he felt a sense of relief she wasn't Mrs. Crisp, but he sure as hell wasn't happy this beautiful and enticing young lady was Sir Phillip's offspring. She was, by far, the most intriguing person he'd met since coming to London.

Shortly after his arrival, Iverson had been introduced to her father, and he'd seen the man at several parties during the winter, though surprisingly his daughter had never been with him. Sir Phillip wasn't at all like the pompous poet Lord Snellingly, who was an irritating fop demanding attention from everyone and constantly wanting some poor soul to listen to him recite his dreadful poetry. Sir Phillip enjoyed the ladies. He was always talking, laughing, or dancing with a lady. In fact, the few times Iverson had been around him, he didn't think he'd even heard the man mention his poetry. He didn't have to, because his poetry was actually good.

Unlike Keats, who had recently been ridiculed in *The Examiner* as a "complete failure," and by *Blackwood's Magazine* as an "unsettled pretender who had no right to aspire to poetry," Sir Phillip was constantly being lauded and praised for his poetic genius. Iverson certainly had no reason to think the man would ever write a parody about him and his twin brother.

Clearing his throat and his thoughts, Iverson said, "In that case, Miss Crisp, I would like to speak with your father."

"My father is not here."

"Yes, your maid told me he was gone," he muttered under his breath and rubbed the back of his neck in frustration. "And as I told her, I'll wait for him to return."

She gave him an understanding smile. "First, Mrs. Wardyworth is my housekeeper, not my maid. And second, my father has been gone almost a week. If you plan to stay until Papa returns, you will have to take up residence, and I'm afraid I can't allow that because it would shred my reputation."

"On that point I will agree with you." Iverson took in a deep breath. "So tell me, when is he expected back?"

"Sir, I can't possibly tell you what I don't know."

"And if you don't know," Iverson echoed, "then how can you be certain he won't return tonight?"

"I'm not." She looked thoughtful for a moment before adding, "There are times when my father simply packs his trunks and follows his dreams and his muse. It often keeps him away for days at a time, but whatever road he takes, it eventually leads him back home. Perhaps you could check again in a few days to see if he has returned."

That gathering storm of anger rose in him again. Iverson wanted to see her father now and put a death scare in him so he wouldn't have any desire to print more of that sensational, obnoxious, and completely false drivel about his family.

"No, no, Miss Crisp." Iverson shook his head impatiently. "I'm afraid that answer is not good enough."

She sighed softly, folded her hands together in front of her and pleasantly said, "I don't know where he is, so I don't know what more I can do for you."

A wave of sweet anticipation swept over Iverson, and his lower body hardened. Iverson knew exactly what she could do for him. He had an intense desire to pull her into his arms, press her soft breasts against his chest, and kiss her delectable lips. Impulsively, he took a step toward her with that in mind, but the reality of what he was about to do raced through him like a wild fire through dry brush, and he stopped just as he went to reach for her.

What was he thinking?

Kissing her would be madness.

Iverson was treading on unfamiliar ground here. He'd never been so enchanted by such a strong and determined young lady. She was the daughter of the devilish man he came to turn into mincemeat. The last thing he needed to do was kiss her inviting lips. Iverson had done some rash things in his lifetime, but thankfully someone was watching over him just now and stopped him from creating even more scandal. It was enough of a thorn in his side that he found her immensely attractive.

Emptying his mind of wayward thoughts, he said, "There is a lot you could do for me, Miss Crisp." He stopped and cleared his throat and his thoughts again. "But I'll not mention what that is, because even though I'm not always a perfect gentleman, as you no doubt have noticed, I'm the last person to want to take the shine off your pristine reputation."

Another knowing smile played on her lips. "I'm sure you have done plenty of that to innocent young ladies in your time."

He started to let her remark go unanswered and not say more on the subject but realized he couldn't let her have the last word. The temptation to best her was just too thrilling. Besides, there was a reason he was the aggressive twin in the Brentwood's Sea Coast Ship Building Company, and his brother Matson always the peacemaker. They had set up their business that way years ago, and it had served them well, playing off each other as the good brother and the bad brother.

Some habits were just too damn hard to break.

"To a number of ladies, I'll admit, but to none who weren't willing."

"And no doubt you still have a few of them waiting in line for a chance to be the one who conquers the heart of the Rake of Baltimore."

She won't give up.

"Actually, yes, I do. And coming from you, Miss Crisp, I'll take that comment as a compliment that you even know that much about me."

"As I said before, it would be hard not to have heard or read about you and your two brothers."

"Yes, but for now, let's get the subject back to your father. Surely, at the very least, you know if he's in London."

"My father never tells me where he is going."

A smile fluttered the corners of her mouth again. He was amusing her, and rather than it irritating the hell out of him as it should, for some reason he couldn't fathom, he enjoyed it. Being tall and broad in the shoulders, his size alone intimidated most people, but it was clear Miss Crisp didn't have an ounce of fear in her. She was strong, seductive, and every ounce his equal. Iverson didn't know how a man who could spew such garbage from his fingertips could have spawned a daughter as lovely and captivating as Miss Crisp.

"Sir Phillip's daily poetry column still continues to appear in *The Daily Herald* each morning. His…story, if anyone can call it that, *A Tale of Three Gentlemen*, just came out in today's newsprint, so he has to be nearby."

"Your guess is as good as mine on that. However, I will tell you that the daily poetry is often sent in weeks in advance, and the piece you referenced was turned in several days ago."

"So you have read it?"

She hesitated, and he wondered why. It was an easy yes or no answer.

"It doesn't change the fact I don't know where my father is or that he has no control over when his writings are published. The scheduling of his printed work is always at the pleasure of the publisher."

Iverson folded his arms across his chest in a nonchalant manner before saying, "Perhaps your father ran off to Scotland like Keats did when *The Examiner* vilified him a year or two ago."

Miss Crisp tilted her head back defiantly. "My father's work is praised and respected by his peers, and he has never been vilified by his critics."

"No? Then maybe he's absent because one of his colleagues slandered him. Keats was certainly upset when Lord Byron referred to an article about him and his being 'snuffed out' as a poet."

He watched anger fly across her face. Her back bowed with indignation, and he thought he'd finally found her breaking point, but almost just as quickly, he watched in awe as her lovely, calm countenance returned quietly and without her fury erupting. Somehow she had managed to compose herself and not express her outrage over his damning words. Iverson could take a lesson or two from her on how to do that.

"You know your poets, Mr. Brentwood. I'm duly impressed by your knowledge."

"Compliments of my mother." Iverson smiled as he fondly remembered his mama and the many winter nights she sat her sons before the roaring fire and placed a book in their hands. "She was a firm believer in being well read and saw to it that her sons were, too. She was always quoting someone. She didn't care if it was Shakespeare, Lord Byron, or the Bible, and poetry was always her favorite reading."

"She's to be commended on your education in the literary arts."

"Yes, she is," he said softly, feeling a sudden sense of grief. "I didn't see her often in the last few years of her life, but she was a sweet, beautiful woman. She doesn't deserve to be characterized in print as a *fallen woman* for a fleeting fling of passion that happened almost thirty years ago."

Compassion quickly filled her eyes, and she took a swift step toward him. "Mr. Brentwood, I want you to know that my—"

Miss Crisp paused and stepped back when, at the rattle of cups and saucers, Iverson glanced down the corridor. The tallest woman he had ever seen was coming toward them, carrying a tray she held balanced in one hand and holding a cane to help her walk with the other. She was gangly, with slightly hunched shoulders. Her large, bulging eyes stared directly at him, and she wore a wide, giddy grin.

"Mrs. Wardyworth was right, missy," the woman said as

she approached. "I see you do have a gentleman caller, but by the dead saints, she didn't tell me what a handsome, tip-top man he is."

"No, Nancy," Miss Crisp said too quickly, her gaze glancing from Iverson to the servant. "You must have misunderstood her. The gentleman is here to see Papa, not me."

"Nonsense, missy," she said, stopping in front of Miss Crisp and leaning heavily on the cane. "You know that can't be true. Your papa's not here."

"Yes, that's just what I was telling Mr. Brentwood. Papa is not here."

Nancy continued to smile at Iverson and look directly into his eyes as if she were mesmerized by him. If he didn't know better, he'd think the woman was infatuated with him.

She held the tray perfectly steady as she leaned against the cane. "Oh, don't mind that, missy. It's perfectly fine for him to use your father as an excuse to come see you. That's what a true gentleman who wants to court you would do."

Momentarily flustered, Miss Crisp shook her head and said, "Here, Nancy, let me take that tray from you. It's heavy." She turned to Iverson and said, "May I offer you a cup of tea before you go on your way, Mr. Brentwood?"

The tightness in her voice and stern set to her full lips let him know the offer was made merely out of politeness, and she didn't want or expect him to accept. It was on the tip of his tongue to be chivalrous, oblige her, and decline, but unlike his twin brother, he had never been known for always doing the right thing.

Iverson wasn't quite ready to leave Miss Crisp. It wasn't something he could revel in, of course, but he was intrigued by Sir Phillip's daughter. With her, he believed he'd met his match. He wanted to know more about this lady who stood up for her father with such vigor, allowed her servants more latitude than would be accepted by anyone else of means, and had the audacity to tell him to his face his name had been dragged through every respectable home and snickered about in every tavern in London.

He was more than happy to spend a few more minutes in her company. So for now he would put aside what he wanted to say to her father, and even though he didn't care a fig for the taste of tea, he would take advantage of her "slip of the tongue" and accept her invitation.

Iverson gave her what he hoped was his most charming smile and said, "Yes, thank you, Miss Crisp. I believe I would like a cup before I go."

Her mouth rounded in surprise. He relaxed. At last, for the first time since he knocked on the door, he felt he had the upper hand, and it felt damn good.

"Allow me to take that tray from you," he said, using some of the same words she had spoken to the servant. "It's heavy."

She bristled perceptibly and sucked in a long breath. He took hold of the tray, but she didn't release it.

"No, I can't allow you to do that," she said, doing her best to pull the tray from his grasp.

"Of course you can," he said. "I insist."

The cups rattled in their saucers as the tray shifted between them. Iverson wouldn't let go and neither would she. He could see she was more than mildly miffed at him for accepting, and was searching her mind, trying to find a polite way to uninvite him. Iverson sensed vulnerability in her. For a moment, that rare glimpse softened him, and he thought about letting go, but only briefly.

Iverson admired her show of determination, when she finally accepted defeat genially and let go of the tray.

She stepped back, and with a graceful lift to her shoulders and chin, politely said, "Very well. In that case, follow me."

"Should I go with you, missy?" the affable servant asked while keeping her smiling gaze locked on Iverson.

"That won't be necessary, Nancy. Don't worry, Mr. Brentwood won't be staying long at all."

Iverson followed Miss Crisp down the corridor and into a spacious drawing room. She quickly removed scattered pages of newsprint from an oval pedestal table that stood between a gold-colored, brocade-covered settee and two large, tufted-back armchairs.

He glanced around as she handled her task. It wasn't the most fashionably decorated drawing room he'd seen in London but certainly bigger than most. There was a low-burning fire in the fireplace, and he smiled to himself, thinking it wasn't nearly hot enough to take the chill off Miss Crisp's disposition.

A lamp had been lit on the desk portion of a finely polished mahogany secretary. It, too, was littered with newsprint, papers, ink jars, and quills. Over the fireplace hung a gilt-framed, large piece of aged parchment that had something written on it. The ends of the paper were rolled like a scroll, and the writing was elaborately styled with swirls, sweeps, and curly lettering throughout. Iverson harrumphed to himself. No doubt it was some long and well-received poetry written by the master of the house. He could see the man displaying his work in such a boastful manner in his own home.

Obviously, Sir Phillip was better off in his pockets than

most poets. His house was larger than many of the homes in Mayfair, so it had to cost him a fortune to keep it and all the servants required to maintain it superbly.

Iverson placed the tray on the cleared table and looked at Miss Crisp. She motioned for him to take a chair.

"After you," he said.

She sat on the settee, not letting her back touch the plush cushion behind her, and began pouring the tea. Iverson leaned back in the upholstered chair and made himself comfortable. He watched her delicate hands as they held the china pot. Her fingers were slim and her nails neatly trimmed. Suddenly he imagined her hands gently gliding across his bare shoulders and down his naked chest. He had a sudden urge to lift her fingers to his lips and tenderly kiss each one.

When she extended the cup to him, her gaze met his and held. He wondered if she had any idea where his thoughts had wandered. Iverson knew when a woman was aware of him, not only as a man but also as an object of her desire. And Miss Crisp had that look. He had never minded it, and certainly not with this lady. He took the tea and was certain she saw in his eyes he wanted something far different from her than tea.

"You looked deep in thought for a moment, Mr. Brentwood."

Oh, yes, she knew where his mind had been.

"Somewhat," he admitted and cleared his throat. Wanting to get back to the reason for his presence, Iverson asked, "Where exactly does your father usually go when searching for his muse?"

She smiled. "I said he follows it, not that he searches for it."

He acknowledged her correction with a nod. "Pardon me. Where does he usually go when he follows it?"

A wistful expression stole over her face. Iverson caught another quick glimpse of vulnerability in her, and for a brief moment, he had a desire to protect her.

"I have no idea, for I've never been with him. I stay here and take care of the house and the staff."

He gave her a genuine smile. "Yes, I would say you definitely take care of the staff. Tell me, why is it that I haven't seen you at any parties I've attended?"

"I have no idea why you haven't seen me," she said softly. "I was at several this past winter."

She shifted her cup and saucer to her other hand and lowered her long, velvety lashes as if she didn't want him to see her true feelings. For the second time, he had the feeling she was hiding something. Outwardly, she appeared strong and capable, but instinct told him that inside, she was feeling far differently. Something troubled her.

But what?

Again he wondered if she was hiding her father's whereabouts, but her servants seemed to back up her claim that the man was gone.

And why did the thought of her hiding anything intrigue him so? No doubt because most young ladies he'd been acquainted with in Baltimore, and the ones he'd met since coming to London, enjoyed talking about themselves. It was easy to grow weary of a young lady constantly telling him how adept she was at running a household, how talented she was on the pianoforte, or how she had been praised for her stitchery.

As if feeling a little guilty about her short answer, she added, "I do tend to arrive early at a party and leave early."

"That must be the reason we've never met. I usually arrive

late and stay late. So will you be attending parties when the Season starts?"

"Yes, my father will probably insist that I make some of them, but there are so many, it would be impossible to make them all." She cleared her throat and asked, "Is your tea to your liking, Mr. Brentwood?"

Iverson took the hint that she didn't want to talk about herself and looked down at the cup he hadn't touched. There was a small tart of some kind on the side of the saucer. He decided it might make the tea tolerable.

"Quite," he said and popped the small refreshment into his mouth. It was very tasty.

"Mr. Brentwood, why don't we put an end to this idle chitchat, and you tell me what it is you want from my father."

His eyes searched hers before he said, "I don't think I should do that, Miss Crisp."

"Why not?"

He grimaced, remembering why he had come over. The anger he had felt for the slander to his mother's memory. "What I intended to say was for your father's ears and not yours."

"But I am here, and he isn't. I'm somewhat familiar with my father's business dealings. I may be able to help you."

Should he tell her the truth? He was tempted.

No.

Whether or not he was a gentleman, she was a lady. He was in her home. He had probably already shocked her enough for one afternoon.

"Please, Mr. Brentwood. I insist you tell me why you seem so desperate to see my father."

Iverson tensed. Miss Crisp could get his back up faster

than anyone else ever had, and that included both his brothers.

"Me? Desperate?"

"You appear that way to me. I don't think I've ever met anyone quite as determined as you to see my father."

Suddenly he was really tempted to tell her why he was there.

There was a reason he was called the Rake of Baltimore by the city's social elite. When he first came to London, Iverson was determined to shed his image of the bad twin, but Lord Waldo had taken the rose off that stem a week after Iverson had hit Town. At that point, it appeared there was no hope to change his image or to be seen as refined and even-tempered as Matson. Furthermore, Miss Crisp just seemed to be daring him to shock her. What would this beautiful, self-assured young lady do if he told her the truth?

There was only one way to find out.

He set his cup and saucer on the silver tray and leaned toward her. "All right, since you insist. I intend to grab him by the neckcloth and tell him if he writes another word about my mother or my brother, I'll break his fingers so he won't be able to write anything for a long, long time."

Miss Crisp gasped.

Two

*Poetry is boned with ideas, nerved and
blooded with emotions, all held together
by the delicate, tough skin of words.*
—Joseph Joubert

An ominous shiver stole up her back.

Catalina Crisp stared at the handsome man with blue eyes, trying to decide if she'd heard what she thought she'd heard. And if she had, did he really mean he would do her father bodily harm for writing a parody of the Brentwood twins' arrival in London a few months ago?

She swallowed hard. Not from fear, or even outrage at his bluntness, but from sudden awareness. She didn't know why, but it had never occurred to her that her father's story had cast an unmistakably shameful light on the Brentwood twins' mother, even though she was never actually mentioned in the story.

No wonder Catalina was now looking into the stony face of a very angry man.

Why hadn't she thought about what the story of the two handsome gentlemen, looking so much like a man who was not their father, said about their mother? And what would Mr. Brentwood say or do if he knew it was *she*, and not her father, who had written the ending to that story? And more important, what would he do to her father if he knew there were two more installments at *The Daily Herald* waiting to be published?

How should she deal with Mr. Iverson Brentwood? What should she say?

Catalina wished she'd been more intuitive about the people behind the story, but at the time, all she could think was that she had to finish the parody and turn it in so Mr. Frederick would pay her father. Ever since they had moved into the larger home three years ago, it seemed there was never enough money to keep up with the mortgage, buy food, pay her father's ever-increasing staff, and numerous other expenses.

Oh, yes. She was in big trouble.

But she couldn't worry about herself right now. No one knew she had helped her father complete his writings, and she had to keep it that way. It would ruin her father's reputation as a poet if it were made known. He would be ridiculed, and no one would publish his work again. It must remain their secret.

When she had first seen Mr. Brentwood glaring at Mrs. Wardyworth, he had appeared hard and menacing, but after she'd gotten a closer look, she knew neither she nor her staff was in jeopardy from him—though she would do well to be wary. He wore the demeanor of a harsh and ruthless man as if it was a matter of honor, but Catalina was a good judge of people. Mr. Iverson Brentwood didn't raise any fear in her at all. Even knowing he was most likely the man who had given Lord Waldo a black eye a few months ago, she had no worry for herself, but he could very well make good on his threat to do harm to her father.

That she couldn't allow. He might be a fierce protector of his family, but so was she.

Collecting her thoughts, she reached over and placed her cup and saucer on the tray beside his before looking into his fathomless, icy blue eyes. With a calmness she didn't know she was capable of, she asked, "Are you trying to frighten me, Mr. Brentwood?"

He looked at her with hot intensity that made an unfamiliar but delicious sensation spiral through her. Her breath grew uncomfortably shallow as sudden heat flared inside her.

"Absolutely not," he answered her as calmly as she had spoken.

"Then what were you intending by your previous remark?"

His gaze held steadily on hers. "To threaten your father."

"And you don't think a comment like that would frighten a gentle-born lady in her own home?"

He smiled and nodded. "Most ladies, I agree, but not you."

Mr. Brentwood relaxed into the comfort of the armchair, and a sudden gleam shone in his eyes. Catalina's breath caught in her throat again. He was a devilishly handsome man when he was so at ease. A true gentleman would never be so crass as to say such a thing to a lady, but she didn't have time to ponder why she wasn't offended by his remarks.

"I've watched you closely, Miss Crisp."

Oh, yes, she knew how closely he had looked at her. Her skin had tingled responsively more than once when she caught his gaze skimming down her face. It was as if he was caressing her with his eyes. Even now, she knew he found her as attractive as she did him.

He continued. "I've not seen a flicker of fear cross your lovely face."

He was obviously good at reading people, too.

"What have you seen?" she asked, and the moment the words were out of her mouth she wanted to clamp her teeth together tightly and take them back.

Why was she trying to engage this man and discover how he felt about her? She wasn't a coquettish female trying to gain his attention or his favor. By his own admission, he intended to threaten her father with physical harm. That was all she needed to know. He was not even a man she needed to converse with. She should have asked him to leave her house the moment he made his reasons known to her. No, the moment she saw him in the vestibule and knew this man had touched a place inside her no other man had been near. Instead, she foolishly chose to match wits with him because she found him so deliciously stimulating.

"I can't say right now, because I think you are hiding something, Miss Crisp, and I can only assume it is the whereabouts of your father."

Oh, he was good.

She *was* hiding something: the fact that when her father had left without finishing the story he had promised to Mr. Frederick, she had been forced to finish it so he would be paid.

And it wasn't the first time she'd had to do it.

In the past couple of years, she'd had to complete at least half of her father's work. Sometimes he could get so enthusiastic about a story or a poem, he would write all day and night, never stop for food, drink, or sleep. And at other times, like with *A Tale of Three Gentlemen*, he would

get bored or lose interest and never make the time to finish
it. Half-finished work would not pay their obligations. Sir
Phillip Crisp was a good father, a loyal friend, and a compassionate employer, but he had absolutely no head for business
matters, deadlines, or duties.

Catalina was the practical one in the family, and someone
needed to be. She had taken over managing their business
and household affairs when she was only sixteen years of age.
Her father had no use for keeping account books balanced
or even paying their debts on time. She had tried to explain
to him that their expenses were increasing and he needed to
write more often. They needed more money coming in each
month. She might as well have been talking to a statue in the
garden for all the good it did.

Sir Phillip was a dreamer whose head was always in the
clouds. For him, life was a lark. She had never seen her father
angry or even mildly upset. He would not be hurried or
interrupted when he was writing or doing anything else. If
a fanciful notion struck him, he would take off on one of his
"idle loafings," as he liked to refer to trips, saying only that he
had to follow his muse.

One glance at Mr. Brentwood told her he was a far different man from her blithe father. Clearly, Mr. Brentwood was
arrogant, authoritative, and impatient. She couldn't imagine
he would ever shirk a duty. And she was certain she'd never
met a man as intense, challenging, or as maddening as he.

Now she wished she hadn't turned in the other two
installments of *A Tale of Three Gentlemen* to Mr. Frederick.
But she had. So the only thing that could be done now was
to go to *The Daily Herald* and ask the man to give them back
to her.

Trying to appear more relaxed, Catalina leaned against the settee and smiled at Mr. Brentwood. "You are not a very good gambler, sir."

The edges of his eyes narrowed, and he bent toward her again. In a suspicious tone, he asked, "I'll admit, you have me curious. I'll take the bait you've thrown out and ask the obvious question. Why do you say that?"

"The first thing is because you wear your feelings on your face."

He gave her an appreciative nod. "It's true my anger showed when I entered your house. Reading that travesty of a story and then spending a few hours trying to find out where Sir Phillip lived proved extremely frustrating for me today, not to mention my unsatisfactory conversation with Mrs. Wardyworth when I arrived."

She smiled. "I do believe you had her in a dither when I walked into the room."

He gave her a relaxed smile as he said, "The feeling was quite mutual, I assure you."

"Are you always so impatient with servants?"

He took his time answering her. "I've never had a reason to be until today."

Catalina picked up her cup and sipped her tea while she watched him over the rim. Mrs. Wardyworth was difficult at times, but Catalina would never admit that to Mr. Brentwood.

"You gave me one reason why you think I'm not a good gambler," Mr. Brentwood said. "I'm curious. Do you have another?"

"Yes," she said and nodded. "You laid all your cards on the table for me to see."

He gave her a comfortable grin and said, "That's a low blow to a man who considers himself a fairly good gambler."

"Well, you know what they say about 'if the cap fits.'"

A short burst of derisive laughter was his only answer. He was much too sure of himself.

She lifted her eyebrows a little and said, "You do realize now that I know what you want with my father, when he returns I can tell him to avoid you at all costs and save him from your temper."

"Please do that, Miss Crisp," Mr. Brentwood said, keeping his gaze on her lips. "That way, at least, Sir Phillip won't be able to say he didn't have fair warning of my intentions. I will not allow him to slander my family's good name again for the sake of a few laughs from a sordid story."

If only Mr. Brentwood knew it wasn't for laughs or recognition for her father that she finished the story but for the sake of their livelihood. As it was, she constantly received letters demanding payments from her father's tailor, her aunt's apothecary, the milliner, and countless others. She lived in fear that one day everyone would know they were always one step away from destitution.

"The name Brentwood was never mentioned in the story," she felt compelled to say.

"It didn't have to be," he said with defensive resolve. "How many sets of adult twins have come to London in the last year and have an older brother who is a viscount?"

"I believe the older brother was an earl in the story."

"You're splitting hairs, Miss Crisp," he said, his tone and demeanor turning less tolerant than before.

"Not in the least," she added. "Furthermore, there was never anything scandalous mentioned about the mother. In fact, I don't think she was referenced at all."

"Now you are straining to swallow a gnat. It was implied.

How else could the twins look exactly like another man if the mother hadn't taken a secret lover in her past?"

Feeling guilty because she knew he had some ground to stand on with his complaint, yet not wanting to admit it, she was no longer able to sit still. Catalina rose and said, "Surely, Mr. Brentwood, you know my father's story was not meant to be taken that way. If anything, you are being thin-skinned and making a mountain out of a pebble—no, out of a grain of sand. Surely you know it was not his intention to slander your family."

Mr. Brentwood rose, too, and stepped so close to her she thought she heard his heart beating.

A wrinkle of anger creased his forehead. "No, I don't know that," he said.

"It was only a simple story meant to entertain."

"Yes, to entertain all of London at my family's expense. And you wonder why I am upset?"

"No one takes seriously what's printed in the Society section of *The Daily Herald*. If anyone wants serious news, they will go to the *Times* or *The London Chronicle*."

He leaned his face in closer to hers and kept his voice low and his tone level as he said, "No, you're wrong, Miss Crisp. Most everyone who reads that rubbish assumes every word of it is true, and seeing it in print gives legitimacy to the hogwash. What your father wrote revives the gossip that had finally settled down and fuels the scandalmongers to keep it going."

"I believe you are wrong, and time will prove that to you. In less than a month this story will be all but forgotten."

"I hope you are right, Miss Crisp, because it amazes me that anyone could actually think Matson and I would approve of a parody that casts a shameful light on our mother. Tell me, Miss Crisp, how would you be feeling right now if some fashion of *A Tale of Three Gentlemen* had been written about your family?"

"Oh, but my mother wouldn't—" Catalina caught herself and clamped her mouth shut quickly.

He leaned in so close his nose almost touched hers. "Your mother wouldn't what, Miss Crisp?"

"Nothing, nothing. I was just… I mean, I wasn't thinking."

Suddenly her entire body seemed to go still. She couldn't believe what she had almost said. Surely it went beyond the pale of decency to say her mother never would have taken a lover. She was horrified she had allowed his goading to rile her to that point. She was usually so calm, knowing exactly how to handle the biggest of problems without getting flustered or angry. Mr. Brentwood was right. The parody should never have been written, and she was sorry and upset for her part in seeing it published. She was going to do everything possible to see that the rest of the story never made it to the streets.

He watched her, studied her hard as if he was absorbing every detail of her face, before slowly letting his gaze sweep down her neck to the crest of her breasts rising and falling with each choppy breath. His eyes lifted to hers again, and for a brief moment, she had the distinct feeling his lips were going to touch hers.

He quietly asked, "Does your father know what a strong advocate you are for him?"

She appreciated that, for the time being at least, he was letting her insensitive remark pass.

"What do you expect of me when you say you want to harm him?"

"That's not what I said. It's not that I *want* to, but that I *will* if he publishes anything more about my family. I protect my own."

She believed him but couldn't back down from her strong stance now.

"And I will protect my father as fiercely as you protect your family."

All of a sudden, he reached out and caressed down her cheek with the backs of his fingers before letting his knuckles lightly skim back and forth across her lips. His hand was warm and his touch tender. A thrilling tingle of something she'd never felt before swept across her breasts and then tumbled its way down into the depths of her abdomen. She inhaled the clean, fresh scent of shaving soap that lingered on his skin. Her chest tightened, and her stomach felt like it fell to her feet.

Catalina knew she should shrink from his touch, but she couldn't. It was as if she wanted and needed him to touch her so softly to prove he was a gentle man in spite of his tough talk and angry expressions. And for a fleeting, bewildering moment, her heartbeat raced and her throat went dry as she thought about the possibility of dallying with the rake. She had always wanted to be kissed by a man who stirred her senses the way this man did. It took all she could do not to throw her arms around his neck, place her lips on his, and give in to the madness of the intriguing man.

"Understood, Miss Crisp…"

"What's this? I just heard there's a gentleman in the house."

Catalina spun at the sound of her aunt's voice and saw the petite woman dressed in a flowing, puce-colored gown breeze into the room with all the fanfare of a young maid at a cotillion.

Aunt Elle's face was flushed, and several strands of her dark brown hair had fallen from the chignon at the back of her head. The delicate lace fichu wrapped around her slim shoulders hung askew, and she wore only one large pearl earring. Catalina had no doubt her aunt had spent the afternoon lying on the settee in her bedchamber reading poetry and sipping wine.

Holding a fine linen handkerchief in her hand, Aunt Elle said, "Catalina, my dearest, have you forgotten all your upbringing? You simply cannot entertain a gentleman without me or a suitable chaperone of some description present. What in heaven's name were you thinking?"

After rushing to Catalina's side, her aunt stumbled to a halt too quickly and almost toppled over.

"Careful, Auntie," Catalina cautioned, trying to catch hold of her aunt.

As if sensing a disaster in the making, Mr. Brentwood reached out and gently grabbed hold of her aunt's waist to keep her from falling and to steady her. Aunt Elle clutched his upper arms as if she were hanging on to him for her life.

She smiled up at Mr. Brentwood but made no move to dislodge herself from his grasp. Her hands squeezed the muscles in his arms, and she said, "My stars, you are a strong young man. Just like my Mr. Gottfried was."

Catalina purposefully kept her gaze from meeting Mr. Brentwood's, but there was no way he didn't know that by five o'clock in the afternoon, Eloisa Lucinda Gottfried had already had at least one glass of sherry too many.

Catalina took her aunt's wrist and gently pulled her away from Mr. Brentwood and helped her to stand up straight.

"Auntie, I am not entertaining Mr. Brentwood."

"Of course you are, dearest. I'm tipsy, not blind." Aunt Elle paused to put her handkerchief over her mouth and hiccupped as she looked down at the tray. "I can see you were having tea with him. I know what you were thinking, but I won't have you risk your reputation over it no matter how worthwhile a plan it seemed at the time."

"Nonsense, Auntie. I wanted only to find out if I could help Mr. Brentwood. He is looking for Papa."

"Didn't you tell him we don't know where Phillip is? Oh, never mind. Both of you sit back down and finish your tea. I'll handle this, Catalina." She turned back to Mr. Brentwood and smiled. "But first, we must be properly introduced."

Catalina quickly made the introductions while her aunt swayed on her feet and smiled at Mr. Brentwood.

After greetings were exchanged, Aunt Elle said, "Mr. Brentwood, you should have made known your intentions to court my niece."

"Auntie, no," Catalina said, her frustration mounting as she continued to avoid Mr. Brentwood's eyes. She could imagine what he was thinking and didn't need to see it written on his face.

"Mrs. Gottfried," Mr. Brentwood said, "I would have done so if that had been the case. Miss Crisp and I had never met until a few minutes ago. She was right when she said I came here to see her father."

Aunt Elle rubbed her temple as if she had a headache. "Oh, but he isn't here."

"Yes, I've been told," he said, speaking kindly to her, "and more than once, so I think perhaps it's time I took my leave. I'll come back another time to see Sir Phillip."

"Well, I don't know why you'd want to come see him when our beautiful Catalina is here," Aunt Elle said, her gaze darting from Catalina to Mr. Brentwood. "Unless this is a ruse, and if it is, that's so romantic." She smiled at Mr. Brentwood. "My Mr. Gottfried was a romantic man like you, too."

Heat started at Catalina's throat and rose up her neck to her face. Her gaze flew to Mr. Brentwood's, but she realized she didn't know what to say to him about her aunt's behavior.

"Auntie, we just told you there is nothing going on between us."

"Yes, yes," Aunt Elle continued, suddenly looking confused. "I know, I know. It would be wonderful for you to come another time, Mr. Brentwood. You should hear our Catalina play the pianoforte. It's breathtaking."

"Auntie, please."

"Well, it's true. But I'll tell him about that another time. My brother doesn't usually stay away very long. How long has he been gone now, Catalina? About a week?"

"Yes, Auntie, that's right. I'll see Mr. Brentwood out and then be back to help you to your room."

"Oh, yes, I remember now. He'll return most any day now. But you are more than welcome to come back and visit with our Catalina anytime." She paused and smiled at Mr. Brentwood. "Just let me know, and I'll arrange it."

"Yes, madam."

"This way, Mr. Brentwood," Catalina said softly, and started for the door.

Catalina would have given anything for Mr. Brentwood not to have seen her aunt in such an unfavorable light. Mrs. Wardyworth must have alerted her aunt to the fact there was a man in the house. Thankfully, even the times when Auntie dipped too deeply into the wine, she was still always in a good and playful humor, like today.

As soon as they were out of the drawing room and in the corridor, Mr. Brentwood touched Catalina's arm. That same thrilling sensation as before spiraled through her. He must have felt it, too, for he slowly lowered his hand and took a step away.

His expression was the softest she'd seen since he arrived. Gone were the anger, the distrust and suspicion, and in their place understanding had taken root. She was grateful.

"I know where my hat and coat are, and I know the way out, if you want to go back to your aunt."

"Yes, thank you, that will be fine," she said, realizing she really didn't know what to say to excuse her aunt's outlandish behavior.

Catalina turned away but spun back to face him when she heard him say, "Miss Crisp?"

Their eyes met and held, and somehow she knew he was not appalled by Aunt Elle and she had no reason to be embarrassed. And suddenly, she liked Mr. Brentwood even more than before.

"Yes?" she said.

"It was indeed a pleasure to meet you."

"Thank you, Mr. Brentwood," she said and turned quickly and headed back to the drawing room.

Catalina stood just inside the doorway, holding her breath until she heard the front door close behind him. She exhaled a deep sigh of relief and leaned against a chair. She didn't think she had ever been that stimulated in her life. How could a man be so refreshing, so invigorating, and such a challenge all at the same time?

"But he's gone now, and I'll probably never see him again," she whispered.

"What did you say?"

Catalina looked over at her aunt. She was lying against the arm of the settee with her handkerchief covering her face.

"Only that I think the next time Mr. Brentwood seeks my father, he will look for him at a club or on the street. Not that it matters to us, Auntie, but I don't think he will be coming back here."

"That would be such a shame. He's a very handsome man. And I disagree with you. I think he will be back."

Catalina smiled to herself. If her aunt knew just how handsome Catalina thought the man was, she'd have them married before noon tomorrow. "Come, Auntie. Let me help you back to your room."

"No, no, dearest, I'm going to stay here and gather my wits together and have dinner with you tonight. Would you like that?"

"Very much. You know I hate eating alone. But are you sure you're up to it?"

Aunt Elle took the handkerchief off her face and rose up on her elbows. "I will be by the time Nancy has dinner ready. Did I make a complete fool of myself in front of your nice young man?"

Yes.

"No, no, Auntie," Catalina said with compassion, refusing to feel guilt or shame for the prevarication. She sat down beside her aunt. "And I told you he is not *my* young man."

"Oh, yes, yes. You explained that." She smiled knowingly, and her eyes sparkled with innocent mischief. "Your secret's safe with me."

"Auntie, you shouldn't drink so much sherry late in the afternoon."

"Port, dear, it was—" She hiccupped. "Port. You know that nice young apothecary I've been seeing?"

"I've not actually met him, Auntie."

"Well, there's no need you should. He assured me a drink in the evening was good for me." Aunt Elle's eyes widened as if she'd just remembered something. "No, he told me a drink in the evening would be good for what ails me."

"Yes, one drink in the evening," Catalina said, trying to keep her voice from sounding like a reprimand. "Not an entire bottle in the afternoon."

Her aunt smiled and patted Catalina's cheek. "I wish I could still fool you the way I could when you were younger."

"So do I, Auntie, so do I," Catalina said, feeling a little sad. During the past year, her aunt had come to rely too often on her tonics, elixirs, and spirits.

They sat in silence for a few minutes, and Catalina thought about the man who had just left her house. When she'd first seen Mr. Brentwood standing in the vestibule, so confident and commanding, she knew immediately he could easily be the hero of all her dreams. There was a strange quickening in her lower stomach and a catch in her breath.

He'd looked magnificent. Adonis in the flesh. Broad through the shoulders and chest, he'd worn a starched white shirt of fine lawn beneath a coat of the deepest shade of blue. His neckcloth was simple and tied into a casual bow. Thick brown hair was stylishly brushed away from his high brow and held in a queue at his nape with a strip of black braided leather. His cheekbones were wide, high, and aristocratic. His face wasn't classically handsome like her father's, and he certainly didn't have her father's smooth charm and even temperament, but there was no denying Mr. Brentwood's stirring appeal to her senses and to her intelligence.

She remembered the solid, uncompromising look to the set of his chiseled jaw and chin, giving him an arrogant attractiveness only a man of power and prestige could achieve. When she'd looked at him, she had felt the stirrings that always came over her when she read her favorite William Shakespeare play, *Romeo and Juliet*. She had always dreamed about and wondered what it would be like to love someone with the deep intensity of those two lovers. She often wondered what this madness called love was all about.

Catalina shook her head and laughed to herself. There were so many more important things to think about than that elusive emotion called love. Starting with the fact that she no longer had all the money *The Daily Herald* had paid her father for the story. She had to go to Mr. Frederick's office and do something to keep those last two installments from being published. She would have to promise to pay them back as soon as possible—as soon as her father returned and decided to write again. Though right now, she had no idea when that would be. Her father had already been gone longer than usual. She had no choice but to believe Mr. Brentwood when he said he'd harm her father if more stories about his family were printed.

She turned to her aunt and said, "I need your help."

Aunt Elle rose to a sitting position and put her hand to her head as if she was dizzy. "You just tell me what. You know I'll do anything for you."

"I need to see Mr. Frederick at *The Daily Herald* first thing tomorrow morning. I don't want to wait until afternoon. Can you rise and be ready to go with me by noon?"

"Of course, dearest, of course. I'll have my maid wake me so I'll be ready before noon."

"Thank you, Auntie," Catalina said, making a mental note to tell Sylvia herself. In her aunt's current condition, Catalina couldn't trust Aunt Elle to remember to tell her maid.

Catalina rose. "Now, you lie back down for a little while. I'm going to take this tray to the kitchen and ask Nancy to make you some hot tea. How does that sound?"

"Wonderful."

Aunt Elle sighed and covered her face once again with her handkerchief.

Catalina picked up the tray and headed toward the kitchen, her thoughts drifting back to Mr. Brentwood. What an impression he had made on her. He was so commanding, so confident, and so angered by what she and her father had written. It surprised her she wasn't more offended by his harsh manner and tone. She understood his feelings. To him, his family had been wronged, and he was looking for revenge.

But she couldn't comprehend the reason she was so enamored of him. Just thinking about him made her breathless with unexpected pleasure. Of all the gentlemen she'd met at parties during the past year, not one had mentioned poetry to her, even though her father was a poet. But Mr. Brentwood admitted to reading it. He even knew about Lord Byron's slight against Keats. How many gentlemen would know so much about the men who filled their days with songs of the heart?

It was no wonder Mr. Brentwood fascinated her.

Catalina loved to read, and all her favorite stories, poetry, and plays were about love. She knew a hero when she saw one, and there were many things about Mr. Brentwood that reminded her of the hero of her dreams.

She wondered if she would ever see the intriguing man again. And as much as she hated to admit it to herself, she knew for certain she wanted to see him again.

Three

*Start by doing what's necessary, then what's possible,
and suddenly you are doing the impossible.*
—St. Francis of Assisi

CATALINA FELT RESTLESS.

It was the sunniest day they'd had in weeks, and she wished she could close up her parasol and throw it down. Even though there was a cool breeze, she wanted to unbutton her pelisse, take off her bonnet, and let the sunshine drench her. She wanted its calming warmth, shining from a cloudless blue sky, to heat her back and shoulders as the carriage rolled along. But she couldn't do that. Her aunt, not to mention anyone else who might see her, would be horrified to see a hatless young lady riding down the crowded streets of London.

Aunt Elle was just as eager as Catalina for their first outing in the landau without the top since last autumn, and apparently all of London felt the same eagerness to enjoy some of the first sunbeams of spring. The roads were jammed with rigs, coaches, curricles, and high-perch phaetons, which made the ride to *The Daily Herald* building longer than usual. But Catalina didn't mind. It gave her time to think.

She had slept fitfully, knowing what was before her today. Mr. Frederick wasn't an easy man to deal with on a good day, and she had no idea how he was going to react to what she had to ask him this morning. But if she were honest with herself, she had to admit that most of her fretfulness while she lay in the darkness of her bedchamber last night came from her thoughts of Mr. Iverson Brentwood, not the publisher of *The Daily Herald*.

During her wakeful hours, she'd realized she'd had several firsts with Mr. Brentwood yesterday afternoon, starting with his being the first man she couldn't get off her mind once he left her. He was also the first man to display anger toward her. Her father certainly never had. Sir Phillip Crisp was the gentlest, most kindhearted person she had ever known. He had a smile for everyone, and he laughed often. She had never seen him even mildly upset or in a bad temper with an untrained servant. Though he had certainly brought home several over the years who had tried Catalina's patience more than once. Sir Phillip didn't believe in lectures, reprimands, or criticisms, but many times she wished he'd been a little stricter with the staff, as well as in his own life.

To abide by her father's never-changing example, she had simply tried to hold on to her temper, take everything in stride, and to be kind and helpful to those he liked to deem less fortunate than the Crisps. However, when he was away, Catalina often fell short of her father's high expectations on the way to live one's life, as was reflected in her conversation with Mr. Brentwood late yesterday afternoon. The man had just made it impossible for her to hold her tongue as much as she would have liked.

Mr. Brentwood was also the first man she'd met who didn't seem to care a whit whether or not she found favor with him. That surprised her immensely. In fact, at times when she was talking with him yesterday, it was as if he wanted to make sure she *didn't* approve of him. Most of the gentlemen she'd met at parties and balls during the past year were tripping over themselves to win her praise and approval so they could call on her. It was clear Mr. Brentwood had only one person on his mind yesterday—her father. And Catalina was certain if her father had been there, Mr. Brentwood wouldn't have paid her the slightest heed. And for reasons she couldn't begin to fathom, she had wanted Mr. Brentwood to notice her—as a woman.

It was outrageous!

The man clearly was not someone she could be interested in as a suitor. He was too brash, too commanding, and much too comfortable with himself. If she ever met a man she wanted to court her, he would be a gentleman who had a gentle, likable, and easygoing nature, like her father.

Catalina reached up and touched her cheek and remembered another first for her. Mr. Brentwood was the first man, other than her father, to touch her cheek. It surprised her that his touch had been so tender, languorous, and curiously comforting, coming from so strong and forceful a man. Even now, the warmth from that touch seemed to seep into her soul, bury itself there, and make a home.

Maybe it moved her so because it was not an ordinary touch. He had intended for it to be a very sensual caress. And it was.

He had used the backs of his fingers to gently stroke her cheek, rather than his palm as her father always had whenever he'd affectionately patted the side of her face. And he had lightly raked his knuckles across her lips, too. Her stomach curled and tightened again just thinking about the way his forward touch made her feel. She had never had anyone be forward with her until Mr. Brentwood.

"What is it, Catalina? You keep rubbing your cheek with the back of your hand. There's nothing there I can see. Though you know my sight isn't as good as it used to be."

Catalina jerked her hand down to her lap. "Oh, sorry, Auntie. No, nothing's wrong. I was just deep in thought about what I must say to Mr. Frederick."

"Truly?" her aunt asked with a sparkle in her light-green eyes. "By the look on your face, I would have thought you were dreaming about dancing with that handsome Mr. Brentwood who called on you yesterday."

Catalina hoped no telltale blush gave her away. She didn't like getting caught thinking about that man. She looked at her aunt, thinking to tell her one more time that Mr. Brentwood was not there to see her, but instead, she simply smiled. How did the woman do it? She was a completely different person this morning from who she was last night. Her hair was perfectly coiffed beneath the wide-brimmed straw hat, and her light-brown carriage dress and accessories were impeccable. Her speech was well-bred, and her cheeks naturally rosy. Catalina always loved her aunt, but this was the one she adored.

"The truth is, Auntie, that I didn't sleep well last night and awakened with a pain in my neck and my stomach feeling like it has a ball of yarn rolling around in it."

"You should have told me," Aunt Elle admonished. "I would have gone to my cabinet and chosen one of my tonics for you. A generous dose is what you need. You would have felt better in no time at all."

Catalina laughed. "I don't ever want to taste any of your tonics again. You can keep them all for yourself."

"But I have a cure for almost anything that ails you."

"I know, and you can keep them. One sip all those years ago was enough for me. I'd rather be sick than take your medicine."

Catalina smiled and refrained from saying more. Aunt Elle had a bookcase in her room crammed from top to bottom with bottles filled with tonics, elixirs, and more concoctions than Catalina had a desire to know about.

She owed the knot in her stomach to Mr. Brentwood, and probably the pain in her neck, too. Medicine couldn't take away those kinds of feelings. Mr. Brentwood had put her in an untenable position. He had been very brave to come into her home and threaten her father. That was something no gentleman should ever do, even if he had just cause. She probably wouldn't believe he was serious if it weren't for the rumor that Mr. Iverson Brentwood had given Lord Waldo a black eye. For that reason alone, she had to take the man at his word that he would seek out her father and harm him if anything else were printed about the Brentwood family.

Her aunt's eyes softened, and she patted Catalina's gloved hands. "I'm sorry you don't feel well, dearest."

"I'm fine, Auntie. Really, I'm enjoying looking at all the people, elegant barouches, and post-chaises we're passing."

"That's my young lady. Keep your chin up. Now, I know you told me last week you didn't want to do this, but I truly need you to go with me to Lady Windham's party. All the others this week we can skip, if you insist. Even though she has been my dear, dear friend for many years, she will feel I have snubbed her if I don't put in an appearance at her home. You know how easily she gets her stays bent out of shape."

Eloisa Lucinda Gottfried spoke the truth. She never went

to a party alone anymore, and Catalina didn't want her to. She teased her aunt by asking, "Are you trying to say that because you have come with me today I should go with you to Lady Windham's party?"

"Heavens no!" Her aunt laughed. "I'd never say that, but if you take what I said that way, I suppose it's all right."

Catalina laughed, too. "Of course I will go with you, Auntie."

"Good. You can wear one of the new gowns we had made for the Season."

The laughter died in Catalina's throat, and her smile slowly faded. She hadn't yet told her aunt that she didn't have new gowns for the Season. By the time Catalina had paid for her aunt's and her father's new clothing, along with everything else, there simply wasn't the money for her. Catalina didn't mind. She had made do with buying lace and other trimmings. Her modiste had done a lovely job of remaking her old dresses to look new by using contrasting fabrics to make flounces, bows, and ruffles. Hopefully, only the most discerning eyes would know the gowns were last year's.

Catalina breathed in deeply as the carriage came to a halt in front of the tall, imposing building. A moment of dread seized her, but she quickly shook it away. She would not go in to see Mr. Frederick lacking confidence. If she could withstand the intimidating Mr. Brentwood, she could certainly handle the publisher of *The Daily Herald*.

"Are you ready, dearest?" her aunt asked. "Briggs is waiting to help you down."

Catalina saw her footman holding his hand up for her, his toothless grin as happy as always in spite of the fact the old, gray-bearded man couldn't hear very well and could say only a few intelligible words. She held up one finger, and he nodded.

Briggs was fairly good with using hand signals to let people know what he was saying. When her father had brought him home five years ago, all he told her was he found Briggs walking on the Old Post Road. He had been beaten by his last employer and sent off without food, water, or clothing other than what he had on. Her father had offered him a job. In order to help the man communicate better, Catalina had hired an old schoolmaster to work with Briggs. Over the course of a couple of years, he'd learned his letters and how to read and write a few words. He always kept a sharpened pencil and piece of used parchment in his pocket.

Catalina turned to her aunt. "I'm ready, but before we go, I want to ask that you let me do all the talking."

Her aunt smiled indulgently and patted her hand again. "I wouldn't have it any other way. Besides, I'm not even sure why we are here, so you'll have no cause to worry about what I might say."

"Thank you, Auntie. Let's go."

She and her aunt entered the building and asked to speak with Mr. Frederick. They waited for almost an hour before being escorted to the office of the short, rotund man.

"Come in. Come in, Miss Crisp and Mrs. Gottfried. This is certainly a pleasant surprise. How are you two lovely ladies doing on this fine day?"

"We are quite well, thank you, Mr. Frederick," Catalina replied affably. He held out chairs for them and then walked around to his desk and eased his bulky frame into a squeaky leather chair.

He clasped his hands and laid them on his desk. His smile and friendliness seemed a little forced as he said, "What can I do for you?"

"I have a favor to ask of you," Catalina responded.

"I'll be happy to help you if I can. What is it you need?"

"I've come to ask you not to publish the last two installments of *A Tale of Three Gentlemen*."

His eyebrows scrunched together. "What? Surely you can't be serious."

"Oh, but I am. I want you to return them to me."

Mr. Frederick leaned back in his chair and laughed. "I don't know what kind of trick you and your father are trying to come up with, Miss Crisp, but I really don't have time for this. My schedule is hectic, but because I thought you might be bringing me more of your father's work to consider, I agreed to see you. That is all that interests me. So unless you have something else he has written, I'm very busy." He started to rise.

"Wait," she said, tamping down the panic that wanted to control her. "Mr. Frederick. This is not a trick of any sort. Let me explain. It's come to my attention, and my father's, of course, that some persons have found the story to be in poor taste and insensitive because it so closely resembles a very well-respected family in Town."

"That is precisely the thing that makes the story so appealing, Miss Crisp. It's humor. It is always in poor taste. That is why it is a parody. Now, tell me who thinks *A Tale of Three Gentlemen* isn't humorous. I should like to have a word with them myself."

"It wouldn't be polite or proper for me to use names."

He smiled again. "I thought so."

"But please know that the story needs to be suspended indefinitely."

"Nonsense. I don't know of anyone who hasn't been absolutely delighted with the story. That's what we've heard from our vendors. It was the talk of the Town yesterday."

"And that, sir, is most of the problem."

His eyes widened. "Certainly not for me or *The Daily Herald*. I don't know whom your father is talking to, Miss Crisp. Everyone I've heard from considers the story a masterpiece of humor and can't wait to read the rest of it. Your father should be eager for the next installment to come out, not trying to stop it. It adds to his distinction as a renowned poet and writer."

Catalina's back stiffened, and her shoulders tightened, but she managed to smile pleasantly and say, "I agree with all you said about my father, and we don't want to seem unfair about any of this, but for reasons I am not at liberty to confide in you, we need the rest of the story back in our possession. Now, I'm sorry to say we can't, today, return the money you paid us, but you can trust we will in due time. My father is currently writing another story, and he's working on some poetry, as well, that should be ready soon."

"Miss Crisp, our newsprint had record sales at all our vendors yesterday. There were no heinous murders reported in the city, the Lord Mayor is not in any kind of scandal, the Prince is in good health, and the King's is still questionable. Nothing but the story of *A Tale of Three Gentlemen* could account for the rapid rise in yesterday's sales." He shook his head fast to emphasize his point. "No, Miss Crisp, we must finish printing the rest of the story or our readers will never forgive us. Giving them back to your father is not an option."

"You must," she said desperately. "My father insists," she added, unable to avoid the prevarication.

Mr. Frederick pushed his chair away from his desk and glowered at her. "Let me make something refreshingly clear to you and your father, Miss Crisp. I don't want the money back. Even if you laid it right here in front of me, it would not change the fact that I am not going to return the story. First and foremost, the story no longer belongs to your father. *The Daily Herald* bought it, owns it, and is not willing to sell or give it back to Sir Phillip."

Aunt Elle moved to the edge of her seat and said, "But you must, sir. You must understand that Catalina has asked for it, and as a gentleman, you should comply with a lady's request."

Mr. Frederick's wide-eyed gaze jumped from Catalina to Aunt Elle. "I don't have to understand, Mrs. Gottfried. We paid for the entire story. I told your brother if the first part of the story was a success we would consider printing the rest. And by all accounts, so far it has been. We'll do a final assessment in the next day or two, and if all goes as I think it will, I will give the order to start copying it so printing can begin sometime in the next few days." He stopped and gave her a victory smile. "We don't want people to lose interest in it."

Mr. Frederick rose, marched from behind his desk over to the door, and opened it. "The next time you talk to your father, Miss Crisp, tell him for me I'll look forward to more stories from him in the future. And while you are at it, please tell him I'd rather he come in next time. I prefer dealing with him." An insincere smile formed on his thin lips. "Now, if you'll excuse me, Miss Crisp, Mrs. Gottfried, I have others waiting for my time."

Catalina's hands curled into fists of disappointing frustration, but she held her head high as she walked toward Mr. Frederick, nodding to him as she passed. She hated admitting defeat, but she didn't know what more she could say to change the man's mind. Her father would be home soon, and she had no doubt that with his smooth charm he would be able to talk Mr. Frederick into returning the final two installments.

Her stomach felt as if it was sinking to her feet as she and her aunt made their way out of the building. She paused and glanced up the street to see if she could spot their carriage but didn't, so she looked down the street and suddenly inhaled a sharp breath. Her heartbeat surged.

Not far away, Mr. Brentwood was leaning against a lamppost, watching her intently. He wore a black, single-caped greatcoat and held his hat in his hand. He looked the devilishly handsome rogue, and for the first time in her life, she knew what it felt like to want to run and throw herself into the strong arms of a man.

Four

One may have good eyes and yet see nothing.
—Italian Proverb

WHAT WAS HE DOING HERE?

Catalina tried to restrain the unexpected pleasure that filled her at seeing Mr. Brentwood. Of all the gentlemen she had met, why was this man the one who made her breath quicken, her chest tighten, and her knees go weak at the sight of him?

"It's not fair," she whispered.

"Of course it isn't, dearest," her aunt said, patting her back affectionately. "It's your father's work, and you would think if he wants it back, then Mr. Frederick should give it to him. Mr. Frederick is simply a horrid man with no manners, and he hasn't a thimbleful of knowledge about being a gentleman. Perhaps we should ask your father to take his writings elsewhere. I should think that nice man at *The Examiner* would be happy to publish his work and probably pay him more money, too. They've always said wonderful things about his poetry and writings."

"I wasn't talking about Mr. Frederick, Aunt Elle. Look who is standing by that lamppost."

Her aunt gasped with delight. "Why, it's that strong and handsome Mr. Brentwood. What do you suppose he is doing in front of *The Daily Herald*?"

Catalina had a feeling she knew, but turned to her aunt and said, "I don't know why he is here, but I have a feeling we are about to find out. He's walking toward us."

"Good morning, Miss Crisp, Mrs. Gottfried," Mr. Brentwood said as he stopped in front of them.

"So nice to see you again so soon, Mr. Brentwood," her aunt greeted with a smile. "This is a pleasant surprise, isn't it, Catalina?"

Catalina pinned Mr. Brentwood with a questioning gaze and in a low voice murmured, "For now, I'm willing to admit only to it being a surprise." It simply was too much of a coincidence for her to believe they ended up in front of *The Daily Herald* at the same time. But why would the man be following her?

Her aunt gave her a disapproving look, while Mr. Brentwood gave her a chuckle so attractive it felt as if all her senses started dancing.

"If you're looking for your carriage, it should be coming along any moment now. Your driver is making the block."

"Thank you for letting us know, Mr. Brentwood," Aunt Elle said.

Catalina wasn't as easily taken in by the handsome man as was her aunt, so she said, "I'm curious as to how you knew which carriage belonged to us."

"I talked to your driver," he answered.

"Really? That surprises me. Briggs doesn't hear or speak very well."

"I didn't notice," he said charmingly.

"Well, it certainly doesn't matter to me that he's not sitting here on the spot, waiting for us," Aunt Elle said. "It's such a fine day to be standing outside, don't you think, Mr. Brentwood?"

"The best we've had in a long time."

"I hear you've spent several years in Baltimore," Aunt Elle said. "Mr. Gottfried and I wanted to go to America, but there was always so much fighting going on and such ill will between here and there that we never made it. I know things have settled now between the two countries, but I've never been brave enough to set sail. Tell me, sir, is it very different from England?"

"So some say. The winters there are only a little milder than here, but summers are much warmer than London. I found little difference in the landscape or the people. To me, most all seaport towns look alike."

"Nevertheless, I'm sure it's fascinating to be so well-traveled. I would love to hear about that new land sometime."

"It would be my pleasure, Mrs. Gottfried."

"Good. Perhaps you can join Catalina and me for tea again soon."

He glanced at Catalina. Amusement glittered in his eyes. She had the feeling he was letting her know if he couldn't win her over, he would settle for her aunt.

"I'll look forward to an invitation."

Briggs pulled the landau to a stop and set the brake. He started to jump down from the driver's box, but Catalina shook her head to let him know they were not ready to board and leave.

"Splendid," Aunt Elle said, turning back to Catalina with a huge, satisfied smile. "Now, would you mind helping me into the carriage? We had a long wait at Mr. Frederick's office, and I feel in need of a sip of tonic."

"Auntie, I didn't know you brought your tonic with you."

"Of course I did." She smiled and patted Catalina's

cheek affectionately. "I always have a dram or two with me. Unfortunately, not the kind you need for the neck pain you're experiencing. You know, I'm not as young as I used to be, and I never know when I'm going to need a sip of something to invigorate me." She took hold of Mr. Brentwood's hand, and he helped her into the carriage. "Oh, and Mr. Brentwood…"

"Yes, madam?"

"In case Catalina forgets to tell you, we will be at Lady Windham's party. Catalina's dance schedule fills rapidly. Perhaps you should ask her to save a dance for you."

"Thank you, Mrs. Gottfried."

Aunt Elle smiled. "You two stand where I can see you. I'll chaperone you from here. We can't have any of the nosy mamas passing by and starting gossip about courting, now can we?"

Mr. Brentwood turned back to Catalina as her aunt opened the satchel she'd brought with her and began digging through its contents.

"You had neck pain?" he asked with a playful grin lifting one corner of his mouth.

His teasing attitude was infectious, and even though she didn't want to, she had to smile at him. "Yes, and I'm sure you won't find it surprising to hear the pain started late yesterday, shortly after I met you."

He laughed softly, causing a teasing prickle of something wonderful to tighten her breasts. It was maddening that she found him so attractive.

"You're right. I don't find that surprising. I felt a little roughed up myself after I left your house."

Her smile turned into a comfortable grin. It annoyed her that he could be so delightful. "I'm glad to hear it. Now, can you tell me what you are doing here?"

"I was waiting for you to come out."

"Mr. Brentwood, does that mean you are following me?"

His deep blue eyes watched her carefully as he shrugged. "I suppose I am."

Her heartbeat quickened at his bold admission. "That's not the sort of thing a gentleman is supposed to do."

An expression of devilment flashed across his face. "After our meeting yesterday, I'm amazed I left you with the opinion that I'm a gentleman."

Winning a battle of words against him was almost impossible. "Actually, you didn't," she said, keeping her humorous tone. "And obviously it was for a good reason, because you are not."

"So most say."

"And that causes you no anguish?"

For the briefest of moments, Catalina thought she saw a flash of regret in his eyes, reminding her that this man was not as tough as he wanted to appear. And suddenly she realized she had wanted to get the rest of *A Tale of Three Gentlemen* back as much for Mr. Brentwood as for her father. She didn't want to cause this man any more anguish concerning his family.

He glanced down at his hat in his hands before meeting her gaze and saying, "None whatsoever. I freely admit to following you here. I arrived at your house in time to see you and Mrs. Gottfried getting into your landau. I told my driver to stay behind your carriage."

Catalina didn't know if she should be worried or flattered. A chilly breeze whistled past her ears. She welcomed the wind to cool her heating cheeks. She felt flushed and a little disconcerted. "That is how you followed me here, but why were you coming to my house today?"

Mr. Brentwood bowed and smiled at two young ladies and a chaperone who walked past them, and then gave his attention back to her. "I wanted to see if your father had returned after I left last night. I've not hidden from you the fact that I want to speak with him as soon as possible. When I saw you leaving today, I knew if there was any chance you were on your way to meet him, I wanted to be there."

"When we stopped in front of this building, it should have been your first clue that we were not meeting my father, yet you chose to stay out here and wait. Why?"

"To see you. I wanted to talk to you again."

His gentle gaze fluttered softly down her face, lingered on her lips before tipping over her chin and sailing down her neck to the hollow of her throat. Catalina's heart drummed. His gaze took a lazy path up to her eyes again, and she felt a quickening of awareness curl, tighten, and then open and blossom inside her. At that moment, she wondered again if Mr. Brentwood was not only a danger to her father but also to her. She had danced, laughed, and flirted with gentleman after gentleman all last Season, waiting, hoping, and wanting to meet a man who could make her feel all the sensations this man stirred inside her, but none had come close.

Trying to counter her betraying body, she said, "We don't have anything more to say to each other, Mr. Brentwood. I think it would be best if you stayed away from me and from my house."

"That's going to be hard to do, Miss Crisp. You can lead me to something I want."

"My father."

He nodded. "I won't rest until I've spoken with him and had my say."

Catalina took a step toward him, intent on demanding he stay away from her father, when on the other side of the street she saw Mrs. Hildegard Whipple staring at her as she strolled down the boardwalk. Catalina cringed. That woman was the biggest gossip bag in London. The last thing Catalina wanted was to have her name linked with Mr. Brentwood's.

Knowing she needed to get away from him before more people saw them talking, she took a deep breath and simply said, "Good day, Mr. Brentwood."

"Allow me to help you into your carriage?" He held out his hand for her.

Catalina looked at his strong hand and was tempted to reach for it. She remembered how gentle his touch had felt on her cheek and lips, and how inviting the scent of shaving soap was to her senses. She would love to know just how much strength that hand held, but she didn't need any more disturbing memories of him to keep her awake at night. He had already left her with quite enough.

She met his gaze and said, "Thank you, but my driver will do it."

"In that case, until we meet again, Miss Crisp."

He placed his hat on his head and turned and walked away.

On impulse, Catalina called to him. He stopped, removed his hat again, and looked back at her. She lifted her chin. "My aunt spoke out of turn. I will not dance with you at Lady Windham's."

Mr. Brentwood gave her a devilishly handsome grin, and her stomach tightened.

"I wasn't planning on asking you."

She gasped, stunned he would be so bold as to tell her that, even if it was true. As his gaze moved sensually over her face once again, Catalina flushed with heat. And all of a sudden, she realized she felt cheated, bereft. She wanted to dance with him, and she wanted him to *want* to dance with her.

"Mr. Brentwood, I do believe you pride yourself on seeing just how often you can shock me."

He bowed. "I do. I would consider it a great loss to miss an opportunity, even though you make so many available to me. However, dancing with an innocent maiden like yourself might ruin my reputation as a rake. I worked hard to earn it. I can't have anyone thinking I've changed my debauched ways."

"Have no fear of that, sir."

He gave her an appreciative smile. "But you will dance with me one evening, Miss Crisp, so plan on it." He placed his hat back on his head, nodded once, and turned away.

Mr. Brentwood was a man who needed to be put in his place in the worst way. And she would love to be the person to do it. The problem was she hadn't had enough dealings with men to know how to do it.

Unfortunately, Mr. Brentwood knew that.

Catalina forced herself not to stomp her foot as she watched his retreating back. She refused to let him goad her into such childish behavior, though it would feel very good right now to do so. He was by far the most infuriating, stimulating, and arrogant man she had ever met.

She was still watching Mr. Brentwood's imposing back when she heard a horse nicker in alarm. Curious, she stepped closer to the street to see what was going on.

Harnessed to a lightweight carriage, a frightened horse jerked its head and reared in its traces, bucking the young gentleman driver backward off his seat and nearly toppling the gig. Powerful front hooves slammed down on the packed ground a second before the horse crabbed sideways into a passing curricle. That startled the bay even more. He chinned the sky again and screamed, then bolted from the hocks.

At the same time, Catalina saw a small dog limping across the road and heading straight into the path of the runaway horse and gig. She reacted without thinking.

Catalina barely heard her aunt and Mr. Brentwood shout her name over the panic roaring in her ears and the frantic rattle of harness and wheels, but she paid them no mind. She sprinted into the road, leaned over, and scooped the mutt into her arms on the run.

But her success was short-lived.

The toe of her shoe tangled in her hem, and she stumbled to her knees.

Five

The better part of valor is discretion.
—William Shakespeare

IVERSON SAW THE DOG AT THE SAME TIME CATALINA DID, and he started running. His heart hammered. Damnation, he knew she was going to try to save it.

"No, Miss Crisp, don't!" he yelled, dropping his hat and racing toward her at breakneck speed.

But she paid no heed to him or her aunt who was repeatedly shrieking her name.

He watched as Miss Crisp grabbed the dog. It looked as if she was going to get out of the way in time, but suddenly she pitched forward and fell to her knees, clutching the dog to her chest. The horse and carriage barreled straight toward her. Fear like Iverson had never known erupted inside him and spurred him to move faster.

As Iverson grabbed her under the arms and shoved her forward, she flung the dog out of harm's way. A second later, the rig careened by, but not before the big wheel caught his hip a glancing blow, spinning him around. He recoiled from the jolt and pain splintering through him.

"Are you all right?" he asked breathlessly, gently helping Miss Crisp to stand.

"Yes, yes, I'm fine," she said, holding onto his forearms to help steady herself.

She didn't look fine. Her face was pale, and he could tell by the tremble in her hands she knew just how close she'd come to being killed.

Ignoring his pain, Iverson looked around as her aunt came rushing up to them. He saw the Corinthian had finally brought the horse and gig to a stop a short distance away. Not saying a word to anyone, he turned and stomped over to where the young blade sat. Iverson grabbed him by the neckcloth and unceremoniously hauled him down from off of the gig.

"You reckless greenhorn! You almost killed her."

"I'm sorry, sir," the wide-eyed young man mumbled. "I was trying my best to stop the horse. It wasn't my fault."

"Of course it was your fault. You're the driver."

"No, some little street bugger threw a rock with what looked like a slingshot and hit my horse's flank, causing him to bolt."

Iverson tightened his hold on the man's clothing and yanked him up close to his face. "I don't care what happened to the horse. You should have been able to control him. Now get yourself over to a side street and stay off the main roads until you learn a lot more horsemanship than you have now."

Iverson shook his hands free of the man and headed back over to where Miss Crisp and a small crowd had gathered around her. He had to force himself not to limp from the pain in his hip.

"That was an amazing feat of gallantry, Mr. Brentwood," said Mrs. Gottfried. "I can't thank you enough for saving Catalina."

Iverson didn't acknowledge Mrs. Gottfried's praise. He had eyes only for Miss Crisp. "Are you sure you're not hurt?" he asked her.

She lifted her chin and her lashes as she drew in a soft breath. Her beautiful green eyes glistened. He knew she had been as frightened as he. Suddenly, Iverson had a desperate urge to pull her into his arms and hold her until she stopped trembling. He wanted to kiss away the fear that lingered in her expression.

"I'm happy to say only my pride is damaged. I thought I had time to save the dog and get out of the way."

He would have liked to tell her that was a damn foolish thing for her to have done, but he could see she was already admonishing herself, so he tempered his words and said, "You would have, if you hadn't stumbled."

She gave him a grateful smile. "So I like to tell myself. I looked around for the dog. He must have run away. I hope he's all right."

"Don't worry about him. Street dogs learn early how to take care of themselves."

"Do excuse us, Mr. Brentwood," Mrs. Gottfried said. "I think I should get Catalina home now."

"I agree, madam," Iverson said, but he kept his gaze on Miss Crisp.

"Thank you, Mr. Brentwood."

Iverson nodded once before Miss Crisp was ushered away by her aunt. His hip was hurting like hell, but suddenly he felt very good. He didn't mind receiving Miss Crisp's gratitude. He didn't mind it at all.

———

Night had fallen by the time Iverson made it back to his house. His afternoon had been busy, going over monthly account books with his solicitor, and he'd just finished meeting with the gentleman who was looking for a summer home for him in the country. He was hoping to find an estate for sale somewhere close to his older brother's home. But so far, that project was proving difficult to accomplish.

He stepped down from his carriage and winced as his weight landed on his leg. His hip would be sore for a few days, but thankfully, he'd saved Miss Crisp. And she had saved the dog. A shiver of fear shook him when he thought about how close she had come to being trampled by the horse and carriage. He didn't know how, but he'd known the moment he saw the dog that she was going to try to save it. Maybe it was because of how kindly she'd treated her staff, speaking to them gently, helping them do their jobs. Maybe it was just that same perplexing connection he had with Matson. Sometimes he just knew what his brother was going to do and say.

He smiled to himself as he started up his stone walkway. Miss Crisp had been crowding his thoughts off and on all afternoon. He couldn't remember how long it had been since he was this attracted to a young lady. She reminded him of a sunny spring morning: warm and cool at the same time. He liked that about her. He liked a lot of things about her. No, he liked everything about her except the fact that she was Sir Phillip's daughter.

The door opened as Iverson's foot landed on the first step. He swallowed a groan of pain.

"Good evening, sir," Wallace said, holding his hand out for Iverson's hat.

Iverson smiled to himself again. How difficult would it have been yesterday for Mrs. Wardyworth to have greeted him even half as properly as Wallace? He doubted that woman even knew how to hang a coat, let alone how to take one from a guest.

"Your brother is here, sir," his butler said, reaching for Iverson's coat.

"Thank you, Wallace."

"He's been here for quite some time, too. I suggested he wait for you in the drawing room. I had a fire lit to take away the chill, and gave him a book and a drink."

"Good," Iverson said, taking off his gloves.

"Should I pour a glass for you?"

"No need. I'll do it."

"I asked Cook to set a place at the table for him just in case you asked him to stay for dinner."

"I'm sure he'll stay if he doesn't have other plans."

Wallace reached for Iverson's gloves. "May I do anything else for you, sir?"

"No, that will be all for now," Iverson said and turned toward the drawing room. "I'll call if I need you."

Matson had tried to dissuade Iverson from looking for Sir Phillip yesterday, even though he knew it was a lost cause. Iverson had to go. It was a matter of honor.

It was bad enough Sir Phillip's parody implied that his mother betrayed his father; the story also made it seem as if the twins in the story were oblivious to the fact that they looked so much like a well-respected man in town, and of course they weren't. Talking about it—or worse, writing about it—only kept the gossip alive. He was damn ready to put the matter to rest for good. Iverson had to stop Sir Phillip, or he feared others would follow suit. He had to find the man and let him know he meant business, and as much as he hated the thought of it, if need be in the same way he'd let Lord Waldo know his family was not to be discussed.

Their older brother, Brent, had prepped them well for what to expect when they arrived in London, even thinking they might be outcasts in Society. But that couldn't have been further from what happened. From the moment they'd arrived in London, the *ton* had welcomed them with open arms. They were invited to and even celebrated at party after party over the autumn and winter, but that didn't mean people weren't gossiping about them. They were. It was human nature. But most members of the *ton* respected their privacy and didn't bring it up to Iverson and Matson. Not to their faces, anyway. And now that the Season was only weeks away, the invitations to parties, balls, and high-stakes card games had already started stacking up on Iverson's desk.

When Iverson walked into the drawing room, his brother was sitting in a chair by the fire, sipping what looked like a glass of port.

Matson rose quickly when he saw Iverson and said, "Damnation, Iverson, what are you thinking?"

"About what?" he said and strode over to the side table behind the settee to pour himself a glass of the port Wallace left out for him.

"Don't play innocent with me."

Iverson grunted a laugh and said, "In that case, I won't."

"Tell me what happened."

"I thought we had grown past telling each other our secrets, Brother."

"It's not a secret if all of London is talking about it, and I sure as hell don't like being the last one to hear about it. Now,

I can either talk some sense into you or knock some sense into your head right now, if need be."

"You choose," Iverson said, completely unconcerned about his brother's ire.

"What you are doing is not acceptable."

Iverson had had enough of their tit for tat. "Look, Matson, I've had a hellish afternoon, so just get on with it and tell me what you are talking about, because I really have no idea." Making sure he showed no signs of his injury, he walked over to Matson and, without asking, added a splash or two of port into his brother's glass.

"I'm talking about your courting Miss Crisp."

That brought Iverson up short. He frowned. "What are you talking about? I'm not courting Miss Crisp."

"According to several men at the club this afternoon, you are. They all but have you already publishing the banns."

"What the devil?" He might get a hitch in his breath every time he thought about her, but he wasn't planning on marrying her.

"The word is that you two were out for a cozy stroll when she ran into the street to save a dog from certain death, and then you had to save them both."

Iverson laughed ruefully. "What nonsense. We weren't strolling, we were talking. And I didn't save the dog, she did." Iverson replaced the decanter on the table.

"Who saved whom is not as important at the moment as your courting Miss Crisp. I thought you were going to give Sir Phillip a black eye, like you did Lord Waldo, not go after his daughter. That's beyond the pale, even for you."

Matson retook his seat, and Iverson eased down into a comfortable chair to rest his hip. First he had to put up with a servant, and then Mrs. Gottfried thinking he wanted to court Miss Crisp, and now his own brother was giving him trouble.

"Well, what do you have to say for yourself?" Matson asked.

Iverson took a sip of his drink before saying, "I'm not courting Miss Crisp."

"So you just happened upon her on the street and introduced yourself and then proceeded to save her life in front of more than half a dozen people."

"That's fairly close to what happened."

"Don't give me that drivel, Iverson. Yesterday you wanted to ram Sir Phillip's teeth down his throat."

Iverson frowned. "Did I actually say I wanted to do that?"

Matson grimaced and swirled the dark liquid in his glass. "Yes, you did."

"And I probably meant it at the time, too, but I won't do quite that much damage to him when I finally find him. I want only to break his fingers now."

"What?"

Iverson grunted a laugh at the concerned look on Matson's face. He relaxed his shoulders and said, "Don't take me so seriously, Brother. I don't intend to do any physical harm to the man this time. Everyone deserves a warning."

Iverson took a sip and looked at his twin over the glass. He held the port in his mouth for a moment and let it sting his tongue and the back of his throat before swallowing. It was amazing how much he and his brother looked alike, and how much they resembled Sir Randolph.

Only recently had Iverson started wearing his hair much longer than Matson's and pulled back in a queue. There were a few times in his life when it had pleased him to be the mirror image of his brother. Over the years, he and Matson had switched identities more than once to fool playmates, tease young ladies, or confound business associates, but those kinds of games no longer interested either of them. After almost thirty years of being a twin, Iverson needed his own identity, and never more so than when he'd come to London and discovered he not only was the spitting image of his brother, but of Sir Randolph Gibson, too.

Now, though he hated to admit it even to himself, the longer hair and queue was his way of trying to look less like his brother, and if that made him look less like Sir Randolph Gibson, even better. Matson had made subtle changes in his appearance, too. He'd grown a closely cropped, chinstrap beard less than a fourth of an inch wide. It wasn't something he and Matson had spoken about, but since coming back to England they were developing their separate lives, developing different interests and different friends. Even when they were at White's, Matson preferred billiards, and Iverson a game of cards.

"Tell me what happened yesterday after you left our offices," Matson said.

"Sir Phillip wasn't home, so I spoke with Miss Crisp."

"Where is the devil?"

"Miss Crisp didn't know. She said he may not even be in London right now."

"I didn't know the man had a daughter until this afternoon."

"Yesterday she told me she had attended some recent parties, but she always left early."

"Must be why we've missed her. It sounds as if you might have had a lengthy conversation with her if you were talking about parties. And you did meet with her again today. Tell me about her."

She's stunning, lively, alluring, exciting, and delectable.

"I found her challenging to talk to," Iverson said and took another sip of his drink.

"Challenging? That's a rather odd thing to say. Most of the ladies I've met are not challenging in the least."

"How well I know. However, Miss Crisp took one look at me and knew I was quite angry. I couldn't get a straight answer out of her or any of her staff about her father's whereabouts."

"I'm sure that's understandable, considering the temper you were in yesterday. Did you think about finding the groom or footman and exchanging a few coins for a few answers?"

I was too preoccupied with the daughter to think about much of anything except her.

"Not at the time, and judging from the rest of the staff in that house, I'm not so sure either of them would have been much help."

"Why's that?"

Trying to explain Sir Phillip's household to his brother would take more effort than Iverson was willing to expend at the moment. "They were all very protective of the poet."

"Well, I can't say that is a bad thing," Matson muttered. "That's what servants are supposed to do for their employers. Tell me more about Miss Crisp. How old is she?"

"I'd say nineteen, or possibly twenty."

"Lovely?" Matson questioned.

Iverson felt his breathing kick up a notch just thinking about Miss Crisp. "Quite."

"So how was it you happened upon her on the street today?"

"I followed her from her house."

Matson gave him a wary look. "You didn't."

"Oh, but I did."

"So, tell me this, are you going to try to get back at Sir Phillip by ruining his daughter?"

"Of course not." Iverson looked hard at his brother. "You know me better than that."

"I thought I did, but Lord Waldo did end up with a black eye. Come to think of it, I don't think you ever admitted to doing that."

"I've never had a reason to address it, and I still don't. Furthermore, I don't have any intentions of doing anything to harm Miss Crisp or her reputation. I was following her in hopes she would lead me to Sir Phillip. Does that settle everything for you, Brother?"

Matson sighed heavily. "Of course. I suppose I jumped to conclusions when I heard you were courting Miss Crisp."

"Good. I told you I would handle this with Sir Phillip, and I will."

"And speaking of brothers," Matson said to change the subject, "I'm glad Brent wasn't here to read *A Tale of Three Gentlemen*."

"I'm sure he will as soon as the mail coach can get the newsprint to him."

"Let's hope he gets only the *Times* and not *The Daily Herald*. Or if he gets them both, we'll hope Gabrielle keeps him so occupied with other things he hasn't the time to read them."

Iverson chuckled. "Now that is quite possible. I do believe he worries more about our parentage than we do. Last I heard, they are still planning to come to London for the Season."

"That's what I heard, too."

"Wallace had Cook set a place for you. Are you staying for dinner?"

Matson seemed to relax. "I might as well, since I'm here. Afterward, we can head over to Harbor Lights or White's for a hand or two of cards and a game of billiards. It's been a long time since I've won any blunt off you."

Iverson smiled. "And it will be a long time before you do because you're not as good as I am."

"Those are fighting words, Brother, and I'm going to have to prove you wrong on that."

They both laughed, and then Iverson said, "You can try."

"You know, I just thought of something."

"Something worth sharing, I hope," Iverson teased.

Matson picked up his glass from the floor and drained it as he walked over to the side table. He poured himself another splash and said, "Have you thought about paying a visit to the owner of *The Daily Herald*?"

"It crossed my mind. I can do that, if I have to, but for now I think the better approach is to keep Sir Phillip from writing anything more. It can't be published if it isn't written."

"True," Matson said and added port to Iverson's glass. "You can also consider making a visit to Bow Street and hiring a runner to find out where the man is holed up."

But neither of those would put him in touch with Miss Crisp again, and right now, seeing her was almost as important as finding her father.

"Hopefully, Sir Phillip will return in the next day or two, so it won't come to my doing either of those things. In fact, I'm definitely going back to the man's house tomorrow to see if he has returned."

"And no doubt you will see his daughter while you are there."

Iverson smiled. "Of course." He couldn't wait for her to skewer him once again with her flashing green eyes and sharp words.

Matson chuckled and shook his head. "Just stay out of trouble."

"I intend to."

"Now, tell me what's wrong with your leg. You're not limping, but I know something is wrong."

Iverson slowly shook his head and rubbed his forehead. It was hell being a twin.

Six

You may conquer with the sword, but
you are conquered by a kiss.
—Daniel Heinsius

CATALINA FELT WONDERFUL.

She woke to glorious sunshine filling her room. London had its third day in a row of mild temperatures and blue skies. All night she had dreamed about Mr. Brentwood's Herculean effort to save her yesterday. He left her feeling protected, and that was a heavenly feeling. She would never forget his strong and gentle hands grasping her arms, lifting her to safety, and helping her to stand. She'd never forget the concern she saw in his eyes when she was in danger or the relief on his features when she was out of harm's way. But more than those, she would remember that he didn't admonish her for risking her life to save a mongrel.

After she'd dressed and gone below stairs, Catalina asked for her morning tea and biscuits to be served in the garden so she could enjoy the too-infrequent sunshine. She was in the back parlor gathering up the morning's newsprint to take outside with her to read when Mrs. Wardyworth called to her from the doorway.

She turned to her housekeeper and said, "Yes?"

"Miss Mable Taylor and Miss Agatha Harris are here to see you."

Catalina wrinkled her nose in surprise. Mable usually sent a note when she was going to visit. She didn't like wasting time stopping by someone's house only to find they weren't available. She liked people to know she was going to pay a call, so they could respond if it was an inconvenient time. And Catalina really didn't know Miss Agatha Harris very well at all. She remembered talking to her a few times during last Season, but that was almost a year ago. Agatha always seemed a sweet person and the complete opposite in looks and manner from the bold, blond, and petite Miss Mable Taylor. Agatha was a tall, broad-shouldered, and quiet young lady. Catalina often thought of her as a gentle giant.

Catalina looked at the clock and saw it was well past noon, so it was perfectly acceptable for them to call on her to see if she was accepting visitors. No doubt they'd heard about the incident in the street yesterday and wanted to make sure she was all right.

"Show them into the drawing room, Mrs. Wardyworth, and tell them I'll be right in."

Catalina laid down her newsprint and looked at her dress. She had donned a long-sleeved, sprigged morning dress that wasn't one of her best, but she supposed she looked presentable enough in it, considering she wasn't expecting anyone. With funds always so tight, it had been more than a couple of years since she'd had any new morning dresses made.

Placing a smile on her face, she walked into the drawing room, saying, "Good afternoon, ladies. What a pleasant surprise to see you. I'm glad you made yourselves comfortable. Mrs. Wardyworth, please have Nancy prepare tea and tarts for us."

As soon as her housekeeper cleared the doorway, both girls jumped up from the settee and started talking at once.

"Oh, aren't you simply devastated?" Mable said.

"Will you ever be able to show your face in Society again?" Agatha asked.

Mable took hold of Catalina's hand. "We came as soon as we could to comfort you."

Catalina glanced from one lady to the next. They looked so distraught she knew something terrible must have happened to her father.

"What's wrong? Has something happened to Papa? What have you heard about him?"

"Your father?" Mable asked curiously. "How would we know anything about your father?"

"Oh, dear, no," Agatha said. "I pray there's nothing wrong with him. That would be too much to bear on top of this morning's news."

A wave of relief washed through Catalina. "Thank goodness for that. You had me frightened."

"I don't think she's seen it," Agatha said, looking wide-eyed at Mable.

"I agree." A sharp gleam appeared in Mable's eyes. "I'm sorry we have to be the ones to tell you about this, but, well, maybe it will be better if we show it to you."

"Show me what? You two are making no sense whatsoever. Tell me what you're talking about."

Mable jerked open her reticule and pulled out a sheet of newsprint and thrust it toward Catalina. "Read this from Lord Truefitt's column in today's edition."

Catalina tensed. She hadn't read it. But she had a feeling she knew exactly what the famous gossip columnist had written about. Swallowing her trepidation, she took the paper, looked down at it, and read:

> Roses are red
> Violets are blue
> Look who's walking
> Shoe to shoe.

It's on excellent authority I can be the first to report to you that Miss Catalina Crisp and Mr. Iverson Brentwood were recently seen standing so closely together on a street corner that the toes of their shoes touched, and in the next moment, he was gallantly rescuing her from certain death by a runaway horse and carriage. One has to wonder if the poet's daughter thinks she can be the one to leg-shackle the Rake of Baltimore? She seems to already have him by his toes!

—Lord Truefitt, *Society's Daily Column*

"Oh, that's an absolutely dreadful attempt at poetry!" Catalina said as she handed the newsprint back to Mable.

"Poetry?" Mable questioned with eyes wide in disbelief. "Your name is linked to the Rake of Baltimore's in the scandal sheet and all you can say is the poetry is dreadful?"

"Well, it is," Catalina insisted. "I do wish the man had been a little cleverer with his verse."

By the shocked expressions on both the ladies' faces, Catalina knew she didn't give them the reaction they were expecting. She continued, "But, no, that's not all I can say about it. I mean, I don't appreciate Lord Truefitt's mentioning me in connection with Mr. Brentwood. In fact, I suppose I am quite bothered by it, but if he was going to write poetry, he could have at least made it worth reading."

"You don't sound bothered," Mable said in an almost accusing tone.

Catalina looked from one lady to the other. She had never been any good at fibbing. She wasn't bothered by it, and she supposed she should be. After all, Mr. Brentwood had threatened her father. But how could she be too upset with a man who had risked his own life to save hers?

"Of course I am," she said, trying harder to sound affronted and please the ladies. "Besides, everyone knows violets are purple, not blue."

Agatha gasped. "You're still talking about poetry. And violets are violet and not purple at all!"

"You both are talking about uninteresting poetry and flowers!" Mable exclaimed in an annoyed tone. "Catalina, Lord Truefitt makes it sound as if you were having a tryst or an assignation with the Rake of Baltimore and you got caught when you were almost run down in the street."

"Oh, don't be ridiculous, Mable. I certainly haven't had a tryst with Mr. Brentwood or anyone else for that matter."

"Then perhaps you are allowing him to court you," Agatha suggested.

"That must be it, because all you seem to care about is the verse and the color of flowers."

Catalina didn't like feeling as if she had to defend herself to Mable, but she supposed she needed to try again. And use a different tactic.

"Mr. Brentwood and I just happened to be on the same street at the same time. I was trying to save a dog from being hit by a runaway horse. If I don't seem as concerned as you think I should be, it's probably because I've never been in a gossip column before. I don't quite know how to take it or what to make of it. Perhaps I feel if I don't talk about what Lord Truefitt's written, it will be as if it wasn't written."

"Everyone knows why he ran out into the street, to save you, of course, but why were you standing so close to him on the boardwalk that your noses touched?" Agatha asked.

Catalina gasped in outrage. "It didn't say our noses touched. It said our toes. And not even our toes touched. Lord Truefitt wrote nothing about our noses. No doubt that's how gossip starts, Agatha."

"But you were with him?" Mable asked.

"No, I wasn't with him. We met quite by accident, and we were just talking. My aunt was with me, and my shoes never touched Mr. Brentwood's," Catalina reiterated again, becoming quite perturbed that she had to explain herself to these two ladies who were supposed to be her friends.

"Well, you know the only thing Mr. Brentwood does is break innocent ladies' hearts. My cousin told me all about him in a letter. He ruined more than one young lady in Baltimore and rightly deserves the title that marks him." She paused and turned to Catalina. "Court him if you like, but remember he's a confirmed bachelor and not the marrying kind."

"Marry?" This was getting more exasperating. "No one has said anything about courting or marriage, Mable."

"But of course you were thinking about making a match with him?" Mable said with a sly smile. "Ladies always dream about marrying a rake."

Suddenly Catalina knew what this visit was all about. Obviously the girl had set her cap for the handsome Rake of Baltimore and was jealous Catalina's name was the one linked to his by the gossip.

Thankfully, Catalina heard teacups rattling and knew Nancy was coming with tea. She would do her best to change the subject and hurry these ladies through their refreshments and out the door.

———————

By the time Catalina got rid of the chatty girls, her nerves were frayed and all she wanted to do was sit in her back garden by herself. She had a comfortable cushioned chair placed in the center of the lawn, where she wouldn't be shaded by the yew hedge, shrubs, or trees, and made herself cozy. She had thought to read, but when she laid her head back, her eyes closed, and even though she knew her aunt would have a fit of hysteria if she saw her, Catalina lifted her unprotected face to the warm sun.

She relaxed into the chair and let the heat bathe and soothe her. She didn't want to think about Lord Truefitt's gossip, her absent father, the mounting debts, the next installment of the story, or the handsome and intriguing Mr. Brentwood. She wanted only to sit quietly, alone in the garden, and enjoy the sunshine.

It felt so glorious and relaxing, she soon felt drowsy. She thought she might even take a nap. What a luxury that would be.

"All that sun will make your skin blotchy."

Catalina wrinkled her forehead but didn't open her eyes. She smiled to herself. That sounded like Mr. Brentwood, but it couldn't be he. He hadn't been announced, and there was no way he could get into the garden. She smiled and rolled her shoulders reflexively and sank deeper into the plush cushions of the chair.

That man was like a bad penny. Always showing up and invading her thoughts. Now she was thinking she heard him talking to her. No matter that he was the hero of her dreams, she wasn't going to let him disturb her tranquility.

She laughed softly and said, "Good. If I look red and freckled, maybe you won't devour me with that charming, intense blue gaze that tries to see inside my soul."

"Is that the way you feel when I look at you?"

"Yes, and it's quite maddening. You are disturbing my peace. Go away and leave me alone with my quiet and my thoughts."

"Are your thoughts about me, Catalina?"

"Right now, they are."

"What are you thinking?"

"That you are a handsome, brutish rogue who has no boundaries."

Suddenly, a soft, manly chuckle sounded very near to her ear and very real to her senses. She tensed, and her throat went dry. All at once she had the feeling she wasn't alone. And she wasn't dreaming or just thinking she heard Mr. Brentwood's voice. Her lashes fluttered up, and against the bright glare of the sun she saw Mr. Brentwood towering over her.

"Oh," she exclaimed and jumped to her feet. "What are you doing here? How did you get in the garden?"

He smiled. "I'm here to see you, of course. Your aunt told me you were in the garden and to come on out, and she would collect a shawl and bonnet from her bedchamber and join us directly."

Catalina was mortified she had been talking to him when she thought she was only daydreaming about him. "Why didn't you let me know you were here?"

His head quirked to the side, and his brow wrinkled. "I believe I just did. When I spoke to you, you answered."

"That's because I was thinking, I mean dreaming, or something," she said, desperately trying not to become flustered. "I didn't know you were actually standing beside me."

One side of his mouth lifted in a half grin, and he looked a devilish brute. A handsome, intriguing, and alluring devilish brute who seemed to get the best of her time and time again.

"So which is it? Were you dreaming about me or thinking about me?"

A teasing sparkle shone in his eyes. It was maddening, but Catalina was an easy target for his charm. She inhaled deeply and said, "Neither, I'm sure. I must have been napping, so I have no idea what you said or what I answered."

"Then I'll tell you."

"Please don't do that. I'm quite embarrassed enough. Just allow me to thank you one more time for your heroic effort yesterday. If you hadn't been there—" She paused.

He gave her an understanding smile, and she appreciated it more than he would ever know. She supposed she was a lot like her father after all. She couldn't allow even a stray dog to be hurt if there was anything she could do to stop it.

"If I hadn't been there, nothing would have happened. You would have gotten in your carriage and been gone long before the Corinthian lost control of his horse. But I didn't come here for more gratitude from you."

She laughed, knowing she sounded a little nervous and not sure why. "Ah, yes, I should have known. You are here because you want to know if my father has returned, and he has not."

A teasing light glistened in his eyes. "Yes, I was going to ask about your father, but that's not why I came over, either."

"No?" she questioned, feeling a moment of unease.

"I'm here because I thought you might be disturbed about today's edition of Lord Truefitt's column. You did see it, didn't you?"

"Yes, but no, it didn't upset me."

"Really?" His eyebrows rose a little. "And here I thought I would be needed to soothe your ruffled feathers."

She smiled at him. "Not in the least. I know I have no designs on you, so what the man wrote is of no interest to me. Furthermore, anyone who knows me would never believe I have set my cap for someone like you."

He laid his hand on his chest and made an expression of shock. "Someone like me? The much-maligned Rake of Baltimore? You wound me to the core, Miss Crisp."

His antics were so dramatic. He looked so stricken Catalina laughed freely, even though she truly didn't want to. If only he wasn't a threat to her father, she would be free to enjoy his humor, his attention, and the wonderful feelings he created inside her. "If I could, believe me, I would."

He chuckled, too, and she liked the fact that she'd made him laugh.

"You do like to tell me exactly what you are thinking, don't you?"

Not all the time.

"Someone needs to, Mr. Brentwood, and I am up to the task."

"Immensely so, and one of the things I find impressive about you is your honesty."

Catalina's laughter fell silent in her throat. Oh, why did he have to say that? She was not honest with him about *A Tale of Three Gentlemen*. She wondered again if she should tell him about the other two parts of the story. She wanted to hold out hope her father would make it back to Town and speak to Mr. Frederick before the rest of the series was published. Was she being foolish by waiting, or was she being prudent and avoiding unnecessary problems?

She lowered her lashes. "It's not my intention to impress you concerning anything."

"Perhaps that is why you do. And perhaps since you are not upset about Lord Truefitt's column today, it won't upset your father, either."

"My father?" she asked, lifting her gaze to his once again. "Oh, I hadn't thought about it, but I suppose he will be livid when he reads it."

"That would be welcome news," Mr. Brentwood said.

"Oh, but he would never show it."

"Really?" he questioned. "Why not?"

"He's much too kind. He would never tell Lord Truefitt or anyone else they should try harder to write better poetry. I mean, starting a verse with 'roses are red, violets are blue' shows he has no talent for poetry. He should leave that to distinguished poets and stay with his gossip, which he does much better."

Iverson laughed heartily.

Catalina was disconcerted for a moment. "What has caused you so much amusement?"

"You."

Her eyes widened. "Me?"

"Yes. I was hoping when your father saw your name linked with the Rake of Baltimore in the gossip pages he would fear your reputation was in jeopardy and come running home to protect you. But you didn't see past the bad poetry."

Catalina's breath shortened in anticipation of what his words implied. She hadn't thought about the possibility of the article bringing her father home. But it had been impossible to think at all earlier with Mable and Agatha's constant chatter. But Mr. Iverson could be right. No doubt scandalous gossip about her would bring her father home quickly. And then he could convince Mr. Frederick to return the last of *A Tale of Three Gentlemen*.

Her spirits lifted.

"Perhaps you are right. This might be just the ticket to bring Papa home. He's never been away this long before."

"Perhaps his muse has led him on a merry chase, and he can't find it."

She smiled again. "I think that is a given, Mr. Brentwood."

"Well, if Lord Truefitt's column today doesn't bring him rushing back, we can always up the stakes."

"What do you mean?"

"I can make sure several people overhear me saying I intend to make you my next conquest. Or I could make it even worse by pronouncing we will be married before the Season starts."

Catalina's heart started pounding. "You wouldn't dare."

"On the contrary, Miss Crisp, by now you should know I will dare anything."

"But that would be outrageous. Clearly Lord Truefitt has already written enough."

He stepped closer to her and then looked down at his feet to make sure the toes of his boots touched the toes of her light-brown slippers. Catalina looked down, too. Suddenly the friendly atmosphere around them changed to something very intimate.

When they both looked up again, their gazes met, and he said, "Maybe, and maybe not."

He was so close she felt heat radiating from his body. She suddenly felt as if a swarm of butterflies had been let loose in her stomach. "No one would believe you if you spoke such rubbish."

"Oh, I think they might if I was caught stealing a kiss from you right here in your garden."

Catalina suddenly felt mesmerized by him. *A kiss?* Why did the thought of a kiss from him leave her breathless?

"You wouldn't," she whispered, knowing she very much wanted him to do just that.

He reached up and caressed her cheek with the backs of his fingers as he had that first day they met. And his touch sent sizzling tingles all through her.

"You know I would," he said huskily.

"But Aunt Elle could come out at any moment."

"She probably will, but right now I want to kiss you, and it's a chance I'm willing to take."

His tone, his closeness, made her stomach quiver deliciously. She had no desire to move away from what he was promising. Teasing warmth tingled across her breasts and spiraled down to the deepest part of her abdomen.

He lowered his head and leaned his body forward until his lips lightly grazed hers with the merest amount of pressure. The contact was sweet, light, and enticing. Catalina didn't know why, but her eyes closed and her lips parted naturally the moment his touched hers. She felt the strong beat of her heart in her ears. His lips were warm, soft, and moist. They lingered over hers as if he were savoring something deliciously rare. A small sigh of wonderment escaped her lips. She drank in the moment and enjoyed all the sweet sensations that bubbled up inside her at the momentous occasion of her first kiss.

He lifted his mouth no more than an inch from hers. His gaze locked on hers, and he whispered, "That sounded like a very satisfied sigh."

He raised his head only a little and said, "Did you know I've wanted to kiss you since I saw you walking toward me in your home?"

She lowered her head as she shook it. Could she be as truthful and tell him he had reminded her of the hero in all her romantic dreams?

"Look at me," he said and tenderly placed his fingertips under her chin, lifting her head. "It's true. You are a very desirable lady."

Something amazingly inviting seemed to curl protectively around her, and she felt comfortable saying, "I've been reading about kisses since my father gave me my first book of romantic poetry when I was fourteen years old, but I—"

"But this was the first time you've been kissed, right?"

She nodded. "I didn't know it would be so..."

"Tell me." He smiled sweetly. "So what?"

"Delicious and thrilling. I wanted to savor it."

"So it was everything you expected it to be."

"No, more. I didn't know I would be so eager for another kiss."

He chuckled softly. "I didn't expect you to say that, but I'm glad you did."

She moistened her lips and then said, "The kiss was also softer than I expected it to be."

He raised his hand and traced the curve of her upper lip with his middle finger as his forearm rested gently, softly on her chest between her breasts. The intimacy of his touch made her abdomen tighten.

"Ah," he said. "I can fix that. A first kiss should always be soft, tender, and memorable, but the second can and should be passionate."

"Passion?" she whispered. "I've read about it so many times."

"And now you want to feel it?"

"Can I?" she asked eagerly.

"Oh, yes. I'll show you."

His lips came down to hers again, but this time with confident, commanding pressure. She responded by instinct and parted her lips. His tongue darted inside her mouth and explored with slow, sensual movements. Catalina's stomach tightened, and her heart fluttered erratically.

The kiss deepened as his lips moved urgently, seductively over hers. She loved the feel of his lips, the taste of his mouth on hers. She couldn't seem to stop herself from sighing again, because the pleasure was so immense.

Now she knew why Juliet didn't want to live without Romeo's kiss.

Without thinking, Catalina leaned into his body. His hands circled her waist, slid to her back, and suddenly she was caught up against his strong chest. Her arms automatically wound around his neck. Wondrous curls of unexpected pleasure came instantly alive inside her, and she melted against him. She had often dreamed of being held in a man's powerful embrace, her breasts flattened against his wide chest, but she hadn't been able to imagine just how heavenly it actually felt.

Catalina gasped over and over again as his tongue brushed hers, teasing her with featherlight contact. His gentle hands and strong arms pressed her closer and closer to the warmth and hardness of his body.

It was a heady, powerful experience, but all too soon his lips left hers. His arms relaxed around her.

With a ragged, husky voice, he whispered, "I think we may have tempted fate enough for one afternoon."

He let go of her slowly. The magic of the moment was broken. Catalina inhaled a deep breath and stepped away from him, too, quickly putting the lawn chair between them.

Had she actually told him she was eager for another kiss? She cringed inside. What had made her say such a thing? And to this man!

She cleared her throat and said, "Why did you say you came to see me?"

A half chuckle whispered deeply from his throat. "A kiss will do that to you."

"What?" she asked with genuine curiosity about what he thought.

"Make you forget everything but the moment of the kiss."

"Yes, I believe that's true."

"But to answer your first question, remember, I wanted to make sure you weren't too upset about Lord Truefitt's column."

"Yes, right, and no, as I've told you—" She realized

she was mumbling. "I'm…curious about something, Mr. Brentwood."

"Yes?"

"Did you—?" She cleared her throat. "I mean, do gentlemen feel the same extraordinary sensations women do when they are kissed?"

He stepped closer to the chair that separated them. "You are asking if I felt the same way you did just now."

She swallowed hard, not sure she really wanted to know the answer but nodding her head anyway.

His gaze locked onto hers. "Yes, Catalina. My God, yes."

"I've read about this, this magic, this desire between a man and a woman, but I never could have imagined how it actually feels."

"It's quite intoxicating, is it not?"

"Exhilarating and invigorating, too," she answered softly. "Thank you for kissing me."

"It was my pleasure."

Iverson's gaze swept easily down her face and then back up to her eyes. His smile was so sincere she started to reach for him.

Catalina heard the back door open. She looked up to see Aunt Elle coming down the steps, wrapping her shawl about her shoulders. Catalina let out a wispy breath of relief. Her aunt was just in time to save her from saying something she would regret. She had been just about to ask Mr. Brentwood to kiss her again.

Seven

We have met the enemy and they are ours.
—Oliver Hazard Perry

MISS CATALINA CRISP HAD SET HIM ON FIRE.

He really shouldn't have kissed her until his grievance with her father was settled, but her allure had been impossible to resist. Even now, as he stood on her front stoop, pulling on his gloves, he was reluctant to leave. He wanted to find a reason to go back inside, get her alone, and kiss her again. But he would have to wait to see her until later tonight at Lady Windham's party. She drew him as surely as when the hot days of Baltimore's summers had beckoned him to the waters for a cooling, refreshing swim.

When he'd first met her, had he really told her he would grab her father by the neckcloth and threaten to break his fingers?

He shook his head and grunted a laugh. That was not his finest moment. Though in truth, if he'd actually found the man at home, instead of his daughter, he would have threatened Sir Phillip in some way.

Obviously, old habits die hard.

Because of his temperament, being the difficult brother had come easy for him when he and Matson first went to Baltimore. And not from want of trying, that hadn't changed since he'd returned to London. At the time, he and Matson didn't know why, but their father had insisted they move to America and open Brentwood's Sea Coast Ship Building Company for him. In England, it was unheard of for sons of a titled man to manage one of their father's businesses, but no one gave it a second thought in America.

But Iverson and Matson were Englishmen through and through, and the new country couldn't compete with their homeland. Their father had died, and they had gotten older. They wanted to move their business and settle in London.

At first, they had felt as if their father had placed them in exile, even though they had been given a generous allowance. It hadn't been easy to accomplish anything in the new country. Because of continued tensions between the Americans and the British, Iverson and Matson had to hide their roots in British aristocracy. They worked twice as hard for every scrap of business they obtained. There wasn't much time for their own pleasure, because they didn't want to squander the opportunity to form a successful company. Over the course of time, he and his brother had developed a solution that had worked well for them—the good twin/bad twin scenario.

Growing up, Iverson had always been the daring and adventurous twin. He was the first to jump to conclusions and be ready to do battle. It just came naturally to him to be impatient, intense, and impulsive.

In business matters, Iverson would take on anyone and everyone, remaining firm on his stand, arguing his point, and sounding tough as steel when he asked for more than they wanted. He never budged an inch on the issue at hand. Matson would then come in after him, acting in a conciliatory and approachable way, willing to compromise for something less than Iverson had insisted on. Their strategy had worked to get exactly what they wanted almost every time. Now that their business was well established and flourishing, their customers happy, the antics of the earlier days were no longer necessary.

But Iverson's demeanor hadn't changed. He never backed down from a challenge, no matter the stakes, as when Lord Waldo had approached him in the taproom of the Harbor Lights Gentlemen's Club last autumn. The weak-kneed ninny had the gall to ask him why he looked so much like Sir Randolph Gibson.

Without thinking, Iverson had punched the man. It wasn't that Iverson liked being a bullyrag, but sometimes that was the only thing that worked.

Iverson turned to step off the stoop, when he saw a gentleman hurrying up the walkway toward the house.

Sir Randolph Gibson.

Iverson tensed. Why was that dandy coming to Sir Phillip's house?

Iverson had been introduced to Sir Randolph months ago at a ball. He was a tall, robust fellow with a thatch of silver hair that helped give him the appearance of a much younger man. He was still quite dapper and dashing for a man well past his glory days.

They had seen each other at numerous parties around Town, but Iverson had never had a conversation with him. It seemed to be an unspoken truce between them that they left each other alone.

Iverson mentally started sorting through the snatches of conversations he'd heard about Sir Randolph Gibson. The old man was well respected and extremely well liked among the *ton*, especially with the widows. They could always count on him for a dance at the balls, afternoon rides in Hyde Park, or much-coveted invitations to sit with him in his opera box.

Iverson seldom saw the dandy without at least one of three cousins at his side: the Duke of Blakewell, the Marquis of Raceworth, or the Earl of Morgandale. Iverson and Matson had laughingly referred to them as his three puppet bodyguards. There was sensational gossip that the three had saved him from losing his wealth in such risky business ventures as a hot air balloon travel business and a time machine. There was also a rumor that the man had been involved in a boxing match over some lady's honor, though Iverson had his doubts that was true.

He knew there was no bloodline between Sir Randolph and the titled gentlemen. The rumor was that Sir Randolph had had a long-standing relationship with the cousins' grandmother. Iverson didn't know what kind of relationship they had, but he could make an educated guess. No doubt the man's considerable wealth and lack of legitimate heirs were the main reasons the cousins were so eager to step in and watch out for him.

The older gentleman slowed his steps when he saw Iverson. Sir Randolph masked his astonishment at suddenly being trapped under the front portico with Iverson and pleasantly said, "Good afternoon, Mr. Brentwood. Beautiful weather to be out and about, isn't it?"

The man was good at covering for himself and acting as if he wasn't as shocked as Iverson at their chance meeting.

Iverson nodded. "What brings you here?"

The old man eyed him warily, and his brow wrinkled into a frown of curiosity. "I could ask you the same thing, but if what I read in the scandal sheets today is true, I don't have to."

Iverson didn't bother trying to deny the story that he was courting Miss Crisp and said, "I was looking for Sir Phillip."

Sir Randolph's face relaxed a little. "That's what I'm doing, too."

"In that case, I can save you a lot of trouble. The man is not at home."

Sir Randolph cocked his head and scrunched his forehead tighter. "Are you sure? Maybe he's just hiding somewhere in his house, writing more of his poetry and stories."

Iverson grunted a laugh and was tempted to say, *"After what I went through a couple of days ago, hell yes, I'm sure."* But instead, he said, "I exhausted every possibility. I'm convinced the man's not here."

"That's too bad. I would really like to have a few words with the fellow before the day is over. I was at my home in Norfolk when I received my copy of *The Daily Herald* and read *A Tale of Three Gentlemen*. I came back to London early just to have a few words with him. Perhaps I'll wait for him."

Iverson grimaced. "I tried that a couple of days ago, and his daughter wasn't fond of that idea."

Sir Randolph grunted. "I suppose I can understand that. What were you told in regards to when he will return?"

"I wasn't able to get a conclusive answer about that. I was told I should check back at a later time. So that's what I've been doing. Every day."

The old man seemed to consider what Iverson said. He finally nodded and said, "Then I guess that leaves me with no choice but to do the same. He's bound to show up sooner or later."

"After talking to Miss Crisp, it's believable to me that Sir Phillip is an indolent fellow who walks around with his head in the clouds."

"It appears we are alike in our thinking about him."

Iverson's eyes narrowed, and he shifted his stance. He was certain that wasn't something he wanted to hear. "That depends."

Sir Randolph cocked his head again. "On what?"

"Did you approve or disapprove of what he wrote?"

Understanding dawned in the old man's eyes. "It's clear you don't know me, or you wouldn't have to ask that. I don't mind enlightening you. I intend to see that Sir Phillip keeps his stories, parodies, thoughts, or whatever he calls them, to himself from now on. I don't think any more of his nonsense will show up after I have a talk with him."

The old man was full of surprises. "In that case, maybe we do think alike. But you don't have to bother coming back to see him. I have this handled."

Sir Randolph chuckled low in his throat and shook his head. "As I said, you obviously don't know me. This is a matter of honor to me, Mr. Brentwood. I'll have my say with Sir Phillip."

"Understood."

"I would appreciate it if you would let me know when you hear he's back in Town."

There was something to be said for the fact that Sir Randolph didn't let Iverson scare him off. He kept his gaze tight on the old man's eyes and said, "You do the same."

"You can count on it."

The dandy turned and started back down the walkway. Iverson called back to him, "Sir Randolph."

He stopped and looked over his shoulder at Iverson.

"Do you have any idea where Sir Phillip might be?"

"What did his daughter say about why he was away?"

Thinking of Miss Crisp made Iverson give a rueful smile. "Only that he left to follow his muse."

"Ah, that must mean he has a mistress. I'll ask around at the clubs and see if I can find out where he spends his time."

Iverson hadn't thought about the idea he might be with a woman. The old man was sharp as the point of a needle, but that didn't mean Iverson trusted him. "You'll let me know?"

Sir Randolph nodded once and started down the walkway.

Why hadn't it occurred to Iverson that Sir Phillip could be spending a few days with his mistress? Now that he thought about it, it made sense. If that was where the poet was, he certainly wouldn't want his daughter to know.

Eight

*However much we may distrust men's
sincerity, we always believe they speak to
us more sincerely than to others.*
—François de La Rochefoucauld

IVERSON WALKED UP THE STEPS TO LADY WINDHAM'S
opulent Mayfair home, thankful he had no lasting pains from
the injury to his hip. He left his hat, coat, and gloves with
the servant at the front door. He stopped at the doorway to
the drawing room. Staring into the crowded room reminded
him why he always went to parties late.

He hated crowds.

Whether in Baltimore or London, Iverson didn't like
being crushed shoulder to shoulder and elbow to elbow
with people he didn't know well and had no intention of
getting to know well. The music was always loud and lively,
and no matter how cold the nights were outside, inside
the rooms were always hot and stuffy from hundreds of
burning candles and lamps. The reek of cooked foods and
liquor hung in the air, mixing with pungent perfumes,
stale smoke, and scented beeswax. It was enough to turn
any man into a recluse. And even though Lady Windham's
house was one of the largest in Mayfair, it was no excep-
tion to the general rule of a crush. The Society-led lady

couldn't bring herself to be judicious in the number of people she invited.

Ballrooms mobbed with revelers were only a little better in grand places like the Great Hall, so arriving late had always suited Iverson. It usually meant the crowds had thinned. The musicians were tired and played softer and slower music. The reverberation of chatter and laughter of the guests had slowed to a low hum, and the candles had burned low. That was when Iverson liked to enter a party.

But he wasn't at Lady Windham's for the merrymaking this evening, or for the three lovely young ladies who were smiling at him across the crowded way. He was there for one reason only, and that was Miss Crisp. She had told him she always came early and left early. For reasons Iverson didn't quite understand, he was dying to see her again, so he swallowed his desire to leave and walked farther into the house.

After searching every face in the assembly and every corner of the drawing room, Iverson didn't see any sign of Miss Crisp. He turned and strode down the corridor to the next room, which unfortunately was just as crowded with beautifully gowned ladies and impeccably dressed gentlemen, but he quickly spotted his prey. Iverson's lower body throbbed at the sight of her.

She was a vision of loveliness, with her hair loosely swept up, a thin rope of delicate-looking white flowers entwined throughout her shiny dark locks. The alabaster-colored gown she wore was banded at the high waist, the hem, and the short capped sleeves with a wide copper-colored ribbon. A cascade of pearl earrings dangled from her ears, but she wore no jewelry around her neck, leaving the hollow of her beautiful throat and chest bare, sensuous, and ever so tempting.

She stood in the arc of three gentlemen who were vying for her attention. She smiled and talked to all of them.

As he watched her for a few moments, he could see she favored one of the gentlemen over the others, and that made Iverson's stomach tighten. The only thing he knew about the man who had caught her eye was he had become the latest Earl of Bighampton about a year ago.

"Miss Catalina Crisp is beautiful, isn't she?"

Iverson turned and saw Lord Waldo standing beside him. Damnation. Iverson tensed. What had possessed the sap to come up and speak to him, and what was he doing letting a greenhorn catch him watching Miss Crisp?

"Very," Iverson muttered more to himself than to the duke's brother.

"She doesn't come to very many parties. She's very elusive, which is why she's always wrapped up by hopefuls seeking her attention when she does Society the favor of coming out for an evening."

Lord Waldo paused, and Iverson wondered if the man expected him to make a comment. He remained quiet. Iverson had seen Lord Waldo on several occasions since their disastrous first meeting shortly after Iverson arrived in London, but the two hadn't spoken. He had nothing to say to the man. In fact, he was surprised Lord Waldo had the courage to speak to him after Iverson had given him a black eye.

"At first," Lord Waldo continued, "I thought her sporadic attendance at parties was a ploy to keep interest in her high. Some ladies do that, you know. But I gave up on that idea when she never accepted any gentleman's intentions to call on her."

Lord Waldo fell silent again, giving Iverson a moment

to think. Was it true Miss Crisp had never allowed any gentleman to call on her? If so, that intrigued Iverson, and he wanted to know why, but he sure as hell wasn't going to ask Lord Waldo for his opinion on that. Iverson knew it wasn't that she was put off by men in general. The passion and eagerness of her kisses had told him that.

"Is it true," Lord Waldo continued where his conversation left off, "that you are courting her?"

First the man asked him why he looked like Sir Randolph and now this. The blade must be a true nincompoop. "Think about what you just said, Lord Waldo, and then ask yourself if you really want to ask me any more questions." Iverson started walking away.

"Mr. Brentwood?"

Iverson didn't know why but he turned back to look at Lord Waldo. The young man blinked rapidly, and Iverson could tell he struggled with what to say. Iverson remained quiet and waited. Iverson wanted him to know he was utterly indifferent to anything he had to say.

"I want to thank you for helping look for my brother's dog that night in the park a few weeks ago."

"My brother's dog was missing, too. I wasn't helping you. I was helping him."

Iverson left Lord Waldo staring at him with wide-eyed surprise and entered the swirling throng of people. He headed straight toward Miss Crisp. He supposed he should have been a little nicer to the duke's brother. Obviously the man was trying to make amends, but Iverson wasn't in the mood to be forgiving. Not tonight anyway, and especially not if the prig expected him to discuss Miss Crisp. Besides, right now, the more he watched Miss Crisp smile at Lord Bighampton, the more he wanted to get her away from him.

The earl must be at least twice her age, if not more. His hair was thinning, and his waist was thickening. But he had a title, and Iverson knew most young ladies liked to fancy themselves married to a titled man. Somehow he hadn't thought that would matter to Miss Crisp, but maybe he was wrong. She'd said she didn't want to dance with him, so his mind was swirling with possibilities of ways to lure her away from the new earl.

He grunted a laugh to himself. In the past, it had never bothered him to see a young lady he was interested in smiling and talking with another man. Iverson was always confident that if he wanted the lady, she was his, and he didn't mind a challenge from another man because Iverson always expected to win. But he had no such confidence where Miss Crisp was concerned. He hadn't figured it all out yet but he knew his feelings for her were different from any other lady who had caught his attention.

On his way through the crowd, Iverson was stopped by a group of gentlemen eager to tell him how much they enjoyed Sir Phillip's story. It amazed him people actually thought he and his brother would be flattered by their comments. He quickly excused himself but was then waylaid by a young lady eager to talk about *A Tale of Three Gentlemen*, so as soon as he could he left her side, too. He bowed to a countess and smiled at a young lady who winked at him as he continued his trudge toward Miss Crisp. She caught sight of him just before he stopped in front of her. He could have sworn he saw appreciation in her eyes when she looked at him, and that made him feel damned good.

Though it was the last thing he wanted to do, Iverson greeted the earl first, as Society dictated, and then Miss Crisp, and lastly the other two hangers-on before turning back to her, and without blinking an eye said, "Your aunt said if I saw you to please ask you to make a moment for her."

Concern flew into Miss Crisp's green eyes, and he immediately knew he had used the wrong tactic. She was very protective of her father and her employees, and he should have remembered she was that way about her aunt, too.

"Is Aunt Elle all right?" Miss Crisp asked, taking a step toward him.

"Yes, yes," he hastened to say. "There is nothing wrong with her."

"Oh, good," she said, breathing a sigh of relief, though her eyes remained guarded. "All right, I'll go to her at once. Please excuse me, gentlemen."

She turned to Iverson and asked, "Do you know where she is?"

"I'll help you find her."

"Please allow me to do that for you," Lord Bighampton said to Miss Crisp, stepping in front of Iverson and blocking Iverson's view of her. "I've been coming here for years, and I know Lady Windham's house quite well."

Iverson wasn't going to let the bulky man get the best of him.

"No need for you to bother yourself, my lord," Iverson said as he came from around the earl and touched Miss Crisp's elbow and gently propelled her forward and away from the other men. "I know exactly where her aunt is, and it's no trouble for me to take Miss Crisp to her."

Iverson smiled to himself, knowing the earl's eyes were

throwing daggers at his back. As soon as they were far enough away so no one could overhear them, Iverson had to tell Miss Crisp the truth so she wouldn't continue to worry about Mrs. Gottfried.

"I have a confession to make," he said as they threaded their way through the mass of people crowding the doorway.

She glanced at him. "To me? Please, Mr. Brentwood. I'm hardly the person who wants to hear your confessions. Save that for the church."

"This one you'll want to hear."

"Ah, so at last you've decided to repent and tell me you are sorry you threatened my father. That I want to hear."

"No, I'm not that good. The threat stands." They moved into the corridor.

"What else could I possibly want to hear from you?"

"That your aunt didn't ask me to send a message to you. I haven't spoken to her tonight."

An incredulous expression formed on her face, and she stopped walking and moved to stand against the wall. "What did you say?"

"My comment to you about your aunt was merely a ploy to get you away from Lord Bighampton."

Her eyes widened, and her tempting lips parted just enough to make Iverson want to reach over and kiss her.

"That was more than a ploy, sir. That was a bold untruth."

Iverson let his gaze slowly caress her face before he said, "I admit it was, but I was forced to do it."

Concern edged its way into her expression, and she eyed him warily. "Forced in what way, and by whom?"

He took hold of her elbow and guided her to the far end of the dimly lit corridor, near the door where the servants were going and coming from the kitchen. "By the earl," Iverson whispered as if he were telling her a big secret. "The way the man kept looking at you had me thinking he wanted to pounce on you and gobble you up for his dinner. And by the looks of him, he's eaten quite enough already."

Even in the poor lighting, Iverson could see the corners of her mouth twitch in humor as she tried her best not to smile. He was relieved she wasn't angry with him about the prevarication, and an unexpected rush of satisfaction filled him.

She gave an unconvincing sound of indignation and said, "That is a most unkind thing to say about Lord Bighampton and his size."

Feeling comfortable she wasn't really upset by his comment about the earl, Iverson said, "But true, is it not?"

"No, of course it's not true. Portly"—she cleared her throat—"I mean, robust men look very vigorous and healthy, like the Prince."

"Vigorous? Are you sure, Miss Crisp?"

"Yes," she said, sounding more like she was trying to persuade herself than him. "And, I might add, he was behaving like a perfect gentleman—something you know nothing about."

Iverson grinned. She was doing her best to make him think she was outraged, but Iverson could clearly see she wasn't. He had the feeling she wanted to laugh out loud and enjoy their conversation as much as he was. That pleased him immensely.

"I think you are trying to convince yourself of that, Miss Crisp."

She huffed. "Does your arrogance have no borders, Mr. Brentwood?"

He shook his head. "No fences, either. And as we both know, I dare a lot."

"Indeed you do. Too much."

"It's a bad habit."

Iverson was enjoying himself. He could see by the sparkle in her lovely green eyes that in spite of what she was saying, she was enjoying their conversation, too.

"And you don't have to admit it to me or even to yourself, but I know you must have felt the same way about Lord Bighampton every time he looked at you."

"I felt no such thing," she said without conviction. "You have no insights as to what I feel, sir."

She loved to challenge him. "Don't I?" His heart started beating faster, and forgetting where they were, he stepped in closer to her. His gaze fastened on hers, and his voice turned husky as he said, "I know exactly what you were feeling when my lips were pressed against yours today. I know what you were feeling when your breasts nestled softly against my chest, and what you felt when your knees went weak as my tongue explored the warm depths of your sensuous mouth."

"Don't," she whispered, her chest heaving with short, gasping breaths. "You shouldn't say things like that."

Iverson knew he was tempting fate by standing far too close to her, and he was so tempted to lower his head and kiss her delectable lips. More gossip about him courting Miss Crisp wouldn't be a bad thing. Still, if he didn't move away quickly he could sully her reputation, and that he did not want.

He took a step away from her and said, "Why not? They are true. What I shouldn't say is untruths. I didn't intend to cause you any concern about Mrs. Gottfried. And I only said she wanted a moment of your time, so there was no need for alarm over that innocent comment."

"But Aunt Elle can sometimes get—"

She stopped, and all thoughts of teasing her further vanished.

"What?" he encouraged.

"Nothing. I just don't like to leave her alone for too long a time."

Iverson started to press her but decided against it, for the time being. After having seen Mrs. Gottfried deep in her cups, he had a feeling he knew why Miss Crisp wanted to keep a close watch on her aunt. But instead of saying more about that, he simply said, "May I get you a glass of champagne, or punch if you prefer? Your throat must be as dry as a desert after all that talking and smiling you were doing with those three gentlemen."

Miss Crisp smiled at him, and Iverson felt a shudder deep in his loins. He was no better than all the other bucks who lapped up her attention like a kitten drinking warm milk on a cold night. He wanted to pull her into his arms so he would know what she felt like snuggled close to him. He wanted to wipe away that uncertainty he saw in the depths of her eyes. He wanted to feel her soft, warm body next to his again. He wanted to place his lips and nose in the crook of her beautiful neck and breathe in her clean scent and taste her skin.

Suddenly her smile turned confident. "You should be more careful, Mr. Brentwood."

A short chuckle rumbled from his throat. "Caution has never been a big force in my life, Miss Crisp."

"I can believe that. But your comment just now sounded very much like the jealous remark of a lover."

Was he? He was attracted to her to the point that she consumed his thoughts, but jealous? No. How could he be? There were too many women to love to be jealous of just one.

"Did it?" he asked cautiously, knowing her words had a little merit.

She nodded and said, "Quite."

"But you know that can't be true, don't you?"

She quirked her head to the side and asked, "Do I?"

Her question made Iverson pause. She could keep him on his toes as no other lady had, and be charming at it all the while.

Miss Crisp laughed gently and started walking back down the wide corridor toward the drawing room. Iverson fell in step beside her. She was easily the most charming and most challenging lady he had ever met, and he loved every moment he spent with her.

"Mr. Brentwood," she said, "I believe I have teased you enough about jealousy for one evening. You can get me a glass of champagne. And then you can help me find Aunt Elle because I do need to make sure she is all right."

"Good. I'd like to see her again, too."

Iverson saw a servant with a tray of champagne and stopped him. He gave a glass to Miss Crisp and then took one for himself.

While they sipped their champagne, Iverson said, "So tell me, why is it you like to come early to parties?"

"I find I don't like to stay up late. I do my best writing on early mornings when the house—" She stopped abruptly, and her eyes rounded in shock.

Iverson's interest was piqued. For some reason, she hadn't wanted him to know she wrote verse. But why? It wasn't an unusual pastime for young ladies, but it had made Miss Crisp nervous to let him know.

"So you are a writer like your father?"

"Like my father?" she answered quickly. "Heavens, no. I don't consider myself anywhere near the writer or poet my father is. I belong to a ladies' poetry society and we all try our hand at verse from time to time. Most days, I simply move words around on the page."

"Good evening, Mr. Brentwood, Miss Crisp."

Iverson turned to see Miss Mable Taylor standing close to his side, gazing up at him with a sultry smile on her face. She was at least a head shorter than Miss Crisp, though you wouldn't know it because her dark blond hair and flowered headpiece were piled so high on top of her head. Her blue eyes were pretty, and her full bosom, which was so amply displayed beneath her gown, was lovely to look at, but Iverson had already accepted his body's demand that Miss Crisp was the only lady who commanded his attention tonight.

They both greeted Miss Taylor, but Iverson noticed she never even glanced at Miss Crisp.

"I wanted to tell you, Mr. Brentwood, that after we met a few weeks ago, I wrote my cousin who lives in Baltimore and told her all about you, and I received a letter back from her this week." Miss Taylor clasped her hands together under her chin and giggled before she exclaimed, "She remembers you."

"Is that right?" Iverson answered and then sipped his champagne.

She continued to smile eagerly at him, as if she were sharing a well-kept secret. "Yes. Miss Brenda Taylor. You do remember her, don't you? She said you called on her once. Of course, that was long before she married."

"Of course," he lied without guilt.

Iverson must have called on every eligible young lady in Baltimore at one time or another, so he certainly didn't remember Miss Taylor's cousin. He glanced over to Miss Crisp to see if she was as uncomfortable with this conversation as he was, but she was looking away, searching the crowd, he assumed, for her aunt.

"She'll be delighted to know you remembered her. She had some things to say about how naughty you were and that you well deserved the name the Rake of Baltimore."

"I'm sure all she said was true, Miss Taylor."

She gasped loudly and giggled again. "Oh my, sir, you are indeed as wicked as she said, aren't you?"

"Probably."

"She warned me not to let you break my heart."

Iverson smiled politely at her. "Miss Taylor, I try hard never to break anyone's heart. Do excuse me. I was helping Miss Crisp look for her aunt, and we must get back to doing that." Iverson touched Catalina's elbow and quickly ushered her into the crowded drawing room without another glance toward Miss Taylor.

"Oh, please don't leave Miss Taylor on my account, Mr. Brentwood," she said as he walked beside her. "I certainly don't need you to help me find Aunt Elle."

"No?" He grinned. "Fine, but I need you to help me get away from Miss Taylor."

"That surprises me. She looked as if she was just about ready to pounce on you and gobble you up for her dinner."

Iverson chuckled freely. "Now, now, Miss Crisp, be careful. You are picking up my bad habits."

"Maybe, but I'm certain if you had stayed a moment

longer she would have been begging you to call on her and take her for a ride in the park in your fast curricle."

"What makes you think my curricle is fast?"

She sipped her champagne and watched him over the rim of her glass. When she lowered it, she said, "Because you are."

"Ah, I see. I consider that a compliment, and I thank you. But I have no desire to call on Miss Taylor and take her anywhere. But perhaps I can take you for a ride in the park some day." Iverson stunned himself by that comment. Where did that thought come from? He hadn't even thought about the possibility of asking Miss Crisp to go for a ride with him.

"Not me, sir. I don't have time for such idle pleasantries."

Iverson stopped to let an aging dowager pass and then hurried to catch up with Miss Crisp again. "No time for an afternoon social life? Why not?"

"I have a large house and staff to manage, and all of it keeps me quite busy."

"Doesn't your aunt help?"

"Very little. She keeps busy with her own life."

"Then you need a secretary or an assistant so you can have an afternoon or two a week to take a walk in the park and watch all the handsome gentlemen sporting around on their fine steeds or racing their curricles."

Catalina looked at him and laughed again. He loved seeing her eyes sparkle with humor. He remembered Lord Waldo saying she had never allowed a gentleman to call on her. That surprised and bothered him. She was alluring, intelligent, and passionate, as well as compassionate. He thought about their kiss, and his throat tightened. Oh, yes, she needed to experience and enjoy the pleasures in life, and that included having a gentleman in her life—a deserving gentleman, of course.

"I am not interested in seeing how well a young blade can manage four bays or a black stallion, Mr. Brentwood. I have no inclination for such fanciful outings. And I have no need for an assistant. I am well able to take care of everything for my father and our household." She stopped just halfway around the ballroom and said, "Look, there's my aunt."

Iverson glanced over to where she was pointing and saw Mrs. Gottfried sitting along the wall with Lady Windham, sipping from a glass.

"Mrs. Gottfried seems perfectly fine to me," he said.

"Yes, she does seem to be doing well tonight. She and Lady Windham have been friends for years and always have much to talk about."

"I assume there is still no sign of the missing Sir Phillip," he said in a tone much like he would have used if he'd been asking about the weather.

"Not as of the time I left the house tonight."

"Miss Crisp, Miss Crisp."

Iverson looked around to see the pompous Lord Snellingly waving his lace-trimmed handkerchief and hurrying their way. Iverson swore to himself as the earl greeted them.

"Good evening, Mr. Brentwood, and lovely to see you, Miss Crisp. You look divinely beautiful tonight, as always."

Miss Crisp curtseyed, and with a smile said, "Thank you, Lord Snellingly."

"Your father missed our Royal Poet Society meeting last night. I do hope he's not ill?"

"No, he's away for a few days."

"Again? Well, never mind, but I did want him to hear my latest verse." He sniffed into his handkerchief. "He always gives me such encouragement."

Iverson tensed. He knew what Miss Crisp was going to say before the words left her mouth.

"Perhaps I could listen to it for you, Lord Snellingly," she said. "I'm not as talented as my father, and I certainly don't have his ear for verse, but you know I love all poetry."

"Yes," Iverson spoke up. "But you'll have to hear it at another time. Remember, your aunt was looking for you, and you don't want to keep her waiting."

"Oh, but I can see she is doing quite well and not in need of any attention from me at the moment."

Iverson groaned. He didn't know if he could bear listening to the man's uninspiring poetry even for the opportunity to spend a few more minutes in Miss Crisp's company.

"Iverson, there you are."

At the sound of his brother's voice, Iverson turned and saw Matson wading through the swarm toward him. Perfect timing.

"And here comes my brother, Miss Crisp. Perhaps you can listen to the poetry at another time. I want to introduce Matson before I deliver you to Mrs. Gottfried. Please excuse us, Lord Snellingly."

Iverson touched her elbow and ushered her forward, leaving the befuddled-looking earl behind them and feeling as if he'd just managed to dodge the blade of a sharp knife.

He had wondered how long it would take Matson to find him. He knew his brother well, and he was sure Matson was dying to meet Miss Crisp.

"Matson, let me introduce Miss Crisp," Iverson said after his brother stopped in front of them.

"I've heard a lot about you, Miss Crisp," Matson said after proper greetings were made.

"And I you, Mr. Brentwood. But after talking with your brother just now, perhaps it's better you not put any stock in what he has to say about me."

"Are you saying I can't be trusted?" Iverson asked her.

A glint of humor in her eyes made his stomach do a slow roll that thrilled him all the way down to his toes. "That's exactly what I'm saying."

"Actually," Matson said, "most of what I heard about you came from Miss Babs Whitehouse. She said the two of you belong to the same poetry and reading society."

Miss Crisp smiled. "Oh, yes, Babs. She's quite vocal in her opinions on everything."

"And she's a good friend of our sister-in-law, Lady Gabrielle, who is now our brother's viscountess."

"Yes, I had heard about their marriage. I don't know Lady Brentwood well, but she seems a lovely person."

Iverson sipped his champagne and watched how quickly and easily Matson had Miss Crisp talking and smiling at him. As usual, Matson always knew just what to say and how to say it. It hadn't entered Iverson's mind to try to get a conversation going with her about mutual friends.

When he was with her, he had a difficult time keeping his mind from going where it shouldn't go. He looked at Miss Crisp and realized he didn't like seeing her smiling at Matson any better than when she smiled at the portly earl. She had definitely enchanted him. And right now, he didn't know what he was going to do about it.

"Lady Gabrielle was best known by everyone for her dog,

Brutus," Miss Crisp said. "When they walked together in the park, no one came near them."

"Except for Brent, our brother," Iverson reminded him. "Remember, he met her in the park."

"I didn't know that," Miss Crisp added.

"Yes, Brent often mentioned Brutus was the biggest mastiff he had ever seen."

Iverson looked at Miss Crisp, who was thoroughly engaged in the conversation about the animal, and decided you could never go wrong talking about a dog, so he added, "After Brutus's death, our brother gave Lady Gabrielle another mastiff as a gift."

"I hadn't heard," she said. "That was thoughtful of him."

"Yes, they'll be back in Town for the Season, and no doubt they will bring the new dog with them."

"I'm sure I will see her while she is in London. Would you two gentlemen excuse me? I should go and check on my aunt. I heard the clock strike twelve some time ago, so we should be going."

Still unprepared to say good night to Miss Crisp, Iverson took her empty champagne glass and placed it on a table. "I'll walk with you so I can say hello to her."

They said their good-byes to Matson, and then Miss Crisp said, "It's not necessary for you to see me to my aunt. There is a young lady over to your left who is trying desperately to gain your attention. It would be a shame to deny her."

Iverson wasn't falling for that trick. He didn't look to his left. "I'm sure she was looking at Matson, not me."

"Perhaps, but I don't think so," she said as they wound their way around the dance floor to get to where her aunt was sitting. She sighed wistfully. "I kept looking at your brother and thinking it must be wonderful to have a brother."

"I have two," Iverson reminded her.

"Even better. I would have loved to have had a brother or sister. But my mother was very fragile. There were other children for her and my father, but unfortunately, none other than myself survived."

"I'm sorry to hear that," he said and realized he was.

By the look in her eyes, he knew not having a brother or sister saddened her. He supposed it was natural to want a sibling, someone to confide in, argue with, and compete against. Even though there were many times he wished he wasn't a twin, he was glad he had brothers. Perhaps not having a brother or sister was the reason Miss Crisp was so kind and gentle with the odd mixture of misfits she had working for her. They would be unemployable elsewhere.

Iverson smiled to himself. She was an angel of kindness to her servants, but she could be tough as new leather when she was sparring with him. Oh, yes, she definitely had him on her hook, and she was cleverly pulling him in. What he didn't know yet was if she knew it.

Nine

Patience is the companion of wisdom.
—St. Augustine

CATALINA WAS SMITTEN BY THE MAN.

Why and how it happened she had no idea. He was handsome. He was charming. He was an admitted rake and scoundrel who had threatened to harm her father, and still she found herself laughing with him and teasing him. For the first time in her life, she wanted to flirt with a man and dance with him. He delighted her, and even now, though she had left his company mere minutes ago, she was already wondering when she would see him again.

No, she was more than smitten. She was besotted, completely and utterly foolish over him! And she didn't know what she was going to do about it.

Catalina looked over at her aunt while Lady Windham's servant helped her with her velvet cloak. Aunt Elle's face was flushed, but she seemed steady on her feet, for which Catalina was grateful. But it was already later than they usually stayed, and she needed to get her aunt home.

If not for her aunt, Catalina would have stayed longer at the party and found a way to make Mr. Brentwood ask her to dance. If for no other reason than he'd told her he wasn't going to ask her.

She turned so the servant could place her cloak on her shoulders, and she saw Mr. Brentwood leaning against the door frame leading from the drawing room into the vestibule, watching her. He gave her a soft smile, and Catalina's stomach tumbled. Her breath caught in her throat, and she remembered his kisses and all the heady sensations that had erupted inside her when their lips met. She remembered the feel of his soft, pliant lips on hers—warm, moist, enticing. She remembered the sensations that shimmered, spiraled, and surged through her when he caught her up to him and embraced her in his protective, powerful arms.

It had been an overwhelming, breathtaking experience to be held so close to a man that she felt his strength, his warmth, and the beat of his heart. And she had no doubts she wanted him to hold her and kiss her again and again. And by the way he was looking at her, he knew that, too. For the first time in her life, she had the feeling her heart was not safe.

Suddenly, Miss Babs Whitehead appeared at his side, and his attention was diverted to her.

Catalina turned away.

The way Mr. Brentwood made her feel was maddening, Catalina thought as she and her aunt stepped into the chilling night air. She wanted to be free to explore and enjoy all the wonderful feelings Mr. Brentwood created inside her, but how could she when the rest of *A Tale of Three Gentlemen* stood between them?

The music and laughter of the party grew faint as they walked away from the house to where they would wait for their carriage to come around. The night was clear and dry, making the streetlamps on the fashionable Mayfair Street unusually bright. Aunt Elle chattered about some gossip she'd heard from Lady Windham, but Catalina couldn't focus on what her aunt was saying about who was seen in the garden with whom. When Mr. Brentwood was on her mind, there was no room in her thoughts for anyone but him, and that troubled her.

It had been a couple of days since she talked to Mr. Frederick, and she worried about the wisdom of continuing to wait for her father to return. Somehow she had to keep *The Daily Herald* from printing the rest of her father's story. Perhaps she should visit Mr. Frederick and plead her case again. She wanted to keep Mr. Brentwood from even knowing it had been written. She should never have finished it, but at the time, she had no idea how much trouble it would cause her or how it would make Mr. Brentwood feel to read it. This was her fault, and she must get the rest of the story back. Time for doing that was running out.

She kept telling herself there was a reason her father had been gone close to two weeks now. No doubt he'd found a quiet place that inspired him to brilliance and he couldn't force himself to leave. Perhaps he was working on a long poem that would rival Lord Byron's *Childe Harold's Pilgrimage*. But whatever the reason, if her father wouldn't come home, it was time for her to go looking for him. She couldn't wait any longer.

Briggs brought the carriage to a stop in front of them.

After Catalina had settled on the cushion opposite her aunt, she said, "Auntie, I've decided I must find Papa."

Aunt Elle laughed as the landau started rolling. "Where did this idea come from?"

There was no way Catalina could tell her aunt why. And

there was no use in beating herself up anymore for finishing *A Tale of Three Gentlemen*. At the time, she'd had no choice.

"He needs to come home and help me," Catalina whispered into the darkness of the cold carriage.

"Nonsense, I can help you. What do you need?"

"Oh, I wish you could. I've made such a mess of things."

"What things, dearest?" her aunt said, a slight slur beginning to affect some of her words. "I don't understand what you are talking about, but if you'll tell me what to do, I'll do it."

Catalina could see Aunt Elle was ready for sleep. They hadn't left the party a moment too soon. "I know you would, but this isn't anything you can help with. I need Papa. He's been gone so long now. I'm beginning to wonder if something might be wrong."

"And something might be right. He'll be home when he's ready. No one can hurry Phillip."

"Auntie"—Catalina paused and leaned toward her aunt— "I'm not sure I can wait any longer. I need his help now."

"But how can he help you when you don't know where he is?"

"Maybe we can find him if we put our heads together. Now, think. Has he ever mentioned to you where he goes when he takes his leave?"

In the darkness of the carriage, Catalina could barely see her aunt's brows scrunch together as if she were in deep thought. "No. I'm sure I would remember. I have never questioned Phillip about his plans when he travels."

"Neither have I, but I can see where I should have. That information would be most useful right now."

"But he probably doesn't even go to the same place every time he goes away."

"That's quite possible." Catalina shook her head with worry. "I can't continue to let time pass and not do anything to find him."

"Why are you so desperate to find Phillip? You've never wanted to find him before."

Catalina had an overwhelming urge to tell her aunt everything. She wanted to confide in her how she had finished the story for her father, about Mr. Brentwood's anger over its publication and his threats against her father if more was written. She wanted to pour out her heart and tell how Mr. Brentwood made her feel when he looked at her, when he'd kissed her and made her feel the desires of a woman. She wanted to fling herself into her aunt's arms, lay her head against her chest, and feel loved and protected.

For once, Catalina wanted to be soothed with a hug, a brush of a kind hand, and to hear someone tell her there was no need to worry, everything was going to be all right. But just at her breaking point, when she felt herself moving toward her aunt for solace, Aunt Elle opened her drawstring reticule and pulled out her silver flask.

Catalina swallowed hard. A shiver shook her. She forced the weak feeling away and settled back against the cushion. She would have to settle for the rocking of the carriage to ease her troubled mind.

It was odd that just a few days ago Catalina sat in her own home and accused Mr. Brentwood of being desperate to find her father. The tables had turned, and now she was the one frantic for his return.

Catalina sighed and rested her head against the cushion and let the rocking carriage and darkness envelop her.

"Are you all right, dearest?"

"Yes, of course, Auntie," she fibbed.

Aunt Elle moved to the seat beside her and took hold of Catalina's gloved hand, but the time for her to bring comfort had passed.

"I know you feel you need your papa, but you can't go flying off like an injured bird, looking for him."

A rueful chuckle escaped past Catalina's lips. Aunt Elle was more intuitive than Catalina thought. She had indeed felt like a wounded bird for a moment or two.

"Now, there's no need for you to fret because Phillip has been gone longer than usual. I'm sure he's on his way back home. He might even be there by the time we return."

Catalina smiled. "I do like your optimism, Auntie."

"Dearest, you are your father's rock, and you are a guardian angel to me and all the servants, too. If not for you and your skills in taking care of everything, who knows where any of us would be—probably in the poorhouse and your father in debtors' prison."

"Auntie!" Catalina raised her head and exclaimed.

"Well, it's true. Thankfully, you took after your mother's side of the family and not after me or your 'eyes to the sky' father."

Catalina laughed again. "That's 'head in the clouds,' Auntie."

"Well, whatever it is, you can't be as blithe as he is and go chasing after him. Give him another day or two. He'll be back. I'm sure of it. And in the meantime, you'll take care of us just like you always have."

Catalina lightly squeezed her aunt's fingers. "Yes, Auntie, I will take care of everyone. That is why I must find Papa."

"But how?"

"First, I'll search Papa's desk in his book room and look for correspondence where someone might have invited him to come for a visit, or possibly a note or journal where he wrote the name of an inn or an estate where he planned to stay."

"That does sounds like a reasonable way to begin your search," Aunt Elle said. "But what if he doesn't want to be found?"

"I must do it anyway."

"All right, dearest, if your mind is made up and I can't talk you out of it. Do what you must."

"Thank you, Auntie. If I don't find where he is staying written down, I will question Mrs. Wardyworth, Nancy, and all the other servants if need be. Perhaps they know where Papa likes to spend his time. I already know Papa saw Briggs walking along the road from Bath to London. Maybe I can establish that there is one particular house or an inn where he stays most often along that route. I can go there looking for him."

"Since I can't talk you out of it, tell me what I can do to help."

"Your part will come when you have to go with me to find him."

"Of course, you know I will. You don't think I'd let you travel anywhere without me, do you? When I traveled with Mr. Gottfried, he always said, 'Eloisa, don't tell me no. Pack your trunks, and let's go. We'll make an adventure out of it.' And you know what, dearest, we always did."

"You and I shall do the same," Catalina said, feeling heartened.

"Of course we will. I'll look forward to it."

"Thank you, Aunt Elle."

Catalina turned away from her aunt to look at the lighted lamp on the carriage outside the small door window. It was easy for her aunt to say just wait for him to return. Her aunt didn't know how Catalina was feeling.

Mr. Frederick could give the okay to start printing the copies any day now. Her best guess was she had at most a week or two, but maybe only four, maybe five days for her father to return in time to stop *The Daily Herald* from causing him a basketful of trouble from dangerous Mr. Brentwood.

———

It was much later that night when Iverson found himself sitting in White's gaming room with the best damn hand of cards he'd had in weeks, and he was trying hard to keep his mind on the game and off the temptingly delectable Miss Crisp. It was proving difficult. The reason was he felt differently about Miss Crisp than he had any other woman. He felt differently when he had kissed her, and she made him feel special when she looked at him.

That troubled him.

He'd talked and danced with several young ladies, trying to forget about the ever-charming and indomitable Miss Crisp after she left Lady Windham's party. He might as well have saved the breath it took him to dance. Not one young lady came close to intriguing him as much as Miss Crisp.

Miss Babs Whitehouse was lively and voluptuous. He had no doubt her kisses would be saucy, but he had no desire to taste her lips after she told him she enjoyed the quite clever story that had been written about him and his brother in *The*

Daily Herald. Miss Helen Matthews had the countenance of an angel, but the thought of being wrapped in her arms left him cold after she had asked him if it were true that twins could feel each other's pain. And the young and immensely wealthy widow, Mrs. Ronald Anderson, had him almost running for the doorway when she eagerly asked him to call on her tomorrow afternoon at precisely three o'clock. There was something about the look in her eyes that told him if he accepted her invitation, he'd find himself leg-shackled before he left.

It was Iverson's turn, so he played his hand. He didn't blink an eye or move a muscle when a few minutes later he was dealt the card he needed to win the game, though inside he was feeling good. He casually let himself glance at the huge pile of money in the center of the table. The win would be sweet.

Movement in the doorway of the card room caught Iverson's attention. He looked up to see Matson leaning against the door frame. Iverson knew immediately something was wrong. Matson's foul expression said, "I need to see you now."

But Iverson wasn't walking away from this hand. Matson's problem could wait. Iverson looked back at his cards and then one by one, his gaze drifted over the four men seated at the table with him. What he was holding could beat them all.

A cough came from the doorway. Iverson looked at his brother again. A wrinkle of concern marred Matson's forehead, and tightness showed around his mouth. He jerked his head to the right, indicating for Iverson to follow him immediately.

Not this time, Brother, Iverson thought. Matson was just

going to have to wait. One of the men at the table folded, and the one beside him upped the bet generously. Iverson remained calm, matched, and raised the bet again. Another man folded and then another matched the bet and called for a show of hands. Iverson looked up at Matson and smiled before laying down his winning hand.

After congratulations from the other players, Iverson walked up to Matson and said, "Sorry, Brother, but I couldn't walk away and leave more than a hundred pounds on the table."

Matson clapped him on the back. "I wouldn't want you to. Come on. We can't discuss what I have to say in the corridor. Let's get a drink. After that win, you're buying."

Iverson followed Matson into the taproom. He glanced at the large clock on the wall and knew why the place was almost empty. It was near daybreak. They passed a server, and Matson held up two fingers and said, "Ale."

They walked over to an empty table in the corner of the room and sat down. "There is no one close enough to overhear us, so tell me what is so important."

Matson crossed his arms, laid them on the table, and leaned toward Iverson. "Sir Randolph Gibson owns the company we're leasing our warehouse space from."

Iverson's demeanor remained as stoic as it had been in the card game. "How do you know?"

"Lord Waldo told me."

The hair on the back of Iverson's neck rose. "And how does that fop know this?"

"How he knows I have no idea. He was deep into his cups, but I believe he knew what he was talking about."

"What exactly did he say?"

"That his brother the Duke of Rockcliffe, Gabrielle's father the Duke of Windergreen, and Sir Randolph Gibson own or control most all of the land and buildings in the area. And he knows Sir Randolph owns the company we're leasing from. He said he was quite surprised when he learned about who we were leasing from."

"I'll bet he was," Iverson growled. "Hell and damnation. I wonder how many other people know this."

"There's no way of knowing, but I'm certain Sir Randolph knew we were the ones seeking the lease."

"How could he not?" Iverson added, trying his best to control his anger and outrage as well as Miss Crisp controlled hers. He didn't know how she did it. It was damned hard.

They both remained quiet while the server placed two tankards of ale in front of them and then left.

"I don't know about you, but I don't have any desire to be connected to Sir Randolph in any way."

"Neither do I," Iverson agreed.

"Perhaps we should have moved back to Baltimore when Brent told us our mother had an affair with Sir Randolph and we were quite possibly the result."

"Quite possibly?" Iverson laughed ruefully. "Tell me, is that newly grown strip of fine beard because you no longer want to look like me?"

Matson made a fist and let it lightly hit the table. "Damnation, Iverson, I still don't want to believe it."

"Our mother admitted it to Brent. He wouldn't lie to us about that. But whether or not you believe it makes no difference to me. Handle it however it suits you. But know this: As far as I'm concerned, Judson Brentwood was our father and no amount of gossip or resemblance to another man will change that. He will always be our only father. And remember this, too: Brentwoods don't run from anything."

Matson picked up the tankard and took a long drink before saying, "I know, but sometimes…"

"Sometimes what?" Iverson asked.

"Damnation, Iverson, sometimes the gossip and the looks get difficult to take. I think it would have been easier if we'd stayed in America and never come back to London."

Knowing he would never have met Miss Crisp if they had never come to London, Iverson said to his brother, "Easier, yes. But since when have we had it easy, Brother?"

Matson let out a breathy chuckle. "Not since our viscount father shipped us off to Baltimore and forced us to develop a business."

"And this isn't easy, either, but we'll handle it."

"Remember when we used to think Papa sent us away so we wouldn't be jealous of Brent's title—as if we would?"

"I'm sure there are some brothers who are, but I could care less about a damned title. It doesn't make a man a man. Papa gave us a job to do—build a company—and we worked damned hard every day to do it. And we did. That's all that mattered then, and that's all that matters now."

"And I don't intend to be beholden to Sir Randolph for anything, including warehouse space."

"I don't either," Iverson agreed. "Now that Brent is married to the Duke of Windergreen's daughter, the man should have no problem leasing some of his vacant space to us. We'll go see him."

"That's what I was thinking. Our ships are bound to be here soon. We need to get this settled before they arrive."

"Agreed. We'll go see Lady Gabrielle's father tomorrow afternoon."

Iverson picked up his tankard and took a sip. Also, he would think of a reason to visit Miss Crisp. But he wouldn't share that bit of information with his brother.

"Tell me," Matson said, "what do you suppose Sir Randolph thinks about the story Sir Phillip wrote?"

"He doesn't like it any better than we do."

Matson grunted a half laugh. "You really think that?"

"I know it. He was coming to see Sir Phillip as I was leaving Miss Crisp today, and we had a chat."

"A chat?" Matson's brows rose. "That's quite interesting. Perhaps he simply wanted to congratulate Sir Phillip on the story."

"I doubt that, Matson."

"I don't," he said grumpily. "We know nothing about the man. What did he have to say?"

"He's not much of a talker, but it was clear he wasn't happy about the story. He was there to take Sir Phillip to task over it as well. He asked me to let him know if I found out where Sir Phillip is, and I agreed. He said he'd do the same if he discovered his whereabouts."

Matson cocked his head to the side. "And you believed him?"

"At this point, I have no reason to doubt him."

"The story certainly doesn't make him look as bad as it does our mother," Matson said with an edge to his voice.

"No, but remember he's here to endure the blasted gossip, as are we, and we can only thank God our mother isn't."

"True, but I can't say I feel at all sorry for the man."

"Neither do I, but I recall Brent telling us, when he had

talked to Sir Randolph after we first came to London, he seemed very protective of our mother, and that's the way he appeared today."

Matson grunted again.

"As long as he stays away from us, as he has in the past few months, I have no quarrel with the man."

Matson took a long drink from his tankard. "Well, I do. He had an affair with our mother, and as you said, he's obviously our father. That bothers me."

Iverson pushed his tankard away. "It's best we don't think about that."

"You and Brent can be civil to Sir Randolph if you want, but I don't intend to."

"That's up to you, Matson. I don't believe for a moment the man forced himself on our mother, so I choose to assume she had her reasons for whatever relationship was between them, and I'll leave it at that. I suggest you do the same."

Ten

*Nobody makes a greater mistake than he who
did nothing because he could do only a little.*
—Edmund Burke

SHE HAD ONE PURPOSE IN MIND.

And nothing was going to stop her. Catalina had expected to sleep fitfully after her late-night decision to search for her father, but she'd slept soundly, and for much longer than she had wanted. She had awakened with an eagerness to get started on her mission. After a cup of chocolate and a piece of warm toast, she dressed as quickly as she could and went below stairs to her father's book room. It wasn't a place she sought often. She considered it his private domain, and she respected that.

When she had to finish one of his stories or poems, she never sought the solitude of his library but would work at the small secretary in the drawing room. The space was much larger than her father's workplace and therefore had more windows to give the room a lot of light, making it bright and cheerful.

A damp, musty odor assailed her as she entered, even though there wasn't a speck of dust on anything. Catalina knew it was because the room was small and filled with the clutter of things her father had brought home from his many

trips to wherever it was he went. There were various stat-
ues, urns, and candlesticks of all sizes stacked against each
other. A ghastly looking gargoyle stood guard in one corner.
Chairs, footstools, and small tables sat around the room in
no particular order. There were piles of books and stacks of
magazines and newsprint lining the walls and sitting atop
tables and chairs.

No, she could never work in the chaos of her father's
book room.

Because of her father's carefree and idealistic outlook,
he never saw any of the disorder in his life or the havoc it
caused the household when he promised to turn in work
to be published and then wouldn't finish it so he could get
paid. When he wanted to, he could push everything out of
his mind and write beautiful, searing, and breathtaking lines
of verse and prose in the midst of it all. He could stir the
senses and the emotions in his stories with seeming ease
and make a person laugh or cry, depending on the reaction
he wanted. Catalina had often wished she could write half
as well as her father.

She stood in the middle of the book room and knew that
the place to start looking for her father's whereabouts was
his desk. But in order to do that, she needed more light. She
walked over to the window, opened the dark brown draperies, and parted the aged and yellowed sheers. She tied all of
the fabric away from the panes with brown roping.

Early afternoon sunshine spilled into the darkness, chasing away the shadowy gloom of the room. She felt better
instantly. Her father's desktop was a scattered disarray of
papers, quills, ink jars, and books. There was nothing to be
done but to sit down and start looking at the papers and

notes one by one. She decided she might as well organize them while she was at it. She only hoped something in the correspondence might provide a clue about where her father might be. She didn't relish opening the desk drawers and searching through his private papers, but at this point, she had no other choice.

An hour passed and then two, but Catalina found nothing that might tell her where her father was staying. She had tried every drawer in her father's desk. None of them were locked, and they were all filled with sheets of parchment, vellum, and foolscap. On many sheets would be just one line or two lines of poetry she was sure he meant to return to one day and finish.

She didn't know how long she'd been working when Nancy came in carrying a tray with tea and biscuits on it. She rose from the desk and said, "Here, let me help you with that." She took the tray from her cook and smiled at her. "How did you know I needed a sip of tea right now?"

Nancy smiled, too. "Mrs. Gottfried said she thought you might like a cup. She asked me to steep some fresh and bring it in to you."

"Thank you, Nancy. While you are here, I'd like to ask you a few questions before you get back to your work."

Her big eyes danced with wonder and excitement. "You can ask me anything, missy. You know that."

"Good. Do you remember where you were when my father asked you to work for us?"

She laughed. "Well, I was in the kitchen, of course."

Catalina smiled indulgently. "But in whose kitchen were you working?"

"Oh," she said softly, as if just realizing the subject was

of a serious matter. "I was working at the Cooked Goose Tavern and Inn."

"You were the cook there?" When Nancy nodded, Catalina asked, "Was my father just a guest in the tavern, or was he staying at the inn?"

"He stayed at the inn often, missy. He would even send the owner a letter and let him know when he was coming to the Cooked Goose so I could have roast duckling cooking the day he arrived. Sir Phillip always said nobody can cook duck the way I can."

Catalina smiled. "And he's right."

Now Catalina knew why they had to pay Nancy so much. No doubt he had lured her away from her employer with the promise of higher wages, because she was certainly getting more than their previous cook. And at her father's insistence, their former cook stayed on to help Nancy with the lifting and carrying of heavy pots from the fire, work that was impossible for her to do because of her limp.

"Would you tell me where the tavern and inn is located?"

"A small village that's a long day's ride from here called Brighton Hollow."

"Wonderful, Nancy, thank you. This will be a big help. Now when you see Mrs. Wardyworth, would you ask her to come in to see me?"

After Nancy left, Catalina wrote down the name of the inn and the village. She then went to her father's book shelf and looked through the clutter of scattered and stacked books until she found an old and faded map of London and the surrounding townships and villages. Nancy was right. Brighton Hollow didn't look to be more than a day's journey away. Hope surged inside her, and she tried to tamp it down.

Would it be too much to hope that her father was at the inn right now? She poured herself a cup of tea and sat back down in her father's chair. She closed her eyes and wondered how many times she was going to daydream again about Mr. Brentwood kissing her.

"Did ye ask to see me, missy?"

Catalina looked up and smiled at her housekeeper. "Yes, Mrs. Wardyworth, please come in."

The large woman lumbered into the room and said, "Are ye enjoying yer tea, missy? And is that some of Nancy's sugared tarts I see there?"

"Yes to both. I don't have an extra cup, but plenty of tarts to share. Would you like one?"

"Don't mind if I do, if ye're sure it's all right."

"Of course it is."

The housekeeper took one of the small treats Catalina offered from the china serving bowl.

"Mrs. Wardyworth, would you mind telling me where you were when you met my father and he asked you to come to work for us?"

Her hand stopped midway to her mouth, and fear flashed in Mrs. Wardyworth's dark brown eyes. "Ye aren't planning on trying to send me back there, are ye, missy?"

"No, no, of course not. Why would you even think that? You know how much we need you to help manage the house. Believe me, your employment here is safe."

"She won't take me, ye know. She said I was too old, too slow, and too grumpy to work for her anymore, she did. Can ye believe that?"

"That was a most unkind thing for her to say."

"I thought so, too."

"What was her name? I'd like to know where you worked before you came here."

Mrs. Wardyworth's fear was replaced with a cautious wariness Catalina had never seen in the older woman's eyes before, and that puzzled her.

"I'm not at all sure yer papa would want me telling ye where I was when we met. I think I best leave that information for him to tell."

Catalina's curiosity was piqued. Nancy had no qualms about telling where she was when she met her father. Mrs. Wardyworth had always been a little strange, and the woman was acting no differently now.

"Nonsense, Mrs. Wardyworth," Catalina said. "There is no reason for you to be shy about this. You know my father trusts me to manage our affairs for him when he is away, and when he's at home, too. I assure you he will not mind your telling me."

"But this is different, missy."

"How so?"

The woman remained quiet, and Catalina had to force herself not to become irritated with her.

"Mrs. Wardyworth, I wouldn't be asking the question if it wasn't absolutely crucial for me to know."

The housekeeper put the tart in her mouth, and as she chewed, seemed to think on what Catalina had said. "If he ever asks, I'll tell him how reluctant I was to give ye the information."

"If that ever becomes necessary, I will tell him, too."

"I worked for Madame Shipwith at her bawdy house on the north side of London. I managed the front door for her."

Bawdy house!

"The front door?" Catalina almost whispered her words, still trying to assimilate what she'd just heard.

"Yes. Mrs. Shipwith knew she could trust me to check out the gentlemen thoroughly before they were allowed to come into the drawing room. That's where they would meet the girls to decide which one they wanted to spend an evening with."

Catalina swallowed hard. "And you met my father there?"

"Oh, yes. He came often, he did. He always liked to laugh and say Madame Shipwith ran a tight ship. And she did. She wouldn't allow any disreputable gents in her establishment. No, missy, she managed a respectable place and took only gentlemen of quality and means. And because of that, all the young girls I ever heard about wanted to work for her. But the madame was just as particular about her girls as she was about the gents who wanted to purchase their time."

Catalina grew stiffer and stiffer the more Mrs. Wardyworth revealed where she had come from. Catalina prayed her face didn't show just how shocked she was by what the woman was saying. And Catalina had heard enough. She had to excuse the woman before she said more.

"I understand, Mrs. Wardyworth. You've answered all my questions, and I thank you."

The woman slowly rose, leaning heavily on the chair arms to help support her until she was standing straight. "And ye don't think yer father will be upset with me for telling, do ye?"

"I can assure you my father will never know you said a word to me about this. In fact, we'll both make a vow right now never to speak of this again. It will be our little secret."

Mrs. Wardyworth smiled. "My lips are sealed, missy."

"Mine, too," Catalina assured her. She picked up the tray

and thrust it into Mrs. Wardyworth's hands. "Would you please ask Nancy to make some more hot tea, and do enjoy another tart before you give the tray back to her?"

Mrs. Wardyworth smiled as she turned away. "Thank ye kindly, missy. Don't mind if I do have another."

Catalina made herself busy with papers on the desk until she was sure her housekeeper was out of the room. She then sank into her father's chair and stared straight in front of her.

A bawdy house, her mind screamed.

What was she to do? Never in a thousand years would she have suspected her father visited such an establishment as that, or that Mrs. Wardyworth had ever worked at a—a house of ill repute!

No, she would not find him there because she would never go there looking for him. She didn't even want to think about that. She had to put any thoughts of her father going to a place of such reputation out of her mind.

Forever.

Mrs. Wardyworth was right. That wasn't the kind of thing a daughter needed to know.

Resting her elbow on the desk and dropping her forehead into the palm of her hand, Catalina sighed. She had found nothing on the desk to indicate where her father was, but since Nancy said he loved to stay at the inn where she'd worked, Catalina believed it was worth the drive over there tomorrow to see if she could find him. Thinking of that journey brought up another matter. How much money would it take to look for her father?

Catalina rose and headed for her desk in the drawing room. She had limited experience traveling and could only estimate how much it would cost for lodging and food. At her secretary she moved aside the day's mail and opened a secret compartment at the bottom of one of the small drawers. She could look at the red velvet bag and see it wasn't heavy with coins. Hopefully there was enough for a night's lodging and a little food.

"Oh, there you are, Catalina," Aunt Elle said, entering the room. "This came this morning." She handed a piece of paper to Catalina. "It's from my apothecary. It appears we never took care of the man last month for my tonics. I don't know how that happened, dearest, as I know you are quite good with keeping up with everything that must be paid."

"I'm certain I handled this, Auntie." Catalina looked at the paper and was astounded by the amount. "Auntie, this isn't for last month. This is for something you picked up just last week. Did you need this much tonic?"

Aunt Elle's eyes widened with concern. "Yes, of course I did. You know how distressed I get when I don't have my medications in a timely fashion."

"Yes, yes, I know," Catalina quickly said, trying to hide her shock at the amount and not alarm her aunt. "It's not a problem." She smiled. "This is nothing for you to worry about. I'll take care of it."

"Oh, good," her aunt said, looking more at ease.

Catalina laid the paper on the desk. Once she found her father and had the trouble of *A Tale of Three Gentlemen* behind her, Catalina was going to pay her aunt's apothecary a visit and insist on better prices, or convince him she would see to it her aunt went elsewhere for her tonics.

"You know, dearest, if our pockets are light right now, we can always ask your father to write more poetry and stories, and to write faster so he can make more money."

A troubled laugh escaped Catalina's lips. "It's not that easy, Auntie. It takes time to write poetry good enough to be paid for it. Besides, we don't even know where Papa is right now."

"But you said we're going to find him, right?"

Catalina lifted her chin and smiled. "Right. We will find him, and he will come home with us." Just saying that out loud made her feel better. "Now tell me, are you packed?"

Aunt Elle's face brightened. "Sylvia is doing so as we speak. But I suppose I should go check on her."

Catalina sighed heavily as her aunt left the room. She opened the red velvet bag and poured the coins out on the desk and counted them. Her shoulders sagged. If she paid the apothecary, they certainly wouldn't have enough money for their journey, so the man would just have to wait.

She pushed the invoice aside and thumbed through the remaining mail, opening some of it. Most were invitations to parties, as the Season wasn't much more than a week away. But there was also a debt from her father's tailor. She had no idea he'd bought new clothing before he left on his journey.

She broke the seal on the last envelope. Her heart sank when she immediately recognized it as another invoice. She started to just toss it aside, but her gaze landed on the words *The Cooked Goose Tavern and Inn.* The innkeeper was asking to be paid for her father's lodging.

"Oh, yes!" she whispered to herself. Her father must be at the inn. She was on the right track.

Obviously, because her father had stayed much longer than he intended, he was out of money.

It would be wonderful if she could travel alone, but that was impossible. There were other ways she could save money. She would not take her own maid and instead use her aunt's. That way the three of them could share a room and save a night's lodging. And she would have Nancy cook enough food for the two days they would be gone so they wouldn't have to buy food at the inn. She was sure there were other ways to keep the costs of traveling down.

All she had to do now was talk to Briggs and make sure he had the carriage ready to go at first light—and pray her father was still at the Cooked Goose.

Eleven

*One meets his destiny often in the
road he takes to avoid it.*
—French Proverb

HE COULDN'T GET HER OFF HIS MIND.

And sometimes that's exactly what he wanted. He actually enjoyed thinking about Miss Catalina Crisp.

Iverson wiped the last traces of the shaving soap off his face with a cloth and threw it aside. After their first meeting, he'd tried to forget about her, but she just kept threading her way through his thoughts and popping up when he should be thinking about more important matters, such as establishing his ship-building business in London.

But that subject wasn't nearly as inviting as thinking about Miss Crisp and how much he wanted her in his arms again.

And why shouldn't he think about her? He was a man. She was beautiful, intelligent, and challenging. She was strong, compassionate, and more sensual than any other woman he could remember. Men were supposed to be attracted to women like her.

"Damnation," he muttered to himself as he drew his pressed shirt over his head. "Men are supposed to be attracted to all types of women. That is what adds the spice to life."

And Iverson was, or rather he used to be.

But he couldn't deny his own feelings. He'd felt some-thing different inside him when he'd kissed Miss Crisp. A yearning he couldn't explain had taken hold inside him, and he couldn't shake it. He hadn't expected to be knocked off his feet, but he had been. Perhaps when he was a youngster in his teens he'd given a few young girls their first kiss, but certainly not in the last few years. He didn't know how Miss Crisp made it through her first Season without a stolen kiss, but he was damned glad that experience had been saved for him.

She felt like heaven in his arms, and he was eager to taste her lips once again.

Iverson picked up the newsprint again and looked at Lord Truefitt's column. His eyes immediately singled out the part he'd already read several times.

> Roses are red
> Violets are blue
> The Baltimore Rake is whispering
> And Miss Crisp is, too!
>
> Last evening at Lady Windham's opulent home, Miss Crisp and Mr. Brentwood were once again seen huddled toe to toe and nose to nose in a dark corner. Hmm. Does anyone know what they were whispering about? If so, do tell, and it will all be printed here.
>
> —Lord Truefitt, *Society's Daily Column*

He wondered what Miss Crisp was thinking of their latest mention in the gossip sheet. No doubt she was annoyed about the attempt at poetry again. He smiled and threw the newsprint aside, grabbed his collar off the chair, and fastened it around the base of his throat. But as far as he was concerned, he was happy for the mention again. No doubt Sir Phillip would get wind of their supposed courtship sooner rather than later and hurry home to see what it was about.

Iverson couldn't remember how long it had been since the taste of a woman lingered on his tongue, enticing him to want to taste her again. He was going to ask her to go for a ride in the park with him this afternoon. Her aunt would approve, he was certain. He didn't care that she thought she was too busy for such fanciful things. He wanted her to sit by him in a carriage and talk and laugh with him. And he didn't give a damn what the gossips said about his courting her. Let them all write whatever they wanted.

But would he be able to convince her to go? And perhaps the bigger test would be if he were able to convince her that what was between him and her father had nothing to do with the two of them.

Iverson whistled as he picked up his neckcloth, wrapped it underneath his collar three times, and started fashioning a bow with the ends. He chuckled out loud and glanced at the clock on his dressing chest. It was late enough in the day that he could pay Miss Crisp a visit. He wanted to see her green eyes flashing pretend outrage at him when he arrived at her door again. He had as much as told her he'd be back to see if her father returned. He was sure it wouldn't surprise her to see him. She was probably expecting him, and he didn't plan on disappointing her.

The hell of it was it didn't even bother him anymore that she was Sir Phillip's daughter. The poet was the one who wrote that rubbish about Iverson's family, not his daughter. When the man came back to Town, Iverson would settle things with him. In the meantime, he intended to let Catalina Crisp know he wanted to court her and show the scandal sheets they finally printed something that was actually true.

Iverson smiled. Had he just thought of her as "Catalina"? He said it aloud, and then said it again a couple more times. He liked the way the name rolled off his tongue. Even her name was warm and sensuous. He chuckled to himself again as he buttoned his muted-red waistcoat. Miss Crisp was much too cold-sounding, but Catalina heated his blood.

It shouldn't take long for his cook to prepare a basket with some bread, cheese, and fig preserves. And since the days were still a little cool, he'd add a bottle of his favorite port, too.

Iverson whistled as his long, sure strides took him up the stone walkway to Catalina's front door. He rapped the door knocker against the brass plate and waited, tempted to strike it a few more times. He held the urge at bay. A few moments later, the door opened.

Mrs. Wardyworth greeted him with the usual surly expression on her flat, pinched face. For the life of him, he couldn't understand why someone with such a disagreeable disposition was allowed to answer the door.

"Good afternoon," he said in as pleasant a voice as he could muster, considering Mrs. Wardyworth's expression. He wasn't going to let her ill temper put a damper on his expectation of taking Catalina for an afternoon ride.

"He isn't here," she said.

Iverson grunted a half laugh. Clearly Catalina was the only person who had the temperament to employ Mrs. Wardyworth. "Still cheerful as ever, I see," he said. "But this time you'll be happy to know I'm not here to see Sir Phillip. I'm here to see Miss Crisp."

"She isn't here, either."

Having been down this route with her once before, Iverson knew exactly what to do. "Not a problem. I'll wait for her return," he said and brushed past Mrs. Wardyworth much in the same manner as he had several days ago when he first arrived at the door, looking for Sir Phillip. There was just no other way to get past the woman. Wherever she'd worked before this household, she must have been hired to intimidate the faint of heart.

"Ye can't come barging in here," Mrs. Wardyworth admonished.

"Of course I can. I just did."

He took off his hat and laid it on the table where Catalina had put his things the other day, and started unbuttoning his coat.

"Ye can't wait here, I tell ye. I don't know when she's coming back."

Iverson shrugged out of his coat. "Haven't we had this conversation, Mrs. Wardyworth?"

"What's the matter with ye? Ye know we haven't had a conversation before, sir. Ye just got here."

Iverson sucked in a slow, deep breath. The woman was exasperating.

"Where exactly did Miss Crisp go?"

"I have no idea and wouldn't tell ye if I did. She doesn't check in with me about her social calendar before she leaves the house."

"That's quite understandable. But you do expect her back by this evening, do you not?"

"Not hardly," the housekeeper informed him with a matter-of-fact tone. "She took her trunks with her."

A niggle of alarm pricked Iverson, and he swallowed hard. "You mean she left Town?"

Mrs. Wardyworth jerked her hands to her hips. "I suppose she did. I don't know of any other reasons ye'd pack for overnight travel, do ye?"

No, there would be no other reason. And she had to be going to see her father.

Iverson had to hand it to Catalina. She had him believing she didn't know where Sir Phillip was. A tight-fisted knot formed in Iverson's chest, slowing his breathing. She'd had him believing a lot of things recently.

"Mrs. Wardyworth," Iverson said in a much calmer manner than he was feeling, "I'm certain Miss Crisp didn't leave without someone in this household knowing where she was going. I'm not leaving this house until I know where she went."

"What's all the commotion?"

Iverson looked up to see the gangly, big-eyed cook slowly walking toward them.

Mrs. Wardyworth harrumphed. "This man wants me to tell him where missy went. Like I would even if I knew."

"I can tell him," Nancy said, giving Iverson a wide, friendly smile.

Iverson let out a sigh of relief.

"Well, ye better not open yer mouth," Mrs. Wardyworth exclaimed. "Not if ye want yer job. Ye know missy doesn't want ye telling anyone her business. Ye best keep quiet about anything ye know."

Nancy stopped in front of them and leaned on her cane. Smile in place, she looked straight into Iverson's eyes, though she spoke to Mrs. Wardyworth. "I don't think missy would mind Mr. Brentwood knowing. By the dead saints, if you would read the newsprint, you would know he's courting her. She's probably hoping he'll find out where she went and he'll follow her, too. Wouldn't that be romantic?"

Romance wasn't exactly what Iverson had in mind when he found Catalina, but he'd keep that bit of information from the servants.

Iverson gave Nancy a genuine smile. "Thank you, Nancy. I would very much like to know where she went and would appreciate your telling me."

"I overheard her tell Adam they were going to the Cooked Goose Inn in Brighton Hollow. I used to work there, and Sir Phillip often stayed there."

"I see. That's good, Nancy. Do you know if she's going to find her father or how long she plans to stay?"

"Oh, just for the night, as far as I know. And she's hoping to find her father. He's been away a long time."

It was almost laughable. One moment he was thinking Catalina knew where her father was all along, and the next moment he was thinking maybe she was telling the truth when she said she didn't know.

Nancy continued, "She might find him there. Sir Phillip is like a carefree bird. He lands somewhere for a little while, and then he ups and flies away again. He can't stay put in one place for long at a time."

"Tell me, when did Miss Crisp leave today?"

"Not much past first light," Mrs. Wardyworth injected

for Nancy, apparently feeling left out of the conversation. "I heard missy say they should be there before dark."

"They will," Nancy added. "It's not that far away. None of us knew they were leaving until late yesterday. I stayed up most of the night cooking and packing food for them so they wouldn't have to buy any. Besides, no one can cook as good as I do."

"I'm sure you're right about that," Iverson said, but a different thought crossed his mind. Maybe Catalina needed Nancy to cook because she didn't have enough money to adequately make the journey.

Iverson picked up his hat and coat. "Thank you, Nancy. You've been most helpful." He then looked at the sullen housekeeper, and for the life of him, he didn't know why, but he added, "You've been helpful, too, Mrs. Wardyworth."

And then much to his surprise, the woman smiled at him and said, "Thank ye, Mr. Brentwood."

Iverson couldn't help remembering one of the first things Catalina said to him was that a few kind words could brighten a person's day. But he didn't need to be thinking about all the things that made Catalina special. His list of those things was already way too long. If what the servants said was true, Catalina had several hours of travel time on him. If he wanted to catch up with her, he needed to forgo his coach and valet and take a satchel and his horse. He could go much faster that way and be there shortly after nightfall. But to do that, he had no time to waste.

And for once, maybe he could be the one to turn the tables on Catalina.

But the first thing he had to do was find his brother and tell him he was leaving Town. Matson wouldn't be happy, but it wouldn't be the first time he'd done something to upset his brother—and now that Iverson had met Catalina, it looked like it wouldn't be the last. Right now, following her was more important than finding warehouse space that wasn't owned by Sir Randolph Gibson.

Iverson didn't fully understand his feelings for Catalina, and he supposed he didn't have to. But he did have to find her and make sure she was all right. Later he would think about her father. He hadn't lost his desire to put a death scare in Sir Phillip about the parody he'd written.

Twelve

What will not woman, gentle woman dare;
when strong affection stirs her spirit up?
—Robert Southey

THE JOURNEY TO THE COOKED GOOSE INN TOOK MUCH longer than Catalina expected. She hadn't traveled often in her lifetime, as there was never the need. She was fairly unfamiliar with the process. She remembered taking a long journey with her mother and father when she was about the age of seven or eight, but she hadn't been past the outskirts of London in years.

The biggest surprise of the day to her was how often they had to stop and rest the horses. Her aunt and her maid looked forward to the respites from the cramped compartment and would always take the opportunity to get out of the carriage, stretch their legs, and be slow about getting back inside. Aunt Elle was careful not to grumble where Catalina could hear her, but Catalina could tell the hours in the carriage were not to her aunt's liking.

Catalina's father had taken their bigger traveling coach, so she and Auntie had to make do with the landau. The smaller, lightweight conveyance was not built for a long journey over often hazardous roads, but she didn't have a choice. She didn't have the money to hire a larger coach. Since Nancy had packed them enough food for at least two days of travel, Catalina hoped all she would have to pay for was one night's lodging and her father's expenses. After that was paid, there would be no more money until her father wrote another story or poem.

All seemed to be going well until they left central London and connected with the main post road. The way became almost treacherous at times, as the carriage seemed to hit one hole after another. When they made their first rest stop, she had talked to Briggs and his young groom, Adam, about the possibility of going around the holes, but they both assured her they had to stay in the hardened ruts in order to keep the landau rolling safely along.

And if it wasn't enough to worry about the competence of the carriage, Aunt Elle's elderly maid, Sylvia, grunted loudly every time they hit a bump. Catalina could have brought along her own maid but knew her aunt would be more comfortable and agreeable having Sylvia to tend to her. At one point when the road was particularly grueling, Catalina wondered if the carriage or her aunt's maid would make it to the inn. Neither one seemed to be up to the trip.

Sometime late in the afternoon, Aunt Elle had finally laid her head on her maid's shoulder and gone to sleep. Thankfully, her maid went to sleep, too. And for once Catalina was happy her aunt brought along her satchel of tonics. Heaven only knew what was in the little bottles of elixir Aunt Elle sipped during the afternoon, but Catalina suspected they were heavily laced with brandy. But for today, she was glad the mixture kept her aunt happy, and that made the traveling a little easier for everyone.

Catalina was thankful for the peace and quiet but quickly

discovered she couldn't read or work on her stitchery in the bumpy carriage, as it made her stomach feel queasy. She'd been forced to simply stare out the window at the passing scenery. When her mind was idle, she thought about Mr. Brentwood. She had tried to occupy her thoughts with other people, other things, but nothing worked. If she believed in such nonsense as curses, she'd think the man had put a spell on her.

It was dusk by the time the carriage rolled to a stop in front of the Cooked Goose Inn. Catalina didn't wait for Briggs or Adam to help her down. She shoved the door open the moment the landau stopped, held up the hem of her skirt, and jumped down, leaving the men to deal with her aunt and Sylvia. She had to know if her father was at the inn.

Catalina hurried inside and found the innkeeper, Mr. Turner, only to discover a few minutes later her father had been there but had left two days ago. The innkeeper had no idea where he went or if he would be coming back. She whispered a silent prayer that he was on his way home. She thought about turning around and heading straight back to London without a minute's rest but knew that wouldn't be fair to Adam and Briggs. If her father was on his way home, he would still be there by the time she returned tomorrow evening. Hiding her disappointment, she put a smile on her face and secured a room for Aunt Elle, Sylvia, and herself, as well as accommodations for Briggs and Adam. She promised Mr. Turner she would pay for her father's lodging when she settled with him in the morning.

After chatting with the innkeeper about her father and Nancy, Catalina realized how weary she was from the day's travel. She was looking forward to bed, until she went up to her room and realized how small a space she was to share with Aunt Elle and Sylvia. She grabbed her needlework and told her aunt she was going below stairs for a while to sit by the fire in the ladies' parlor and give them time to have their dinner and ready themselves for bed.

The inn wasn't a large or spacious establishment but accommodating enough for the few patrons she'd seen. The taproom was located on one side of the vestibule and the dining room on the other. She heard a smattering of chatter coming from the taproom as she made it to the bottom of the stairs. She found Mr. Turner and asked if she could spend some time in the ladies' parlor. He assured her it would be fine and showed her to the room. As was usual for inns, it was down the main corridor and at the back of the inn, away from any raucous or unsavory language that might be coming from the taproom. And unlike the taproom, which had a large opening with no doors, the ladies' parlor had a single entranceway with a door giving it privacy.

The room was empty, but a small fire and a lamp were lit, making the atmosphere welcoming. Mr. Turner built up the fire and brought her in a steaming pot of tea.

After closing herself inside, she pulled a high-backed rocker in front of the fire and made herself comfortable. She picked up her needlework and began her stitchery. She tried to stay focused on the intricate flower design but found her mind wandering from Mr. Brentwood to her father to wondering what they were going to do for money until her father could sell more of his work. She didn't know how long she'd been embroidering when she heard the door open. Thinking it was the innkeeper coming in to stoke the fire or ask if she needed anything, she looked up, smiling. But it wasn't Mr. Turner she saw, it was Iverson Brentwood.

Her needle fell still in her hands. She was tired and weary from the exhausting coach ride and disappointed she had missed her father, but all the tension she'd felt since she'd started her journey ebbed at the sight of Mr. Brentwood. Catalina experienced the same feelings she'd had when she saw him outside *The Daily Herald* building a week ago. Joy swelled in her breast, and she had an overpowering urge to get up and run into his strong arms.

Looking at him dressed so handsomely in his white shirt, fawn-colored riding breeches, and black, shiny, knee-high riding boots, she knew she wasn't upset with him for following her. She was happy to see him and wanted to have a pleasant conversation with him.

His gaze stayed locked on hers as he stepped into the room and clicked the door shut behind him.

"Good evening, Miss Crisp," he said with amusement lurking in his disarming eyes. "I trust you were expecting me."

She returned the smile. "No, actually I wasn't, though I should have been. I was too busy patting myself on the back because I thought I had gotten away without you knowing I was gone."

He walked toward her with an easy, rolling stride that exuded self-confidence, and a little thrill of excitement raced through her.

"You almost did. You had quite the lead on me."

"But obviously not enough to elude you," she teased lightly. "I'll be more diligent next time. I can assure you no matter where I go from now on, I will look behind me to see if you are catching up."

There was seductiveness to his throaty chuckle, and

Catalina's chest tightened, her stomach fluttered, and her skin tingled. Oh, yes, if not for his threat against her father, this man could be the hero of all her dreams.

His blue gaze stayed on hers. "I'm not sure I want to get to the point where I'm that predictable, Miss Crisp."

Catalina shrugged casually, easily, and laid her stitchery on the table by the teapot. "Too late, Mr. Brentwood, you already have."

"You wound me again. Perhaps instead of admitting I am following you, I will just say I am looking for Sir Phillip at the same place you are looking for him."

"Oh," she said as innocently as possible. "Is that the reason you think I'm here?"

A moment of concern etched its way into his eyes. "Isn't it?"

Catalina laughed softly. She enjoyed perplexing him. "Of course it is. But unfortunately for me, he isn't here."

"Unfortunate for me, as well," he whispered more under his breath than to her.

She smiled again, remembering how frustrated he was that first day she met him because her father wasn't home.

"You know, if I hadn't met Sir Phillip on more than one occasion, I might be tempted to think the man doesn't actually exist."

"I am living proof he does. Now, tell me which one of my servants you bribed."

"Oh, no, Miss Crisp." He shook his head. "A gentleman doesn't divulge his sources. He may have to use them at another time."

"But we've already established you are no gentleman, Mr. Brentwood."

"Oh, I should have known." A teasing light shone in his

eyes. "That's true, but I do have a code of honor I live by. I'd like to think most gentlemen would approve of it."

He pulled a chair over opposite hers and sat down, extending his booted feet toward the fire and making himself comfortable.

"Sir, you can come in to say hello, but you can't stay. You must go to the taproom where all the men are or into the dining room."

"Not to worry, Miss Crisp, everything is fine. I had a talk with the innkeeper before I came in here, and a few extra coins turned the ladies' parlor into a drawing room tonight where everyone is welcome."

Excitement danced through her senses, but she willed it to stay under control. "You didn't."

Mr. Brentwood made no effort to hide his grin. "I did."

"In that case, we shouldn't be in here alone. Someone might come in and see us and start more gossip."

His brows lifted slightly, and a warm gleam sparkled in his eyes. "I don't think that will happen, either."

"We might be a long way from London, but Society's rules still apply."

"I agree."

"What did you do?"

"The innkeeper assured me he wouldn't let the two locals who are in the taproom know the ladies' parlor had been converted into a drawing room."

A feeling of expectancy stole over Catalina. "You paid for that bit of convenience, too, didn't you?"

A possessive smile lifted the corners of his mouth. "Well, the man does need to make a living. I'm happy to help him out however I can."

"You are very sure of yourself. You do know how to get your way, don't you?"

"Most of the time," he said confidently but without arrogance. "It's a rather skillful and useful asset to have. Now, tell me, were you hoping to find your father so you could warn him that I'm looking for him?"

Catalina bit down on her bottom lip and studied on his question. She could answer *yes* and be telling the truth. But she would be admitting to only part of the reason she wanted to find her father. Between *A Tale of Three Gentlemen* and the mounting bills, the reasons for finding her father were multiplying.

"Yes," she finally said, "but there are other, private reasons I need to find him, as well. I believe I've mentioned he's never been away this long before, and I find it a little disconcerting that he hasn't returned."

"I'm sure you would have heard if anything nefarious had happened. He's probably holed up somewhere, writing more of his poetry, prose, or perhaps another parody of some unsuspecting family."

Deciding not to comment on the parody, she simply said, "I keep telling myself no harm has come to him." She answered a little more brightly than she was feeling at the moment.

"How is Mrs. Gottfried?"

"The traveling made her very tired. I'm sure she and her maid are already asleep." Catalina paused and picked up her needlework. "I should be going up to my room, too."

He reached over and touched her arm. "Wait. Don't go yet." He rose from his chair, took the embroidery from her hand, and laid it back on the table. "I'm enjoying sitting here alone with you. Stay a little longer."

Catalina's breaths shortened, and her heart started thudding. She was tempted, but she said, "I'm sure that is not a good idea."

He looked down at her. "I promise your reputation is safe."

"It's not my reputation I'm worried about." She started to add it was her heart that concerned her, but thankfully she caught herself before she revealed that secret.

"What, then?" he asked.

Catalina remained silent.

"I don't frighten you, do I?"

"No, you know you don't."

In an easy, slow motion, he reached down and took hold of her upper arms and gently pulled her out of the chair so they stood face to face. She heard muted voices from the taproom, the crackling of the dying fire, and her own labored breathing, but the thought of protesting never entered her mind.

She watched as his handsome face descended toward hers in an unhurried manner. She knew he was going to kiss her. That didn't surprise her, but that she wanted him to, did.

Her eyes closed, and her lips parted slightly as his warm mouth descended slowly, lower and lower, until his lips settled over hers. She felt magical sensations speeding across her breasts, spiraling through her stomach, and tumbling down into the lower depths of her abdomen, to then spread between her legs.

The kiss was slow, languid, and potent. Sweetness filled her.

His lips moved back and forth over hers with controlled leisure. Brushing, nipping, and sometimes hovering just above hers, making her want to reach up and demand kisses from him. But always just before she did, his lips would claim hers again, sending shimmers of euphoria washing through her.

She tingled with discovery when his tongue grazed hers. She sighed and opened her mouth to him. His tongue searched the inner surface of her lips and then probed the depths of her mouth without hesitating.

His lips left hers, and he kissed her forehead, the corner of each eye, the tip of her nose, and across both cheeks. Catalina closed her eyes, savoring the touch of his lips all over her face.

"It feels like it is raining kisses," she whispered breathlessly.

"It is," he answered huskily. "Are you enjoying it?"

"Very much," she said and arched her neck back so his kisses could flow over her chin and down the slender column of her throat. She leaned toward him and felt him back away.

Her eyes opened to find his blue, blue gaze set on hers, his lips just above hers. His expression was serious. "Tell me you want me to kiss you, Catalina."

His demand confused her. "Why?" she whispered. "Don't you know I do?"

His large hand slipped around her neck and cupped it, while his thumb caressed her bottom lip. "I need to hear from you that you want this as much as I do. I won't kiss you again unless you tell me to. I won't force you to do anything you don't want to do."

"Yes," she answered softly without hesitating. "I want you to kiss me. I want you to show me how to kiss you."

A soft chuckle rumbled from his throat. "So you want to give me pleasure, too?"

She hesitated for a moment. "Is that not the way it is supposed to be?"

"Yes, but few women recognize that. I'm not surprised you do."

He smiled and slowly took hold of her wrists and placed her arms around his neck. Catalina locked her fingers together at his nape. He slid his arms around her waist and gently pulled her tightly to his chest. Cuddled in his arms again, she felt safe, delicious, and very daring.

He bent his head and kissed her temple and then rested his cheek against her hair. He breathed in deeply and whispered, "I love the way you fit into my arms, and the way your hair smells."

Chills of desire prickled across her skin. She gloried in the strength of his body nestled so close to hers.

He ran his hand up and down her back, pressing her tighter against his hard body. Lowering his lips to her ear, he murmured, "You feel so soft and womanly."

He slowly outlined her lips with his tongue. "You taste sweet, so very sweet."

Following his lead, Catalina rose on her toes and placed her cheek against his. She felt the stubble of his day-old beard, but whispered, "I like the feel of your skin against mine." Her hands spread over his wide shoulders and then slid down his strong arms. "I like the power in your embrace." She kissed him gently and then moistened her lips. "I like the taste of your lips on mine."

Iverson smiled with appreciation. "You learn fast."

Catalina returned his smile. "This is not a difficult lesson to learn."

"What about this?" he asked and then placed his hand

over one breast, cupped it in the palm of his hand, and squeezed ever so gently.

Catalina stopped breathing. Her eyes opened wide. He was massaging her breast. Even if she'd known what to say, she couldn't speak. Somehow she felt as if he was settling his claim on her. And more surprising still, she was content with that.

She felt his thumb hunting for her nipple hidden beneath her dress and undergarments, and it tantalized her. A slow ache started low in her abdomen and quickly became intense. Her body trembled with a surging, urgent need that built inside her.

"Have I finally found a way to silence you, Catalina?"

She swallowed hard, and her breath returned. "No. I'm simply marveling at how a man who talks like a brutish rake at times and insists he's no gentleman can have such a tender touch."

For a moment, Catalina thought her compliment might have made him hesitant, but then in a raspy voice, he answered, "You make it easy for me to be gentle."

She raised her head to his and whispered, "Stop torturing me, Iverson, and kiss me again before I faint."

"With pleasure, Catalina," he murmured, and his lips covered hers once again.

The kiss deepened, and their hands found freedom. She explored the breadth of his shoulders and back. He caressed, molded, and flattened her breasts against his hands while his tongue swirled inside her mouth. She felt his body tremble, and it thrilled her to know this passion between them made him weak, too.

His eagerness to kiss her harder, press her closer, fed hers.

She lifted her hips toward him, and he pressed against her softness. His lips left hers and he fluttered kisses down her neck, leaving shivers of pleasure everywhere they touched. With deft fingers, he pulled on the high neckline of her dress, trying to move his kisses lower. She knew there were more than kisses and caresses to explore with him and she wanted to experience everything.

"Oh, God, Catalina," he whispered huskily against her lips before kissing her passionately once again. And then he abruptly let go of her and stepped back.

Catalina heard his labored breathing and her own. Her body yearned for his touch to return, though somewhere in the back of her mind she knew he had done the right thing in stopping this madness. She certainly didn't have the will-power to do it.

She didn't understand the confusion she saw in his eyes, until he said, "I didn't know you would be so sweet, so eager, so tempting. I didn't know you would be so willing. Damnation, I didn't mean to kiss you and touch you like that."

"I was startled by the urgency between us, too," she admitted. "Is it always so thrilling to kiss and touch with such abandon?"

"Yes," he said, and then quickly shook his head and added, "No."

Catalina could tell he was almost flustered. "Are you confused?"

He grunted a laugh and sucked in a heavy breath. "No, no, I'm not confused, but it's difficult to explain to such an innocent."

"I'm sure I can understand if you will just tell me," she insisted softly.

"It's not that simple, Catalina. Besides, feelings and desires are different for a man."

"In what way?"

"It's always thrilling, but even more so if it's…"

"If it's what?"

"With the right person. And that doesn't explain it well, either. This isn't even something we should be discussing, Catalina. I shouldn't have touched you as I did. There are reasons why we can't—"

"Say no more," she said, feeling a great sense of rejection and loss for what might have been if he hadn't suddenly remembered she was Sir Phillip's daughter. She was not the right person for him. "I understand."

"No, you don't understand."

"Of course I do," she whispered softly. "My father stands between us, and I fear he always will." She reached down and picked up her sewing. "Good night, Mr. Brentwood."

Catalina hurried out of the room without looking back.

Thirteen

*Love is lost in men's capricious minds, but
in women's, it fills all the room it finds.*
—John Crowne

THE RATTLE OF HARNESS AND NEIGHING OF HORSES
woke Iverson. He lay still for a moment, letting his eyes
adjust to the faint gray light of early morning that filtered
in from the small, uncovered window. The memory of soft
lips beneath his tumbled through his mind, awakening the
pleasure he'd enjoyed last night. Catalina had bewitched
him for certain. She was now filling his waking and sleep-
ing hours.

His body responded with a throb at the thought. Pleasure
was not near strong enough a word for what she'd made him
feel when he held her, kissed her, and touched her.

His eyes closed again, and he relived the exquisite torture of Catalina's soft body pressed tightly to his. She was
beautiful and so responsive to his teaching. She was a sensual woman and eager to know a man's touch. He would have
loved to be the one to awaken her banked desires and show
her all the many delights that awaited her. But until after he'd
had his talk with Sir Phillip, he didn't need to become any
more entangled with the man's innocent daughter, no matter
how much his body begged him to do it.

He chuckled to himself and threw his forearm over his eyes to shut out the light of dawn seeping into the room. He needed more sleep and more dreams of Catalina. If he was the blackguard he always claimed to be, he wouldn't think twice about deflowering the lovely, tempting Catalina. What better way to get back at the man who had sullied his mother's memory than to ruin his only daughter?

But that idea held no appeal for Iverson. Catalina was not at fault. Sir Phillip was. And Iverson intended to have a very serious talk with the man and impress upon him his responsibility, including the necessity of assuring no further slurs on Iverson's family.

Muted, distant voices broke through his thoughts, and his eyes popped open again. If there was a coach preparing to leave, it had to be Catalina's. His mind came fully and instantly awake. He threw the thin woolen blanket aside and rushed to the window. He wiped condensation off the pane with his open palm. In the swirling fog below, he saw Catalina's driver, Briggs, standing beside a landau, and that was definitely Mrs. Gottfried clutching her satchel beside him. Bloody hell, had they traveled to the inn in that lightweight carriage, and with a driver who could barely speak and couldn't hear at all?

What was Catalina thinking?

Didn't she know the roads between London and Brighton Hollow were watched by thugs and highwaymen just looking for a poorly equipped and unarmed carriage?

There was no time to shave or even to dress properly. They were preparing to leave. As hastily as he could, Iverson stepped into his trousers and buttoned them. He threw his shirt over his head and packed it into his waistband. He grabbed a leather belt holding a dagger on one side and buckled it around his waist.

His boots were not as easy to put on, but he pulled on his stockings and shoved his feet into them as fast as he could. After throwing on his waistcoat, he buttoned it as he searched the top of a small chest and the surrounding floor for the braided cord he used to tie back his hair. But in the near darkness of the room, he couldn't find it. He swore with a heavy sigh and gave up his hunt, leaving the room the way no self-respecting gentleman ever should, with his collar, neckcloth, and coat in one hand, traveling satchel in the other, and his uncombed hair hanging straight.

Iverson made it outside in time to see Briggs helping Mrs. Gottfried into the carriage and Catalina standing next in line to board.

"Miss Crisp!" he called, wondering if she would even speak to him after the way he'd bungled their time together last night. Truly, he'd meant only to give her a few chaste kisses.

"Wait." He set his satchel down and jogged toward her while pulling on his black coat.

Catalina stepped away from the carriage and looked at him curiously. "Mr. Brentwood, what's wrong? Has something happened? You look"—she paused—"disheveled."

"That's because I am, Miss Crisp."

He stopped in front of her and raked his long hair away from his face and forehead with his palm. There was nothing to be done about his hair until he found something to tie it with.

"I woke to hear you preparing to leave and knew if I was going to catch you before you took off, I had to hurry outside."

Humor lurked in her eyes, and amusement twitched at the corners of her lovely mouth. It made him desperate to kiss her. No doubt it amused her to see him in such a state of dishabille.

Evidently, she'd had no unpleasant effects from last night and had slept very well. She looked as fresh and beautiful as an open rose in the middle of July. It seemed as if he was the only one who had gone to bed frustrated and in an ill temper.

He wished he had time to just stand there and feast on her loveliness. He was utterly enchanted by her. He suddenly had the urge to untie the perfect bow of ribbon under her chin and strip off her bonnet. He wanted to unfasten her cape and kiss the hollow of her throat while he listened to her feminine sounds of pleasure.

"I'm glad you caught us," she said. "It gives me the opportunity to thank you."

"For kissing you, I hope."

"Shh," she whispered and stepped closer to him. "Heavens no."

"I believe you thanked me the last time I kissed you."

"Yes, but that was because it was my first kiss."

"Oh, I didn't realize you give thanks only for your first kiss and not the second."

"Mr. Brentwood, I'm not talking about kisses at all. You should have told me last night that while you were paying Mr. Turner to turn the ladies' parlor into a drawing room, you also paid for our lodging."

He shrugged. "I knew you would find out soon enough."

Her eyes softened. And he could see in her expression the small payment of her shot meant a great deal to her. He wondered just how light in the pockets her father had left her.

"You shouldn't have, but thank you. I've not done very much traveling, and I wasn't as prepared for this trip as I should have been."

He gave her an understanding smile.

"Good morning, Mr. Brentwood," Mrs. Gottfried said, sticking her head out of the carriage door.

Iverson sucked in a labored breath and managed to say, "Good morning to you, Mrs. Gottfried."

"I had no idea you were staying at this inn, too. I find that a strange coincidence."

"I arrived late last night," he answered, trying to fasten his stiff collar at the base of his throat while his neckcloth dangled from his arm. "The innkeeper told me you had already retired for the evening."

"Yes, it was a terribly long day for us," she said.

"He's following us again, Auntie."

Iverson glanced at Catalina. A wicked light of mischief danced in her sparkling eyes. No doubt it amused her to see him in such a state of dishabille and at the mercy of her teasing.

"Nonsense," Mrs. Gottfried said. "Why would he want to do that? And how would he know we were here? We didn't even know we were coming ourselves until the day before we left."

"Exactly, Mrs. Gottfried," Iverson countered. He wound his neckcloth under his collar and tied the ends into a hasty bow. "I'm here for the same reason you are. I'm looking for Sir Phillip."

"The innkeeper said we missed him by two days," she offered. "And unfortunately, my brother didn't enlighten anyone here as to where he was going when he left. A bad habit he has."

"So I heard," Iverson said to the woman, brushing his hair away from his forehead again and wishing like hell he had a string in his pocket.

"It's imperative we find him, Mr. Brentwood," Catalina's aunt continued. "Where are you going to look next? Perhaps this time we can follow you?"

Catalina laughed softly. "Stop that, Auntie. We will not follow him or anyone. Besides, he has no more of an idea where Papa is than we do, and probably less."

"That is true, madam. I'm all out of ideas as to where the man could be."

"Then I suppose it is back home for us," the older woman said. "Are you ready, Catalina?"

"Mrs. Gottfried, before you go, may I have a word with your niece?"

"Of course you may."

Iverson and Catalina walked a short distance away, and when he looked back at the carriage, Mrs. Gottfried had disappeared inside. He looked at Catalina and said, "Tell me you didn't come all the way from London in the landau."

Another smile brightened Catalina's eyes, and Iverson wondered how she could look so lovely so damned early in the morning and on such a gray day.

"As you wish, we didn't."

"But you did," he said tightly, wanting to impress upon her his concern for her traveling in such an unsuitable carriage.

"Of course," she said, smiling again and stretching her arm out toward the carriage. "We had no other to use. My father has our coach, and I didn't have—" She moistened her lips. "I didn't want to take the time to hire a larger coach. Why are you interested?"

"Because I know that"—he pointed to the landau—"was not built for long-distance traveling. You could have broken a wheel, and then what would you have done?"

"We would have changed it. Briggs keeps an extra boarded under the carriage."

"And speaking of your driver, please tell me you have someone other than him with you."

"Adam is with us." She pointed to a young lad standing beside the horses.

"That stable boy is Adam?" Iverson felt his anger rising again that she would travel so ill-prepared. "He can't be considered a qualified guard. He looks barely old enough to be away from his mama."

"Adam is not that young, Mr. Brentwood. He's not sure of his exact age. He thinks he is fifteen or sixteen, but he is a young man for sure. He's simply short and has a small build for his age."

Iverson grunted a laugh. It did not surprise him she defended yet another servant. "He might be small and short for his age, but he has certainly learned how to fool you. He's not even shaving yet. That youngster can't be more than twelve or thirteen at the most. You need a guard who is armed with a sword, a pistol, and a musket. You need a driver who can talk and hear other coaches or, God forbid, highwaymen approaching."

Much to his aggravation, Catalina remained unperturbed. "When we were outside *The Daily Herald* you said you didn't notice that Briggs doesn't speak or hear very well."

"At the time, I was trying to be kind."

"Thank you. I appreciate that. But it seems that Mr. Brentwood obviously woke on the wrong side of the bed this morn. Perhaps you should go back to bed and try getting up on the other side to see if it improves your disposition."

Iverson shifted his stance. He didn't know how she remained so calm. "You can't be careless with your safety when traveling, Catalina. You should be worried about bandits waiting to rob you or worse."

"Or worse?" Her eyebrows lifted, and she gave him an exaggerated expression of doubt. "What kind of stories have you been reading, Mr. Brentwood? On our journey here yesterday, we encountered no trouble with our carriage or its wheels. We were not set upon by thieves or any other unscrupulous kind of scoundrels. And even if we had been, why should I be worried? We have no money or jewels with us and very little clothing anyone would want to take from us. You probably have more coins in your pockets than we do."

"That might be," he argued, "but I also have this, should I encounter trouble." He pushed his coat aside with his elbow and lifted his waistcoat, showing the intricately carved handle of a large dagger. "And I have a pistol in my satchel, should I need it."

Her gaze stayed on his as she moistened her lips and then gave him another teasing smile. "You are quite well-armed, and I'm sure it makes you feel powerful and safe."

As she teased him unmercifully, Iverson was having a hard time focusing on his reprimand. And when she looked at him with that shimmering light in her eyes, all he wanted to do was take her into his arms and kiss her.

"As anyone who is traveling outside London should be, Miss Crisp," he insisted.

"You know what I think, Mr. Brentwood?"

If she kept up that wickedly beautiful and amused smile, he would chance Mrs. Gottfried catching them and kiss her before she boarded her carriage. She enchanted him to distraction. "That you are careless with your safety?"

"No, for I am not. Briggs is well-armed, and he is an excellent shot. Adam is his ears and voice. Now why don't you admit you are simply upset because I left to search for my father without telling you about it?"

"Catalina, I will gladly admit that. I am."

"Good," she said with a satisfied smile.

"But I'm also concerned for you."

As if she finally understood what he was telling her, her eyes and expression softened again. "I think you are also upset and quite possibly angry with me because I wanted you to kiss me last night."

A soft laugh passed his lips. "My sweet Catalina, I might be angry and upset, too, but I'm certain it's not because we kissed. Why would I be?"

She blinked several times. "Because I am Sir Phillip's daughter."

"I am not sorry we kissed, Catalina. And I might as well let you know it will not be the last time I kiss you. If your aunt wasn't in that carriage, I would kiss you right now."

The desire in her eyes let him know she would accept his kisses if they were alone.

"We have a long ride ahead of us," he said. "We'd best get started. I'm going to ride beside the coach and see you get into London safely."

"We will be quite fine without you."

"Probably," he added, "but I'll be traveling with you anyway."

Catalina couldn't keep her gaze off Iverson. And she had the
distinct feeling he didn't want her to. He rode his magnificent horse right beside the small window in the door of the
carriage. Throughout the morning, she tried to concentrate
on other things: her aunt's chatter, the maid's grunts, the
scenery, but nothing else held her attention, and her gaze
kept straying out the window to Iverson. Sometimes he
would catch her watching him, and he would smile. He was
enjoying the fact she couldn't keep her eyes off him.

It was amazing how easily she'd come to think of him as
Iverson rather than Mr. Brentwood. She'd have to be careful
and not call him by his Christian name to Aunt Elle or anyone
else. At times, she laid her head back against the cushion and
closed her eyes. It wasn't long before her thoughts turned to
Iverson's kisses, caresses, and his strong embrace. It was no
wonder there were such stirring words of poetry and prose
about romance and lovers. She would never read poetry
again without thinking of Iverson's kiss and touch and the
sensations they created inside her.

Whenever they stopped to rest the horses, he would walk
over and talk to her and her aunt. At midday they ate leftover
cheese and bread covered with some of Nancy's apricot preserves. But by early afternoon, the gray clouds of morning
had darkened, and the skies turned stormy. The wind kicked
up, rocking the landau and whistling around the doors.

Catalina kept hoping they would make it home before the
rain started, but late in the day they ran out of luck. A light
mist started falling and quickly turned into a heavy, slashing
rain that beat against the carriage. Catalina knew Briggs and

Adam had cloaks and hats made especially to keep the rain off them, but through the gray swirls, she saw Iverson hadn't put a rain garment over his greatcoat and had no hat for his head. He was getting soaked to the skin by the downpour. Surely if he'd had the proper clothing with him, he would have put it on.

He had admonished her for not being appropriately equipped for the journey, but he seemed to be the one ill-prepared for the trip. She knew by how chilly it was inside the carriage that the temperature outside was dropping fast. She and her aunt had pulled out blankets long before the storm started.

When Catalina could no longer stand to see Iverson riding hatless in the cold rain, she turned to her aunt and said, "I'm going to ask Mr. Brentwood to come inside the carriage and ride with us. He has no cloak or hat."

"In this weather?" Aunt Elle exclaimed. "What was he thinking? Of course, invite him in here with us."

Catalina hit the roof with the tip of her closed umbrella, signaling Briggs she wanted him to stop.

As soon as Briggs opened the door, Catalina stuck her umbrella out the door and opened it. The wind almost whipped the umbrella from her grasp. She stepped down, and rain immediately drenched the hem of her dress and her soft traveling slippers. Her feet squished deep into the muddy earth. When Iverson saw her walking toward him, he jumped down from his horse and went to meet her. His near shoulder-length hair lay flattened against his head, and the ends were running water. Streams of rain ran down his cheeks. His face was pale, and his lips had lost their healthy color.

"What's wrong?" he asked, stopping in front of her. "What are you doing out of the carriage?"

"Never mind about me. What are you doing riding in this storm without proper clothing?"

"You could have called me over to your window to ask me that. Your feet are getting soaked. Now get back inside."

"I will not go back until you come inside the coach, too."

"No, Miss Crisp. I will ride out here in the rain with your driver and footman."

"But they have rain capes and proper hats to keep the rain off them. You don't even have a hat for your head, and you dared to accuse me of traveling unprepared."

"I came with them," he countered. "It's unfortunate, but in my haste, I left them back at the inn."

"That was unwise, Mr. Brentwood."

"Agreed, but as you know, I thought you were going to leave without me, and so I hurried out, leaving a few things behind. Now, you need to get back inside. I am good with riding my horse."

"Do not be stubborn, Iverson."

He smiled, and her heart tripped.

"Did you call me Iverson?"

"Yes. I can see you are chilled to the bone. You will catch a death cough if you stay out here any longer, and I will not have that on my conscience. Now swallow your stubborn pride and get in the landau."

He grinned, and Catalina's heart felt as if it melted.

"I like it when you call me Iverson. Be careful, Catalina. You sound worried about me. If you don't watch out, I might start to think you actually care about my well-being."

"Don't flatter yourself so much," she said sharply but

knew he told the truth. "I am pressuring you only because Aunt Elle is worried sick about you. She is the one who has grown quite fond of you because you remind her of her dearly departed husband. Now, I can stand out here in the rain as long as you can. I'm not getting back in the carriage without you."

"Ah, you should have told me about Mrs. Gottfried in the first place." He smiled. "Get back inside, Catalina. I will tie my horse to the back and speak to Briggs. I'll see you inside shortly."

"Thank goodness," she murmured and turned around.

Shivering, with her feet feeling like ice, Catalina climbed back into the carriage. She hovered beneath a blanket, waiting impatiently for Iverson to secure his horse. When he opened the door and stepped inside, he immediately filled the cab with his presence. Her aunt and her maid sat on one side, and he had no choice but to sit beside Catalina.

"Come in, come in, Mr. Brentwood," Aunt Elle said. "We've been worried about you."

While he spoke to her aunt, Catalina looked at him. His coat was drenched, and rain dripped from the ends of his loose hair. Obviously, when he raced to leave the inn, his hat was not the only thing he left behind.

With a shake, a jerk, and a rattle, the carriage started moving again. Catalina hoped they weren't too far from London. She knew Iverson needed to get home and out of his wet clothing. She opened the brass catch to her reticule and pulled out a handkerchief with her initials embroidered on the corner and handed it to him. He gave her a grateful smile, took it, and wiped his face.

Aunt Elle opened her satchel and rummaged around

in it until she pulled out a large brown apothecary bottle with a stopper. With bloodshot eyes and a shaky hand, she extended it toward him and said, "Drink this. It will make you feel better and leave you feeling as warm as if you were sitting by a large fire at White's."

"Thank you, madam," he said as he peeled his leather gloves from his fingers. "I don't need a tonic."

"My stars, but you remind me of Mr. Gottfried, God rest his kind soul. You are as stubborn as he was."

Catalina took the bottle from her aunt and handed it to Iverson. "You'll like her tonic, Mr. Brentwood. I think it's mostly brandy."

"Mostly?" Aunt Elle said with a smile. "It's all brandy. I wouldn't give Mr. Brentwood the watered-down spirits."

"In that case, thank you, Mrs. Gottfried." He took the bottle from Catalina and pulled the stopper from the flask and took a drink. He smiled at her aunt and said, "And a very good brandy, too."

"You know, Mr. Brentwood, there is no need for you to continue to follow us. I will allow you to court my niece in the conventional way."

"Auntie, that is not something you should be saying," Catalina admonished.

"Oh hush, Catalina. I'm taking care of this. I just want Mr. Brentwood to know he doesn't have to continue to take such unusual measures in order to see you." She turned her attention to Iverson. "Though I must say I find what you're doing very romantic. Did I ever tell you Mr. Gottfried was a romantic man?"

"No, madam," Iverson said, brushing his hair away from his forehead.

"He was. He never let a week pass without bringing me flowers, even in winter."

"I didn't know. That made him a very thoughtful man."

"Oh, he was," she added wistfully as a faraway look clouded her eyes. She pulled a silver flask from her satchel. "And such a strong man. He was a very solicitous man, too. He's been gone over ten years now, but I still miss him today as much as I did the day he died."

"I'm told true love works that way, Mrs. Gottfried."

"Indeed it does."

Catalina listened and marveled at how caring and attentive Iverson was being to her aunt. He seemed to know just what to say to comfort and appease her, and it touched Catalina deeply. And then suddenly, love for him swelled in her heart.

Love?

Had she just felt love for Iverson?

Who was he? The angry man who'd threatened to harm her father for his writings, or this man who sat before her now, chilled and in rain-soaked clothing, doing his best to gladden the soul of an old lady who'd clearly had too much to drink?

Catalina realized tears had formed in her eyes, and she quickly made herself busy pulling the black silk drawstring from her reticule. She'd noticed Iverson kept brushing his hair away from his face. The cord had small, short tassels on the ends, and he might not want to use it, but she would offer it to him.

"Now, Mr. Brentwood," Aunt Elle said, "I think this might be a fine time for you to tell me about America. Is it truly as uncivilized as I've heard?"

"Perhaps in some places, but not Baltimore," he said as he stuffed his leather gloves into his coat pocket. "It's a thriving city with plenty of industry and social life."

Catalina extended the reticule cord to him. "Would you like to use this for your hair?"

He gave her a sincere smile. "If you're sure you don't mind it getting wet."

She returned his smile. "I don't mind. I don't need it back. Let me hold the tonic for you."

Catalina held the brown bottle of brandy while he tied his hair into a queue. She thought to herself he was just as handsome with his hair hanging straight as when it was pulled back.

For over an hour, Catalina sat quietly and listened to Iverson and her aunt talk with few pauses in between. But when they stopped, it wasn't long before Aunt Elle laid her head on Sylvia's shoulder, closed her eyes, and fell asleep. Her maid fell asleep shortly thereafter.

"You still look cold, Mr. Brentwood," Catalina whispered. "The color has not returned to your lips."

"No matter," he said softly. "I am feeling warm. Brandy will do that for you."

"For once, I'm glad Aunt Elle had it with her."

"I must admit I was glad to get it. It takes the edge off the chill."

Catalina scooted on the seat and moved closer to Iverson, so her side, hip, and leg pressed against his.

"Catalina, what are you doing?"

"Shh," she whispered with her forefinger on her lips. "Don't talk too loudly. Auntie doesn't like to be disturbed when she's snoring."

Iverson chuckled quietly, and keeping his voice low, said, "I don't think she will awaken for a while, and I don't want you to get wet from my coat."

"I am not worried about getting wet."

Catalina shared her blanket by pulling it over his legs. She leaned in close to him, pressing her breasts against the damp sleeve of his coat. "I want to help you get warm."

His eyes questioned her as he said, "You are being very brave, Miss Crisp, with your aunt not two feet away."

"Perhaps, but I don't want you getting a chill. Give me your hands underneath the blanket, and let me rub them."

"Gladly."

He slipped his hands beneath the wool, and she caught them in hers. They felt larger than she expected, and they were still very cold. She placed one of his hands in her lap, and the other she massaged softly and slowly, rubbing the palm and then between each finger. She enjoyed being in his company. She enjoyed talking to him, sparring with him, and most of all kissing him.

Iverson's gaze searched her face while she caressed his hand. "I don't think you know what you are doing to me, Catalina."

She tried to remain aloof, though that was far from what she was feeling. "Of course I do. I am warming your hands."

"You are, and more than just my hands."

She looked at him and said, "Your lips still look pale."

Having no forethought about what she was going to do, Catalina suddenly stretched up and let her lips brush over Iverson's once, twice, and on the third time they stayed on his. He leaned toward her, deepening the kiss. Catalina opened her mouth, and with her tongue, tasted the brandy.

She continued to massage his hand, and wondered if her caresses made him feel the same warm sensations she felt.

"Does this warm you?" she asked against his lips.

"Hotly, Catalina," he said, and pulled his hand from beneath the blanket, and untied the ribbon under her chin.

He kissed his way down one side of her neck and back up the other. The feelings he created in her were exquisite and heady. He then slipped his hand to the back of her neck, pressing her closer to him as his lips came down hard on hers again.

Catalina sighed softly, contentedly, as her breath mingled with his. Desperately, but quietly, their lips clung, and their tongues tasted, stroked, and explored with leisure. She tangled her hands in his wet hair and traced the top of his wide shoulders with her forearms. Being with him like this brought her immense satisfaction but also a yearning for more.

When she realized she wanted him to touch her breasts again and kiss her with wild, unrelenting passion as he had last night, she knew she had to stop before she was completely lost in the moment.

Reluctantly, Catalina broke the kiss.

As if sensing her reticence, Iverson turned her loose. Leaving the blanket with him, Catalina put as much distance between them as she could and looked out the window. The earlier slashing rain had become a drizzle. Through the fog, she saw lighted streetlamps and knew they were coming into London.

Catalina felt an overwhelming need to tell Iverson there were two more parts of *A Tale of Three Gentlemen* yet to be published.

He deserved to know.

But...

Was it so wrong of her to hold out hope her father would return in time so she wouldn't have to? Dare she hope he was at home waiting for her right now?

She had no doubt if she told Iverson the truth he would never speak to her again. If she waited, and by some chance her father had made it home, Iverson would never have to know what she had kept from him.

Fourteen

Our desires always disappoint us; for though we
meet with something that gives us satisfaction, yet
it never thoroughly answers our expectation.
—François de La Rochefoucauld

IVERSON'S THROAT STILL HURT LIKE HELL.

He was sore all over, too, he found as he stepped out of his carriage in front of the well-lighted Great Hall. How did a little cold rain make one so blasted sick?

He'd spent the last three days in bed shaking like a leaf, but finally his fever broke yesterday, and today he was stronger and feeling more like himself. He couldn't miss the first official pre-Season party. He cared nothing for the revelry, but he didn't want to miss an opportunity to see Catalina. On their way back to London, her aunt had mentioned they would be attending the ball at the Great Hall. Catalina would never know the determination and sheer willpower it took for him to brave the early crowds just for her. He knew she'd be gone if he waited until later in the evening.

No doubt the Earl of Bighampton would be there as well, fawning over Catalina, wanting to dance with her, Iverson thought as he climbed the stone steps. He was determined to see that didn't happen.

Matson had come to see him the first day he was back

from the Cooked Goose Inn but stayed only long enough to tell him he had discovered the Duke of Windergreen was out of Town, and his man of affairs wouldn't even discuss the possibility of a lease with them until the duke gave him permission. They had quickly decided to send the duke a letter by private courier in hopes he would agree to their proposal and send back word to his administrator. Now that he was better, Iverson wanted to know if his brother had heard from the duke. And if he stayed long enough at the ball, he would probably see Matson.

There was nothing good about being in bed with chills and fever, but it had given Iverson time to think about Catalina. And think about her he had—night and day. The knot that had settled in his stomach wasn't because he hadn't eaten much the past couple of days but from wanting to see her. He'd never dreamed he'd be smitten by Sir Phillip's daughter. And he had fought it for as long as he could.

He touched his pocket as he made his way up to the entrance. He'd had the handkerchief she'd given him laundered and pressed. It was safely tucked away to return to her tonight.

The tall double doors of the Great Hall were open wide and held back with flower-filled urns. Music, chatter, and laughter roared from the doorway where he left his hat, cloak, and gloves with the servant. He walked to the opening of the ballroom and stood there for a moment, looking at the vast sea of people.

The large hall was flanked down each side by immense fluted columns that had been decorated with flowers and streams of yellow and blue ribbons woven together. Hundreds of candles burned brightly on hanging chandeliers, multipronged candelabras, and tall brass candlesticks placed strategically around the room. The grandeur and scope of the space was tremendous.

After Iverson's eyes adjusted to the light, he scanned the crowd, looking for Catalina. It wouldn't be easy to find her. Unlike the small parties he'd attended all winter in private homes, this event had turned out most everyone in Polite Society. No one wanted to miss the first pre-Season ball of the year.

Iverson didn't see Catalina on his first or second quick glance around the room, so he took his time and gave the stirring mob a slower perusal.

"Mr. Brentwood, what a delightful surprise to see you tonight."

Iverson turned to see Miss Mable Taylor walking up to him with a bright smile on her face. He took an unconscious step backward when she stopped close to him. In her hair she wore an extremely high pointed crown that seemed to be made from some kind of thin gold and silver metal. He assumed she wore it to make her look taller, but to him it made her look ridiculous.

He got the uneasy feeling she'd been watching the door for him, because he'd been standing there for less than a minute when she approached him. He was not up to her idle chatter tonight and would have to think of something quick and clever to get away from her.

"Good evening, Miss Taylor. That headpiece you're wearing is extraordinary."

Her eyes brightened, her smile widened, and her squeal of glee as she clasped her hands together under her chin could have been heard above the chatter, laughter, and music on the dance floor. "I'm so glad you noticed it. It was my mother's artful creation, and my father said it makes me look like a princess. Do you think so?"

"It does. In fact, I know my brother, Mr. Matson Brentwood, would want to see how lovely it looks on you."

"He would?" Her eyes frantically searched the ballroom. "Is he here? Where is he? I haven't seen him come in tonight."

"You must have missed him. He's probably at the buffet table, or perhaps he's already taking a turn on the dance floor. I can't see it from here, so I'm not sure."

She looked back to Iverson and batted her lashes rapidly. "Oh, then perhaps I should go look for him? What do you think?"

"I think he would be disappointed if he missed seeing you tonight."

Miss Taylor reached up, touched her crown, and smiled. "In that case, I should look for him immediately. Do excuse me, Mr. Brentwood."

Iverson chuckled to himself as he watched Miss Taylor skip merrily away. Of course, if Matson were indeed here, he wouldn't be too happy Iverson had sent Miss Taylor his way. But it wouldn't be the first or last time his brother would be unhappy with him.

Iverson took his time and slowly looked over the ballroom once again. He saw no sign of Catalina or her aunt and he was beginning to wonder if they had come. The thought that Catalina might be sick, too, entered his mind. But then he caught sight of Lord Bighampton. He was leading Catalina onto the dance floor.

Iverson's chest tightened.

Damnation. He hadn't been able to see her because the

portly earl was standing in front of her. Obviously, Iverson was too late to keep Catalina from dancing with the oaf.

Iverson walked over to a column and leaned against it. He watched as Catalina's and the earl's hands met and clasped over their heads and held as other dancers sashayed under the arch their arms made. He didn't like seeing that man's puffy hands touching Catalina's, even if she did have on elbow-length gloves. For a moment, Iverson thought about tramping down to the dance floor and pushing the barrel-shaped earl out of the way and taking his place with Catalina.

"Mr. Brentwood, are you hiding behind this column?"

Iverson straightened and smiled at Miss Babs Whitehouse. Unlike Miss Taylor, Miss Whitehouse was a delectable feast for a man's eyes. Her face was beautiful, her bosom full, and she knew how to invite a man to enjoy looking at her. She was also clever enough to know how to get a man interested in her—if he were so inclined.

"No, I just arrived and was looking around."

"The hall is already filled. I think everyone is ready for the Season to begin. I know I am, so perhaps you will ask me for a dance later tonight."

"Why don't I ask you right now?" he said without hesitating. "The current dance started just moments ago, and I'm sure we can find a place to fit in on the floor."

Miss Whitehouse smiled. "I think I would like to dance with you right now."

Iverson led the way and took the longer route around the sides of the hall. He could have elbowed his way through the center of the crush of people and ended up right on the dance floor, but Iverson didn't feel up to wading through the swell of expensively gowned ladies and impeccably dressed gentlemen.

He'd had no idea he was going to ask Miss Whitehouse to dance when she walked up beside him, but he was glad the idea popped into his head. He wouldn't mind at all keeping a closer eye on the earl and Catalina.

With patience, he guided Miss Whitehouse onto the dance floor, and they fell in line with the other dancers. There were several couples between them and Catalina and Lord Bighampton, so he started working his way toward them. He knew the moment Catalina saw him, and the pleasure in her eyes pleased him. Just looking at her made him feel better. She kept glancing his way, and so did Lord Bighampton, but not with the happiness Iverson saw on Catalina's face.

It wasn't easy, but Iverson took his time and made a few calculated moves and eventually stepped his way around and through the other dancers, until he and Miss Whitehouse were right beside Catalina and the earl. Lord Bighampton tried to move away from them but succeeded only in confusing the couple on the other side of them and causing the four of them to miss several steps in the dance and scramble awkwardly to catch up.

Iverson smiled when he saw the sparkle of amusement in Catalina's eyes and the look of aggravation on Lord Bighampton's face. He had no doubt the earl was once again throwing imaginary daggers.

Through the next several steps, Iverson glanced over at Catalina and was satisfied to see she was watching him and Miss Whitehouse as raptly as he watched her and Lord Bighampton. Iverson then divided his attention between smiling at Miss Whitehouse and wanting to growl every time he saw the earl inappropriately let his hand slide down Catalina's forearm, or let his stubby fingers tickle the underside of her wrist before letting go of her. For the first time, he was thankful ladies wore gloves. Iverson had an intense desire to wipe the touch of that man from Catalina and to erase all thoughts of him from her memory.

The time finally came in the dance where he and Lord Bighampton exchanged partners for a series of several steps. Iverson felt an immediate sense of relief as he held up a flat hand and Catalina pressed her palm against his. There was something about her touch that comforted him and eased his longing to be with her. As he looked at her lovely face, he remembered how she had caressed his hands and warmed them under the blanket on their journey back to London.

"Are you enjoying yourself, Catalina?" he asked as they walked in a circle.

"Very much, Mr. Brentwood. I love to dance."

"So it's just me you didn't want to dance with when your aunt suggested it a few days ago."

"Sir, I believe you are the one who said you didn't plan on asking me to dance."

They switched hands and turned and walked in the opposite direction. "That's because I knew you wouldn't accept."

"Ha!" she said with a teasing smile. "You knew no such thing. Besides—"

He knew she deliberately left her sentence unfinished, so he took the bait she threw out and asked, "Besides what?"

"A lady can always change her mind."

In seconds, Iverson would have to turn her back over to the earl, so he quickly whispered, "Meet me on the south terrace in half an hour."

"I will not," she whispered back to him.

"Do it," he commanded gently and turned and caught

Miss Whitehouse's hand without missing a step as he returned Catalina to the corpulent earl.

After the long dance, Iverson was in need of some nourishment, so he excused himself from Miss Whitehouse and went to find refreshment and to rest before he met Catalina. He knew she would join him on the terrace, even though she declared she wouldn't.

As she said, ladies could always change their minds.

He found the food table filled with such delicacies as marinated oysters and clams, pickled fish and vegetables, and carvings of various cuts of pork and beef. He ate his fill, and as he was leaving, feeling stronger once again, he looked up and saw Sir Randolph Gibson watching him from the doorway. Iverson hoped the man was not looking to talk to him. He wasn't in a mood to be nice to him after discovering he owned the warehouse space he and his brother were leasing and hadn't bothered to reveal that bit of information.

Iverson stopped and talked to a group of gentlemen but excused himself shortly after one of the men mentioned how much he'd enjoyed *A Tale of Three Gentlemen*. It still amazed him people thought he approved of the story and wanted to hear they had liked it.

He spoke to Lady Windham, hoping Sir Randolph would be gone by the time he was ready to leave the buffet room, but he had no such luck. The dandy was still lingering around the doorway when Iverson headed that way.

"Were you watching me?" Iverson asked as he walked up to the man.

"No. I was waiting for you," Sir Randolph said.

That surprised Iverson. "And why would you be doing that?"

"I wanted to talk to you."

"Why would you even consider talking to me, seeing as you leased space to me and my brother without us knowing it belonged to you?"

The old man's bright-blue eyes narrowed. "You sound as if that upset you."

"Tremendously."

The man never blinked an eye. "Was I supposed to know it would?"

A half laugh passed Iverson lips. Sir Randolph was a cagey old goat. "Hell, yes. Did you doubt it wouldn't?"

"I can't say I thought about it much one way or the other."

Iverson looked around to see if anyone was close enough to hear before he said, "Most everyone in London already thinks you are our father. The last thing Matson and I need is you doing us any favors and perpetuating that gossip."

"There was no favor to the arrangement from me," Sir Randolph said, seeming unperturbed by Iverson's irritation.

"How can you say that when you knew the Duke of Windergreen shut down all other possibilities for us because he was trying to manipulate our brother?"

"It's easy. You pay the same price anyone else would."

What the man said made sense, but Iverson still didn't like it.

Iverson scoffed. "No one will know what we paid, or if we even paid you."

Sir Randolph folded his arms across his chest and said, "I'm not in control of what other people think, but maybe you are. The way I see it, you needed space. I had it. I don't know what else I can add to that."

"We are trying to get in touch with the Duke of Windergreen. Now that his daughter married our brother, he should be more inclined to lease to us."

"I hope it works out for you. But in the meantime, I have some information you might find useful."

Iverson felt the hair on the back of his neck prickle. "About what?"

"I have a lead on the whereabouts of Sir Phillip."

All thoughts of the warehouse incident vanished. Sir Randolph had told Iverson he would let him know if he found out anything about Sir Phillip, but Iverson had never believed the dandy would.

"That would be welcome news, and I'd like to hear it."

"Apparently he's been known to seek his pleasures at Madame Shipwith's house over on the north side of London."

"Is she a widow?"

Sir Randolph shook his head. "She's a courtesan, a highly paid courtesan."

"Not surprising."

"That's not all. She also runs a brothel."

That didn't surprise Iverson, either. It wasn't unusual for highly paid mistresses and courtesans to start their own businesses after their beauty faded.

"Why haven't you checked to see if he's there?"

"I did, but unfortunately I wasn't judicious in my approach to the madame and I didn't learn anything. It wasn't that I didn't know better, I did. So I wouldn't suggest you go in and ask if the gentleman you're looking for is there, if you know what I mean."

Iverson nodded and wondered if Sir Randolph had offered the woman money for information. Probably not, but Iverson would. "I know what you mean. I'll be careful in how I approach her and see what I can find."

The last place a man wanted to be disturbed was at a brothel, but Iverson had no compunction about bothering Sir Phillip no matter where he was. He wanted the matter with Catalina's father settled. And quickly.

Iverson left Sir Randolph and made his way toward the south terrace. He had to see Catalina before he left. He had intended on asking her for a dance. Now that would have to wait for another night. If there was any chance Sir Phillip was at Madame Shipwith's, he had to go there.

She wasn't on the terrace when he arrived, but several other people were. It was an unusually clear night, and a bright half-moon lit the dark sky. Iverson didn't want to get caught up in a conversation with anyone else, so he moved to the side of the building and waited in the shadows until he saw Catalina walk out.

He eased up beside her and steered her as far away from the other people as possible.

"I'm glad you decided to meet me," he said.

"I hope you at least had some doubts as to whether I would."

Iverson laughed and wished he could pull her into his arms and kiss her until he had his fill. "I have always had many doubts where you are concerned, Catalina. You are an expert at keeping me on my toes."

"Don't you mean toe to toe?" she teased.

"Ah, yes. How could I forget Lord Truefitt's column?"

She smiled at him, and her eyes scanned down his face. "I noticed, when we were dancing, you looked pale. I thought it might just be the lighting, but even here in the moonlight, I can see your color is off."

"Really? I can't imagine why," he said, thinking there was no reason for her to know he'd been sick from his ride in the chilling rain.

"You've been ill. I can hear it in your voice, too."

He'd have to remember it was difficult to get anything past Catalina. Neither Miss Taylor nor Miss Whitehouse had noticed his voice was a bit gravelly.

"You can't hear anything," he protested.

"I knew you had gotten too wet the day we returned from the inn. Why didn't you let me know you had been sick?" Catalina demanded.

He realized he actually liked the idea that she was concerned about him. "What would you have done if I had?"

"I would have sent you some of Nancy's chicken stew."

"I really didn't feel up to eating anything for a couple of days, Catalina."

"Well, if I had known that, I would have sent you some of Aunt Elle's tonic."

He laughed. "Now that might have done me some good. I am much better now and not in need of anything but a kiss from you."

Her gaze searched his, and she whispered, "Perhaps I'd be willing if we were not standing out here in the open where others could see us."

Iverson looked at her lovely face and smiled. "Then I will have to plan a time we can be alone."

"That will be difficult."

"But not impossible." He reached into his pocket and handed her handkerchief to her. "I wanted to return this. It saved my life."

"I'm sure you are overstating that," she scoffed, and then

smiled. "But I see you are still wearing the cord from my reticule."

"I've decided it brought me good luck. You did say I didn't need to return it."

She nodded, and he could see it pleased her that he still wore the black string with its small tassels.

"And I meant that."

"I had hoped to ask you for a dance, but now something has come up, and I must leave right away."

Concern sprang to her eyes. "You're still unwell."

"No, truly. I'm fine, but I just received word from some-one who thinks he knows where your father might be. I'm going there now to see if he is."

She stepped closer to him. "My father? Where? Tell me. Better yet, I'll get Auntie and we'll go with you."

"No, no, Catalina." Iverson shook his head. "What I have to say to your father is only between us."

Her eyes suddenly turned stormy. "Because you want to harm him?"

He saw real fear in her expression, and he moved closer, wanting to calm her. "No. Maybe at one time I wanted to, but not anymore. You have my word I will not harm him, Catalina. But if I do find him, or whenever I do, I must make it clear to him there will be consequences if he should write about my family again."

"But what if—?"

"What?" he asked.

She remained silent, as if she were trying to decide what to say, and that puzzled him. Catalina was seldom at a loss for words.

"Are you thinking, what if you could promise me he would

never do it again? You know you can't make that promise for him. He must do it, and I will have it from him."

"Iverson, I— Will you give him a message for me?"

"Of course."

"Tell him I need him to come home. He's been gone much too long."

Iverson had the feeling there was an unspoken *and* at the end of her sentence. He was sure she wanted to say something more, so he waited and gave her time. But the silence dragged, and she remained quiet, with her gaze gently caressing his face.

"If I find him, I'll make sure he gets your message."

"Thank you. Now if you'll excuse me, I need to check on Aunt Elle."

Iverson watched Catalina hurry inside.

Oh, yes, he intended to find Sir Phillip, and before this night was over.

Fifteen

Make haste slowly.
—Latin Proverb

COULD SHE DO IT?

If so, there was no time to waste.

Catalina's heart pounded, and her skin suddenly felt cold as she turned her back on Iverson. She prayed he didn't try to stop her to say more, for if he called to her she would not turn back. If she did, she might change her mind.

Tension struck her fiercely, and her legs felt stiff and awkward as she cleared the terrace doorway and entered the stuffy Great Hall once again. She picked up the hem of her gown, and trying to remain dignified, she hurried toward her aunt. She mumbled, "I'm sorry," several times as she knocked elbows, brushed shoulders, and stepped on long skirts.

"Catalina," someone called to her, but she kept going and pretended she didn't hear. She didn't have a moment to spare. Thankfully, she knew exactly where her aunt was because she'd checked on her before she'd headed out to meet Iverson.

Moments later, hoping she wasn't visibly shaking on the outside as much as she was on the inside, Catalina stopped in front of her aunt. Trying to sound normal, she said, "May I speak to you alone, Auntie?"

"Of course." Aunt Elle rose from her chair, excusing herself from her ribbon of friends lining the dance floor. "What's wrong, dearest? Your face is flushed, and you're wearing a rather frantic expression."

Catalina tried to relax her face. "I'm afraid I am at the moment."

Aunt Elle touched Catalina's gloved arm and moved her farther away from the ladies. "What's wrong?"

"I don't have time to explain everything, anything. I'm not certain I would if I could, but I need you just to trust me."

Aunt Elle gave her a curious look and chuckled softly. "What are you talking about? You know I trust you. That has never been an issue between us."

"I know, but I've never asked anything like this of you. Auntie, I need you to allow me to leave in the carriage immediately, and you must ask Lady Windham or another friend to see you home."

A frown creased her brow. "What?"

"Please, you must do this for me. Tell whomever you choose that I had a headache and had to leave early. Ask them to see you home."

"There's no need for that. I'll go with you."

"No, I want to go alone. I must go alone."

Fear suddenly clouded her aunt's eyes, and the wrinkle in her forehead furrowed deeper. "In the carriage alone? Why, that's an outlandish idea, Catalina."

"It's necessary," she insisted.

"You know I can't allow that, dearest. It would ruin your reputation if anyone found out. I can't do that."

Catalina inhaled deeply while she waited for a group of ladies to walk by, and then whispered earnestly, "You must.

I will have Briggs with me. I don't have much time, Auntie. Please, allow me the freedom to take the carriage and trust that I must do this."

Her aunt's eyes searched her face. "Catalina, this worries me greatly, but I'll agree," she finally said. "I don't think I have a choice. I can see in your eyes you will do this anyway, no matter what I say. You would just slip out of the house later tonight, and that would probably be worse."

"Thank you, Auntie. I promise I will not do anything that would be harmful to me."

"Then go. Go. But I'll wait in the drawing room until you return. And, Catalina, send Briggs after me immediately if you need me."

"Thank you!" She hugged and kissed her aunt and walked away as fast as she thought she could without drawing unwanted attention or arousing suspicions at her hasty exit.

When Catalina made it to the front of the Great Hall, she saw Iverson walking out the front door, putting on his cloak as he went. She hurried over to the servant and asked for her wrap, telling him to please hurry. When he returned, she grabbed her cloak from his hands and rushed down the steps. She spotted the host's footman and asked him to call for her carriage from the side street.

There were several ladies and gentlemen standing in front of the building, chatting, and two or three others stood nearer the street, waiting for their coaches to be brought around. It was early for anyone to be leaving, so there weren't many people around. The problem was that all the gentle-men wore black cloaks and top hats. She would have to get closer to distinguish Iverson from the others, and she had to keep him from recognizing her.

She pulled the hood of her cloak over her head and held the ends around her chin as if she were chilled. At last she recognized Iverson, and her chest tightened. Suddenly, following him seemed too daunting to accomplish. What had made her think she could do it? And without him knowing? The task was overwhelming.

"No," she whispered to herself. She would not be shaken in her resolve so easily. Iverson had followed her. She could follow him. She couldn't let him meet her father alone. She had to be there to lessen the blow when Iverson heard there was more to the story of *A Tale of Three Gentlemen*. Summoning strength from deep inside herself, she shook off the debilitating feeling of defeat and moved closer so she could board her carriage as quickly as possible.

A few moments later, a carriage rounded the corner, and Iverson started walking to the street. When the coach stopped, he climbed inside. Catalina squeezed her hands into fists, wrinkling the fabric of her cloak in her palms. How would she ever find him if his coach went out of her sight before her carriage arrived?

As soon as Iverson's driver shut the door, she hurried to the edge of the street. She whispered, "Come on, Briggs, come on."

Iverson's carriage took off, and her heart sank. Moments later she heard another carriage rounding the corner. Her heart soared. It was Briggs. She motioned for him to hurry.

Briggs pulled the horses to a stop and jumped down from the box to assist her. Breathing heavily, she pointed toward Iverson's coach and said, "Do you see Mr. Brentwood's carriage leaving there?"

He nodded and opened the door for her.

"Follow it, and don't lose it."

"Aunt?" he mumbled, clearly concerned as he helped her step inside.

"Do not worry about her. A friend will see her home. Briggs, we must hurry. Do not lose that carriage. It is turning the corner up ahead. Now, let's go."

Her faithful servant nodded and slammed the door shut. Within seconds, the landau jerked forward, and they started rolling and bumping along the street at a fast clip. Catalina leaned against the cushion and realized she was shivering from excitement as much as from the cold. She laughed at herself when she realized that she was actually following Iverson. She pulled a blanket over her legs and fitted her cloak tightly around her shoulders, snuggling deep into its warmth. All she could do now was wait and trust that Briggs would keep up with Iverson's driver, and without letting the man know he was being followed.

Catalina had no way of knowing exactly how much time passed, but it was perhaps close to half an hour before they stopped and Briggs opened the door. She threw off the blanket, and wrapping her cloak tighter about her, she cautiously looked out. She didn't want to step down until she knew where Iverson was. She spotted him walking toward a large house, so she climbed out.

The atmosphere of the area seemed a little strange to her. There were no streetlamps, houses, or other buildings of any kind nearby. The only lights came from the windows in the house and from the lanterns on the carriage. They couldn't be in a neighborhood, so they had to be somewhere near the outskirts of the city.

She held back and watched Iverson walk up the three

steps to the house and knock. The door opened presently. He talked to the servant for a moment or two and then was allowed inside. That seemed simple enough. But of course she knew it wasn't as easy for a young lady without benefit of a chaperone to enter a home as it was a gentleman. She would tell the servant she was there to meet her father. She couldn't imagine Sir Phillip Crisp's name would not gain her entrance past any door. Thankfully, she was dressed for whatever party was going on inside the house. It should be easy to fit in with the group. If she hurried, she could possibly find her father before Iverson did.

Catalina turned to Briggs and said, "I hope to be back shortly."

Briggs shook his head and made signs with his hands that meant he did not want her to go. He mumbled what sounded like the word "gentlemen."

The place could be a high-stakes gaming house or an out-of-the-way gentlemen's club and not a party for gentlemen and ladies at all. That could present problems, and she could understand Briggs not wanting her to go up to the house if that were the case, but she couldn't let that stop her. She looked back at the house. Her chest ached from holding herself so rigid. The cold air whipped around her, but she would not lose her courage now.

If there was any chance her father was inside, she had to go up to that door. And if it turned out it was a gentlemen's club, she would simply ask that they tell Sir Phillip she was there and needed to speak to him.

Briggs must have sensed her indecision. He pointed to her and then to the house again, and shook his head vehemently.

He mumbled, "You no go," and jerked his thumb toward the house again.

It was unusual for Briggs or any servant to take her to task over anything. He was a gentle man and always eager to please her. She was surprised he was so adamant. Obviously, he was trying to protect her from following Mr. Brentwood, and she appreciated his concern. But this was her decision. He had to accept that she was the one in charge. No one was going to keep her from finding out if her father was in that house.

"I know what I'm doing, Briggs, and I will be fine. You must wait for me here." He continued to shake his head. "Do not disobey me," she said, allowing her irritation at his insistence she not follow Iverson. "Now tell me you understand."

He looked at the house again and then reluctantly pointed to his chest and then to the ground, indicating he would stay there.

She smiled. "Good."

Briggs nodded.

Catalina lifted the hood of her cloak and pulled it over her head and started toward the house with a new determination to find her father and settle the issue of *A Tale of Three Gentlemen* once and for all. She walked up the steps and stopped in front of the door. Her hand shook slightly as she reached for the door knocker and hit it against the brass plate. It was a timid knock, so she struck it harder.

The door opened and a woman—a tall, buxom woman—looked her up and down and then immediately said, "It's about time you made it here. What took you so long, and where's your friend?"

Startled by her gruffness and confused by her words, Catalina said, "I'm not sure what you are talking about."

"Sure you are. You were supposed to be bringing another

girl with you. But you were expected earlier in the day, too, and we see that didn't happen, don't we?"

Catalina tried to smile. "I'm sorry. I think you must be confusing me—"

"Of course you're sorry," the woman barked aggressively. "Women like you are always sorry. I hear it from you every day. Never mind about what happened to your friend or why you are late. I don't have time to listen to your excuses, anyway. You're here now, and it's past time to get started. Come in and let's get you dressed for work."

"Work?" Catalina asked, surprised, and then it dawned on her the woman apparently thought she was there applying for employment.

She opened her mouth to tell her she was making a mistake, but her mind started swirling with possibilities and she decided to stay quiet. Pretending to be the person the woman was expecting would get her in the house, and right now that was her objective.

Catalina stepped into the expensively decorated vestibule. A tall, ornate mirror hung over a fancy gilt-coated and marble-topped side table. Several red velvet-covered side chairs lined the walls. She heard muted chattering but not enough to indicate a large party going on. She might have thought it was a gaming house or a gentlemen's club of some nature if she wasn't sure she heard feminine voices and laughter coming from down the corridor.

"Stop gawking at everything and acting like you've never seen a nice place before. You're already late, and you need to get started. The night will be over before you know it."

"All right," Catalina said and followed the woman down a narrow, dimly lit corridor.

Catalina glanced inside a room as she passed an open doorway and saw gentlemen and ladies standing around talking. She slowed down in hopes of spotting her father or Iverson, but there were too many people crowded into the room. Everyone seemed to be enjoying themselves, just like all the parties she'd attended. This couldn't be a gentlemen's club or a high-stakes card game. She had never heard of either of those places allowing ladies to join them. That realization allowed Catalina to relax a little.

She expected the buxom servant to lead her to the kitchen, but instead she started up a dark back staircase. Catalina was beginning to wonder exactly what kind of servant work the woman expected her to do. Not that it really mattered. She planned to get away as soon as possible and get below stairs again where all the people were.

They bypassed the first floor and went on to the second, where they walked down to the end of the corridor. The woman stopped and opened a door and said, "In here."

Catalina thought it an odd room when she entered. Against the far wall, there were three dressing tables with ornate mirrors. The other three walls were littered with hooks. Various styles and colors of clothing draped from each hook. It was almost too much for Catalina to take in at one time.

"Take your cloak off and pick out something to wear."

She hesitated as she continued to look around. She just wanted to find her father and avoid Iverson. She didn't want to take the time to change into servants' clothes.

"Here, try this on. It looks like it might fit you."

She handed Catalina a dark red gown with a neckline cut so low Catalina could look at it and know she certainly didn't want to wear it. And the gown was far too fancy for servants' wear. And why would the woman give her such a matronly color as dark red?

"Go on, take your cloak off," the woman barked again. "You don't have to wear that gown if it's not to your liking."

Catalina swung her cloak off her shoulders and laid it over her arm. She looked at the dress again.

"Now I know why you didn't want to shed your wrap." The woman jerked her hands to her hips and said, "Where'd you get such a fancy dress as that?"

Catalina looked down at her pale, coral-colored gown with its scooped neckline and delicate beading of faux pearls on the bodice.

"My modiste made it for me," she said cautiously.

The woman's brow furrowed deeply, and her lips pursed unattractively. "Sure she did, and she made my garment as well. Hog-posh! She made it for your last employer and you stole it from her."

Affronted, Catalina gasped and said, "I wouldn't take anything that didn't belong to me."

Pointing her finger at Catalina, she said, "I'm going to tell you right now, we don't put up with stealing around here."

"No, no, I would never do that," Catalina defended.

"And if we find out you have stolen anything, Madame Shipwith will have you out the door faster than you can blink. And the only thing you can take with you is just the clothes on your back, and chances are that won't be very many."

"I told you I would never...steal...anything." Her words slowed down, and her voice ended almost as a whisper. What the woman said registered on Catalina's mind. Maybe she didn't hear what she thought she heard. Surely there weren't two women by that name.

"Pardon me," Catalina said, "but did you say Madame Shipwith?"

"You know that's what I said. I didn't stutter or stammer. And you need to learn right now, girlie, I don't like having to repeat myself. You best remember she keeps a close eye on her girls, and so do I. But as long as you do your job and keep your gentlemen happy, you won't have any trouble from her or me. You've got to keep the gentlemen coming back for more, or Madame Shipwith won't be keeping you anymore and out you go."

Catalina's body felt stiff and disjointed. Her mouth went dry, and her heartbeat sounded so loud in her ears she thought her head might explode. She looked at the gown in her hands.

What had she managed to get herself into?

Catalina lifted her gaze to the woman. "You aren't expecting me to do maid's work, are you?"

"Maid's work?" The woman let out a hearty laugh. "For a pretty girl such as yourself? Madame Shipwith would never stand for that. Now are you going to put on that dress or stay in what you're wearing?"

As the full reality of where she was hit her, Catalina swallowed hard and looked at the dress in her hands again. She was in a brothel. This woman thought she was a— Catalina couldn't finish her thought. No wonder Briggs was trying so hard to keep her from coming inside. And she had been rude to him. He was trying only to spare her from knowing what this place really was.

She had to get out!

Catalina looked at the large woman standing between her and the door that led to safety. "I'm afraid you've made a terrible mistake." She shook her head. "No, *I've* made a terrible, terrible mistake."

And to think her father and Iverson were here!

"No," she whispered again, her legs threatening to buckle under her. "I can't stay here."

The woman laughed again. "I can see by your face you really thought you were going to be doing the work of a maid, didn't you? Well, you'll be serving up delicious meals, girlie. It just won't be food."

"I must go." Catalina threw the dress to the floor and rushed past the servant.

The woman caught the tail of Catalina's cloak and jerked her backward, making her stumble. "Slow down there. What's the hurry? You've got nowhere else to go, girlie."

Catalina let go of her wrap, leaving it in the hands of the woman. She raced out the door, slamming it shut behind her. She heard the servant calling for her to come back. Catalina held up the hem of her skirt with one hand and held onto the banister of the back stairs with the other. She raced down as fast as she could. The thought of seeing her father or Iverson in this place, or them seeing her, made her stomach quake. She wanted out of the house before either of them knew she was there.

Why didn't I listen to Briggs?

She didn't slow down, and thankfully she didn't miss a step on the stairs. She kept running when she made it to the bottom landing. She quickly rounded a corner that led to the main corridor of the house and smacked right into the arms of a tall, strapping man who was coming out of a side room.

Catalina tripped on her gown, lost her footing, and would have gone down to the floor if the man hadn't caught hold of her.

"I'm sorry," she whispered breathlessly and immediately tried to pull her arms out of his grasp.

"No harm done to me," he said in a friendly voice but didn't let her go. "Are you sure you're all right?"

"I'm quite fine," she answered. "Turn me loose."

"Settle down and take the time to get your feet under you." He smiled. "What's your hurry? Is the house on fire?"

"No, no fire, but I must get out of here."

"You will, but I think you owe me at least a minute of your time for almost knocking me down, don't you?"

He was a fair-looking man, and perhaps the age of her father, so she wasn't frightened by him but she didn't like the feel of his tight hands on her upper arms. And she didn't owe him anything.

"I'm sorry," she repeated.

"That's better." He smiled pleasantly again. "I haven't seen you here before. Where has Madame Shipwith been hiding you?"

At the mention of Madame Shipwith, Catalina's shoulders flew back, and she glowered at the man. "I do not work here, sir. Now turn me loose this instant so I may leave."

His gaze washed down her face to her breasts and then back up to her eyes. "My minute's not up. Now tell me, why would you want to go off in such a hurry? I understand Madame Shipwith reserves a few of her more expensive girls for certain gentlemen. I can understand her not wanting all of you to be available for public utilization, so to speak."

Catalina was appalled by the man's words, by his tight

grip on her upper arms, and she tried once again to wrench herself free. Her movements only made him hold her tighter.

She had had enough of his brutish behavior. "Turn me loose," she said again, grinding out the words from between clenched teeth.

He caught her up to him and reached down and kissed her neck just below her jaw. Catalina gasped and pushed at his chest with all her strength. He leaned closer, and she feared he was going to kiss her lips, so she turned her face away.

"Come now, pretty girl," he said as his dry lips grazed her cheek. "I'm not going to hurt you or get you in trouble with Madame Shipwith. I just want to talk to you—for now."

At that moment, Catalina realized the man wasn't going to let go of her. He didn't think he had to. And in this house, he probably didn't. He had no reason to treat her as if she were a lady because he didn't think she *was* a lady. He thought she was a woman he could pay for. And that thought riled Catalina like nothing she could remember.

Sixteen

Kisses are like grains of gold or silver found
upon the ground, of no value themselves, but
precious as showing that a mine is near.
—George Villiers

"Unhand me now, sir, or I will not be responsible for what I might do to you."

"Please, do anything you wish." He looked down at her and laughed. "It's no wonder Madame Shipwith saves you for only a few select customers. You're a lassie with spirit. I like that."

"Then maybe you will like this." Catalina yanked down hard on one arm and freed it from his grasp. She then jerked back and with all the power she could muster, swung her hand forward and slapped the man's cheek as hard as she could. His head snapped back with a loud crack. He grunted painfully.

"Now unhand me, you ill-mannered oaf!"

He snatched her to him with a force so strong it wrenched her neck. His eyes were wild and his face full of fury. "You are a little hellcat. I think you need to be taught a lesson."

Catalina tried to hit him again, but he grabbed her arm and jerked her up to his chest.

"Let her go!"

At the sound of Iverson's strong voice, Catalina gasped and stopped fighting. She twisted her head around and saw him striding fast down the corridor toward her, looking as angry as the man she'd just hit.

"Who do you think you are?" The man sneered at Iverson as his hands tightened on Catalina's arms. "And just what do you think you will do if I don't let her go?"

"He'll hold you down while I slap you again," Catalina said confidently.

Within the blink of an eye, Iverson closed the distance between them and clamped his tight fist around one of the man's wrists. The stranger grimaced in pain.

"Take your hand off her or I'll snap your wrist and you won't be holding any woman for a long time."

Iverson's tone was so cold, his voice so intense, Catalina shivered. He'd always told her he was a fierce protector, and now she had no doubt.

The man hesitated for only a moment as he looked into Iverson's deadly serious eyes. He turned her loose. A moment or two later, Iverson let him go.

He held up both hands and stepped away from her. "Fine," he spat, pulling on the ends of his waistcoat. "She's yours. Take her. I hope she's worth the money you're paying for her."

Iverson's fist connected with the man's jaw so fast Catalina never saw it coming. He fell to the floor with a thud, writhing like a fish out of water.

Iverson looked down at him and said, "Maybe next time you'll recognize a lady when you see one." Eyes still filled with anger, he turned to Catalina and said, "Where's your wrap?"

"On the second floor, but I'm not going back for it."

"You were upstairs?" he asked incredulously. "How the hell did you get up there?"

That bit of information seemed to make him angrier. "A woman, the woman from the door took me. She thought I was here for...to—"

"Never mind," he said and swung his cloak off his shoulders and lowered it over her head. "You can tell me later. Cover your face so no one will see you, and let's get out of here."

Catalina immediately felt the warmth from Iverson's body in the cloak, and she shrouded herself in its safety. It was clear he was livid with her for following him, and given what just happened, she could understand. But right now, she didn't care about that. He had come to her aid, and she felt immense relief and gratitude.

They rushed out the front door and down the steps. Catalina had to run to keep up with Iverson's long strides, but she didn't mind. She wanted to get away from that house as quickly as possible. Briggs stood by the landau and opened the door when he saw her coming.

"She's riding with me," Iverson told the deaf man.

Briggs immediately started shaking his head and making hand motions for Iverson to back off.

"No, Iverson," Catalina said, "Briggs is right. It doesn't matter where I just came from, I can't be seen getting out of your carriage in front of my house or at the mews."

"All right," Iverson relented. "But I'm riding with you." He looked at Briggs. "Stop at the corner of Whitfield and Madison before you enter Mayfair. There's a high hedge there, and I can get out without being seen."

Catalina nodded, letting Briggs know the plan was all right with her. After Iverson signaled his driver to follow them, they climbed into the carriage, and Briggs shut the door behind them. Catalina took one side and Iverson the other. The coach took off with a jolt before rolling down the deserted street at a brisk pace.

With no warning, Iverson quickly moved to the seat beside Catalina and grabbed her with fierce urgency and wrapped her tightly in his arms, rocking her. She was safe and in his arms. He kissed the side of her face and her hair as he quietly, lovingly said her name over and over again.

Catalina didn't know if he was trying to comfort her or himself when in a ragged voice he whispered above her ear, "You scared the hell out of me."

She felt a tremble in his strong arms. Her throat was clogged with unshed tears. "I'm sorry," she mumbled against his chest.

"Don't ever go off on your own like that again," he said passionately, squeezing her tighter. "You don't know what it did to me seeing that man holding you against your will."

She raised her head and looked into his eyes. Their faces were close together, their erratic breaths mingling. "Iverson, if you hadn't—"

He tilted her head back. "No, don't talk, Catalina. Just kiss me. I desperately need you to kiss me right now."

Passion flared. Their lips touched in a searing kiss that left Catalina feeling as if she had been starving for Iverson. Their mouths and their tongues clung together. Her hands tangled in his hair, and he pressed her close and kissed her harder. The sounds they made were fierce, gasping, and hoarse.

His lips slipped to her neck, and his hands found her

breasts and kneaded their softness. Catalina moaned, glory-
ing in his touch, his need to protect her.

But all too soon, his kisses gentled, his breathing calmed,
and slowly he pushed away from her. Their intense moment
of passion had passed. Sanity returned.

Catalina took in a deep, steadying breath and lowered her
arms from around his neck. There wasn't much light shining
in the landau, but Catalina didn't need to see Iverson's face to
know he was no longer angry.

"I can't believe you followed me," he said into the darkness.
His voice was calmer, his tone surprised.

"Was I following you or just looking for Sir Phillip in the
same place you were looking for him?"

He grunted a laugh. "I'm in no mood to be taunted with
my own words, Catalina. If I'd had any idea you would follow
me tonight, I never would have told you I was going to look
for your father."

"If I had had any idea of where you were going to look
for my father, you can be sure I wouldn't have followed you."

"Do you really mean that?"

She thought for a moment and said, "No."

"I didn't think so."

He caressed her cheek first with the backs of his fingers
and then with his fingertips. Catalina felt a yearning deep in
her abdomen. She wanted to grab his hand and place it on
her breast and beg him to touch her with passion once again,
but she remained still.

"Where is Mrs. Gottfried? I can't believe she let you
come after me alone."

"She didn't know where I was going, and I didn't leave her
much choice other than to allow me to do what I wished."

"I suspected as much. You take care of her better than she looks out for you."

"She's been delicate since her husband passed on, and I have to take care of her."

"You couldn't have been in that house long, but what did you—? Did you see anything or anyone? I mean, you didn't—?"

"No." She shook her head and gave him a grateful smile. "I saw only the woman who answered the door. She thought I was there looking for employment. She took me to a room so I could change into something more appropriate. I thought she was talking about servants' work until she mentioned Madame Shipwith."

His fingertips glided over her chin and trickled down her neck and settled in the hollow of her throat. "You know about Madame Shipwith's establishment?"

"No, no, I mean yes." Catalina sighed, wishing he would take her in his arms and kiss her passionately. "I knew Mrs. Wardyworth had worked for a woman named Madame Shipwith, but I didn't know who Madame Shipwith was. I certainly had no idea that house was hers until I was upstairs."

Iverson's hand stilled, and he stirred in the seat. "Your father employs a woman who used to work for—?"

"Iverson, please," she interrupted. "Do not try to understand my father and the people he chooses to employ."

Iverson shook his head. "Your father never ceases to amaze me."

"Perhaps my father is different from most people you know, but it just seems to be in his nature to collect oddities."

"I will agree with that."

"And keep in mind if I hadn't known Madame Shipwith's

name, there is no telling what I might have seen or heard before I realized I shouldn't be in that house. I was trying to get out when I ran into that odious man." She cupped his cheek with her hand and whispered earnestly, "Thank you for saving me."

"You have no need to thank me, Catalina," he said huskily. "You were doing a damned good job of taking care of yourself. I saw the powerful blow you gave that cock-bawd oaf."

She laughed softly. "What did you call him?"

"Nothing," he said. "Pretend you didn't hear that."

His arms surrounded her shoulders and pulled her close. There was no anger in his touch, only warmth and strong gentleness. Catalina let out a thankful breath and laid her head on his chest, letting her cheek rest against the softness of his waistcoat.

He kissed the top of her head as his hands caressed her back. She snuggled closer to him, and he said, "You're shaking again. There's no need to fear that loathsome man."

"I'm just cold," she fibbed, knowing the man had been too strong and she wouldn't have gotten away from him if Iverson hadn't found her.

"You know, I kept telling myself I wouldn't hit the man, even though I wanted to smash in his face the moment I saw him holding you. I didn't want you to see me be violent, but when he made that inappropriate comment about you, I had to defend you."

She looked up at him. "I'm not sorry you hit him. I slapped him, too, remember."

Iverson's arms tightened around her, and she slipped her arms beneath his coat to circle his waist. She took pleasure in the contented feeling of being comforted in his embrace.

It made her feel safe and, though she had no idea why, it also made her feel loved, cherished, and cared for, and that was a glorious feeling. She took care of so many people every day it was heavenly to know that tonight someone had taken care of her.

Catalina raised her head and looked into his eyes. She wanted Iverson to see into her soul and know what she was feeling. Her emotions were running wild because of what had transpired at Madame Shipwith's, but what she was feeling in her heart was because of Iverson.

She said, "I felt very foolish tonight, Iverson, and I need you to kiss me again."

"You are the least foolish lady I know, and I was hoping you wanted me to kiss you again."

His lips came down on hers with warm, moist softness. Catalina's arms moved up his strong, firm back. She pressed her body to his, while his lips explored hers with an exquisite tenderness that touched the core of her being.

She pulled away from him and placed her hands on each side of his face and looked intently into the depths of his eyes. "I want to think only about you and the things you make me feel when you kiss me and touch me."

"Then think only of me," he murmured softly, "and I will think only of you."

She smiled. "That almost sounds like poetry."

"Like hell it does," he murmured and then chuckled softly under his breath.

His lips quickly covered hers with the same desperate passion they'd experienced earlier. His mouth and tongue ravaged hers in slow, savoring kisses that thrilled her, filled her. His hands brushed down her chest to her waist and back up again. They kissed and touched and embraced, fueling their desires to continue.

"I want to make you mine, Catalina."

"Yes," she whispered. "Yes."

He scooted her down and carefully leaned her back into the corner of the cushion. With gentle hands, he lifted one of her legs onto the seat, and then he stretched his body over her, fitting the junction of his thighs against her softness. Catalina's heart lurched. She'd never felt a man's weight before, and there was something richly sensuous and deeply satisfying about the pressure of it. A new expectancy filled her, and by instinct she lifted her hips toward him.

A long, low sigh whispered past Iverson's lips. It thrilled her that her action pleased him so much. He lifted himself a little, looking down at her. She smiled and kissed him sweetly, lingeringly on his lips, his cheeks, his closed eyes. His lips moved across her cheek, trailing little moist kisses over her jaw and down her chin to her neck, making her achingly aware of every masculine contour of his body. He cupped her backside and pushed her up closer to the hardness beneath his trousers. Something she didn't know how to explain was building inside her, and she was eager to experience it.

With one hand, he reached down the scooped neckline of her gown, and with little effort lifted the swell of her breast from beneath her undergarments, freeing her nipple to his view. He covered it with his mouth and hungrily sucked. Catalina gasped and arched her body toward him as hot, delicious sensations spiraled through her. Her arms circled his head, and she held him to her chest as wave after wave of thrilling desire racked every inch of her body.

Her breathing was shallow. She gloried in his touch as he feasted at her breast.

"Catalina, you shouldn't be this sweet, this eager," he whispered against her heated skin. "I shouldn't want you this desperately."

Though she didn't know exactly what it was, she answered, "But I want you desperately, too."

"Please don't tell me that. That is not what a rake needs to hear."

"But it is the truth," she said, sliding her arms under his coat again and stroking the width of his powerful shoulders, down his strong spine to his slim waist, over the firm swell of his buttocks and back up again. He moaned.

"Your touch is more than I can bear, Catalina," he said on a shaky breath. "I want to, but I can't do this to you. I want you, but you are not mine for the taking."

He pushed away from her quickly, rose, and rapped three times on the roof with his fist.

The carriage jerked, and Briggs started slowing the horses.

Catalina was shocked beyond belief. She rose in the seat, pushing her gown down over her legs as she sat up. "Iverson, what did I do?"

"Nothing." He fell to his knees in front of her, helping her straighten the bodice of her gown. With caring eyes, he touched her cheek with the backs of his fingers, letting them drift across her lips. "That's just it, Catalina. You haven't done anything to me, and I can't take your virtue away from you."

"But it's mine to give," she argued.

"Yes, but this is not the time or the place. And though I have been a rake many times in the past, I don't intend to be one tonight."

The carriage stopped, and Iverson rose.

"I'll follow you in my carriage and make sure you get safely home."

"Thank you," she said softly, knowing she would feel better with him near. "You'd best take your cloak," she said, handing it to him. "I have a blanket to keep me warm."

He took his cloak and opened the door, but before he could jump down, Catalina said, "Iverson?"

He turned back to her. "Yes?"

She hesitated but knew she had to ask. "Was my father in that house?"

"No. He had been there but was gone. I'm still looking for him."

Iverson jumped down and quietly shut the door.

Catalina shivered and wrapped the blanket tightly around her, wishing she could feel the warmth of Iverson's arms once more. For all his rough talk and his reputation as the Rake of Baltimore, he had proven tonight he was a gentleman. The carriage started rolling again. She remembered the first day she had met Iverson. On first appearance, he seemed so tough, so rigid, so aggressive, but somehow she'd known he had a softer, gentler side, too. Tonight she had seen both sides: the strong protector, and the gentle and passionate lover.

Pulling the blanket up under her chin, Catalina knew she was in love with Iverson—deeply, longingly, and irrevocably in love with him. She didn't know when or how it had happened. He certainly hadn't encouraged her.

And because of her love for him, she wouldn't wait any longer for her father to come home and work a miracle. Tomorrow morning she would go to Iverson's home and tell him there were two more parts of *A Tale of Three Gentlemen* to be published.

He deserved to know.

And if he decided never to speak to her again because of it, she would have to find a way to live with his decision.

Seventeen

Oh, what a tangled web we weave,
when first we practice to deceive.
—Walter Scott

HE FELT DAMNED GOOD.

Iverson was up and dressed earlier than usual and down in his book room. He had done a lot of thinking after he left Catalina last night. One conclusion was clear: He intended to court Catalina.

The thought made him chuckle. Everyone in Society thought he was courting her, anyway. Why not make it official? He certainly had Mrs. Gottfried's blessing.

There was no use in trying to fool himself. He wanted much more than just to court Catalina and had for a long time. He wanted her beneath him, to make love to her all night long. And he almost had last night. She was so damn willing it had been sheer hell pushing away from her.

But he was not such a coldhearted rake as to take her in a carriage as if she were a common trollop, and certainly not half an hour after that whoremaster had accosted her in the brothel. She was a lady and deserving of being treated like one.

But there was no doubt he'd wanted her.

Fiercely.

And he was no longer willing to wait until he'd settled

everything with her father. There was no telling when the man might actually come back home.

Iverson took a sheet of vellum out of his desk drawer and opened the ink jar. He dipped the quill into the ink and started writing.

My dear Miss Crisp,

*   I would like the pleasure of your company in Hyde Park this afternoon. I will pick you up at half past three.*

Iverson stopped and looked at what he had written. He laughed at how stiff that sounded. He crumpled the vellum and took out another sheet.

Catalina,

*   I will pick you up at half past three today for a ride in the park.*

*   Iverson*

Much better, he thought, and blew on the paper to dry the ink.

At the sound of a knock, Iverson looked up and saw Wallace standing in the doorway.

"Sorry to disturb you, sir."

"Not a problem, Wallace. What is it?"

"Your brother is here. He wanted to know if you were feeling well enough to see him."

"Of course," he said. "I'm fine now."

"Yes, sir. I showed him into the dining room and offered him a cup of coffee while he waits for you. Should I tell him you will be there directly?"

"No need," Iverson said, folding his note. "I'm almost finished. And Wallace, have my curricle brought around front. I want to buy some flowers."

"Would you like for me to take care of the flowers for you, sir?"

No. He wanted to pick out the flowers for Catalina. Mrs. Gottfried had told him her husband had brought her flowers every week. He needed to give Catalina flowers.

"I'll handle it. Just get the curricle."

"Right away, sir."

"Wait."

Iverson finished sealing the envelope with hot wax and gave the note to Wallace. "It's early still, but in about an hour have this note sent around to Sir Phillip Crisp's house and delivered to Miss Catalina Crisp."

Iverson grabbed his black coat off a chair and shoved his arms into the sleeves as he walked toward the dining room. Rounding the doorway, he saw Matson standing in front of the back window. The draperies had been pulled back, and bright sunshine spilled into the room. Iverson could see his brother was deep in thought. An odd feeling prickled Iverson's skin, and it was more than twin intuition. Something wasn't right. Matson wasn't a daydreamer, but then, Iverson wasn't one to borrow trouble, either.

He walked into the sunlit room, saying, "Good to see you, Brother."

Matson turned and faced him. "You, too. You're feeling better?"

"Yes, I'm good as new."

"Really? Then you must not have read Lord Truefitt's column."

"No, did I make the man's gossip page again today?"

"Hmm. Apparently you were at the Great Hall last night, but I never saw you."

Iverson walked over to the buffet and picked up the silver pot and poured himself a cup of coffee. "I went early and left early."

"Unusual for you. Obviously you can take crowds better than you used to."

"I'm learning." Iverson cleared his throat. "Tell me, what did Lord Truefitt have to say this time?"

"Something along the lines of:

'Roses are red
Violets are blue
Is it the poet's daughter
The Baltimore Rake will woo?'"

"Bloody hell, that sounds awful," Iverson said, amused by the inference.

"Yes, I suppose he likes to fancy himself being as good at poetry as Miss Crisp's father."

Iverson sipped his coffee and watched Matson over the rim of his cup. It was unlike his brother to brood. Something was wrong, and Iverson had the feeling it didn't have anything to do with Truefitt's gossip.

"In that case, someone needs to tell the man he's more in the category with Lord Snellingly," Iverson said, knowing his brother would eventually get around to telling him what was on his mind.

"Yes, he went on to say both you and Miss Crisp were seen leaving the party early and quite hastily."

Iverson set down his cup. "Damn that man! He must have eyes in the back of his head and spies everywhere, too. Someone needs to find out who the bugger is and put a stop to his constant prattle about other people's lives."

"Is what he indicated true?" Matson asked.

Iverson remained quiet. Iverson was still trying to figure out what was bothering Matson. There had to be something more than this silly gossip vexing him.

"Did you have a rendezvous with Miss Crisp last night?"

"Do I hear a reprimand in your tone?" Iverson asked, hoping to lighten the atmosphere between them.

"You hear only concern."

"Good. In any case I wouldn't tell you if I did, but I will tell you I didn't plan a meeting with Miss Crisp last night."

"Perhaps you didn't plan an encounter, but you did see her after you both left the party, didn't you?"

"Is that your brotherly intuition again or are you fishing and expect me to take the bait?"

"I know you well."

"Obviously too well," Iverson muttered. "So you think I had my way with Miss Crisp last night?"

One corner of Matson's mouth lifted with a smile. "Well, it had crossed my mind."

Iverson scoffed. "I'm not always the rake I'm rumored to be."

"I know."

"Good. We'll go no further with this conversation. Tell me, what has you so gloomy?"

"There's more on our plate than gossip this morning. I have other news."

"Let's hear it."

"I received word late last night that our ships have arrived from America."

"That's not good news."

"No, but what are we to do? For now, the only space available to us is what we've been leasing from Sir Randolph all these months."

Iverson picked up his cup again and took a sip of the hot, dark brew. He thought about their options for a moment. "I'm sure we can leave the ships docked at the harbor for a short time. We'll pay whatever fees are necessary to make that happen."

"There shouldn't be a problem with that. We're bound to hear from the duke soon."

"I'm sure," Iverson said. "Our courier has had time to arrive at the duke's estate and return."

"I should think we will hear from him within a day or two at the latest, and hopefully with a letter from the duke giving us permission to lease space from him."

"There's no reason not to, now that everything is settled between the duke and Brent."

"Agreed. Brent said the duke seemed quite happy with his marrying Lady Gabrielle. So I'm thinking all will be settled within a week. That way, we won't have to move our equipment into Sir Randolph's buildings and then move it again later."

"So no need to worry. All is going well." Iverson picked up a buffet plate and extended it toward Matson.

"I'm not staying this morning."

Matson's mouth was narrow, and the corners of his eyes tightened again. Iverson knew that look. There was still

something bothering his brother other than Iverson's relationship with Catalina and the obvious problem with their
ships. A shiver of uneasiness shot up his back. He put the
plate back on the buffet.

"No breakfast," Iverson said calmly. "You have other
plans?"

Matson turned his attention out the window again, and
Iverson's unease turned into apprehension. "What's wrong?
Did all the ships come in? I mean, we didn't lose any men at
sea, did we?"

"No, no, nothing like that," Matson said quickly and faced
him. "I didn't mean to make you think that. All three ships
are in, and from all accounts, everyone is safe."

Iverson's muscles stiffened. "Then what's wrong? It's not
like you to be melancholy."

"Damnation, I hope not," Matson said with a half laugh.

"Then out with what's bothering you."

Matson let out a heavy breath as he pulled several sheets
of folded newsprint from his coat pocket and extended them
toward Iverson. "You are not going to like this, and I hate to
be the bearer of bad news, but here it is."

"I can believe that," he said cautiously. Iverson tensed but
took the pages. He didn't bother to look at them. His fear
was that someone had seen Catalina at Madame Shipwith's
brothel, and her name would be slandered all over the pages.
"I seldom like anything I read in newsprint. If it's more
gossip or scandalous intrigue about Catalina, I don't care to
read the rubbish."

"It's not the scandal sheets, and it's not about Miss Crisp,
but in a way it concerns her. Open it and look at the title.
That will tell you more than you want to know."

Iverson opened the pages, and his gaze immediately fell on the words *A Tale of Three Gentlemen Part II*.

Disbelief clouded Iverson's vision and cloaked his heart protectively. It simply couldn't be. His mouth went dry with shock, but he managed to look up at Matson and whisper gravely, "*Part II?*"

Matson laughed ruefully. "Oh, yes, Brother. There is more to Sir Phillip's outrageous story, telling about how the twins go about their merry way living their lives in London. All the while, Polite Society is whispering behind their backs and they are oblivious to the fact they are the spitting image of a man who is not their father. At the end of this, White's has decided to have a drawing to see who gets to enlighten the Villory twins about their resemblance to their real father, Sir Mortimer."

"I don't believe it," Iverson murmured, his mind running wild with thoughts of Catalina.

Did she know about this? Did she know there was more?

"Believe it, Brother. It's all there in black and white. And there's more. At the end of the piece it says to watch for *Part III* coming in tomorrow's edition."

"*Part III?* How many damned parts are there?"

"That's all, according to the article. There is no telling what the man came up with to end the story, but you can be sure we won't like it."

The sound of pounding drums roared through Iverson's ears, blazed through his chest, and curled and knotted in his stomach. He looked up at Matson and said, "She knew this was coming out, didn't she?"

"I assume you're talking about Miss Crisp."

"You know I am," Iverson muttered from between

clenched teeth. "She had to have known there was more, and yet she never told me."

"Of course she knew," Matson said, anger lacing his voice. "But you really expected her to tell you there were two more parts?"

"Yes," Iverson whispered earnestly, the feeling of betrayal sinking deep into his bones.

"That's only because you are enchanted by her. Her father wrote it, and you told her you would do him harm if he wrote more. Did you really think she would confide in you after that? Can you imagine the amount of money the man must be making off this rubbish?"

Money?

If the man was making a lot of money, he wasn't giving it to Catalina for new clothing or for their day-to-day living expenses.

Iverson's breaths were deep, ragged. Somehow he held onto his temper, because he knew Matson was right. Catalina had no obligation to tell him anything, but it was almost incomprehensible to him that she hadn't. She knew how angry he had been over her father's writings about his family. There were times he'd felt she was hiding something from him, and now he knew what it was. Two more parts to her father's vile parody had already been written.

But how could she have been so sweet, so eager, and so willing in his arms last night, knowing she kept such a damning secret from him?

He shook his head and chuckled bitterly at how she had fooled him with her sweetness, but it felt more like betrayal. He winced inside when he remembered her innocent kisses and how right it felt being with her.

Matson let out a deep sigh. "Iverson, perhaps just as I needed to accept the fact we are Sir Randolph's sons, it's time for you to accept this parody was written and published and nothing can be done about it. Let the rest of the story come out tomorrow so everyone can have their amusement. In time it will be forgotten, and then we can finally be done with it. It's time for you to let this go."

"Why? So the blackguard can write more parodies about us anytime he wants to? Or what if some other poet decides to pick up where Sir Phillip left off? Is that what you want? Do you want the question of our parentage constantly on the minds of Londoners?"

"You know I don't. I want everyone to let us forget we look like Sir Randolph and let us build our lives right here in London as we planned." Matson stepped closer to Iverson. "But I wasn't thinking about Sir Phillip just now or any other poet. I was thinking about his daughter."

"Catalina?"

"So you are familiar enough now to call her Catalina?"

Iverson swallowed hard. He hadn't even realized he'd said her Christian name.

"Yes, I see how conflicted you are," Matson continued. "I've seen the way you look at her, Iverson, and I know there is something there. I saw—"

"Nothing," Iverson ground out tightly, cutting off Matson's words.

"Don't tell me—"

Iverson raised his hand to stop Matson. "You saw nothing, Brother."

Matson stepped back. "All right, if that's what you want me to believe, I will humor you and agree I saw nothing. But

I still say it's time for us, it's time for you to let go of this quarrel with Miss Crisp's father."

"I'm not letting go until I find Sir Phillip and squeeze from his skinny throat his vow to never write about my family again."

Iverson threw the newsprint down on top of the table and walked out of the dining room, calling for Wallace to see if his curricle was ready. Iverson wasn't waiting until a respectable hour to go to Catalina's house. He was going to pay a call on her as soon as he could get there, and he wouldn't be taking her flowers or asking if she would like a ride in the park.

Now he knew what she and her aunt were doing at *The Daily Herald* that day. Delivering *Part II* and *III* of *A Tale of Three Gentlemen*. His stomach wrenched just thinking about it.

After last night, he'd believed they could develop a relationship different from the antagonistic one they had started with. Damnation! He had wanted to court her properly. She was forthright, clever, and captivating. He enjoyed matching wits with her. He enjoyed being in her company. He enjoyed her being in his arms, and oh, how delicious she had felt beneath him. He wanted to teach her all the ways a man could love a woman.

But now he knew he couldn't trust her.

She must have been laughing at how she had managed to dupe him. She certainly had the last laugh.

This time.

Iverson was already pulling his hat and coat off the hall stand in the corner of the vestibule when Matson and Wallace caught up with him.

"Will you at least come down to the docks with me first and greet the men?" Matson asked. "Let's look over our ships before you go off in such a heated temper. It's much too early to call on anyone, and it will give you the chance to cool down and quite possibly save you apologies later."

"The only apologies I'm going to hear will be coming from Miss Crisp. There will be none coming from me this day, I assure you. I trust you to handle whatever needs to be done with getting the proper documents, fees, and bribes handled for the ships."

Matson shook his head. "I can't persuade you not to go see her until you've calmed down, can I?"

Iverson placed his hat on his head and said, "No. I can't calm down until I see her. This has nothing to do with you, and it really has nothing to do with her father right now. This"—he laid his fist over his heart—"this is between me and the lovely Catalina."

———

Catalina hadn't slept well, yet she was up early. She had told Sylvia to wake her aunt, too. As soon as it was an appropriate hour, she wanted to be on her way to see Iverson. She wouldn't feel at ease until she'd told him about the remaining parts of *A Tale of Three Gentlemen* and could be done with it. He may not forgive her for not telling him sooner, but she had to do it now. While she waited for her aunt to come below stairs, she decided to have a cup of tea and look over the newsprint in the drawing room.

She made herself comfortable in a chair by the window and read Lord Truefitt's gossip sheet. Since Iverson had

danced with Miss Babs Whitehouse, she was curious to see
if there would be something written about the two of them
in his column today.

"Dreadful," she whispered to herself as she read the trite
"roses are red, violets are blue" words. She was surprised he
chose to write about her again, too, until she made it all the
way down to the bottom. With so many people at the Great
Hall last night, how in heaven's name did that man or anyone
else know she and Iverson had left the party early? The man
must continually walk around parties and spy on people.
And to imply they might have left in order to meet up later
for a tryst was definitely beyond the pale.

"Lord Truefitt could use a few lessons in the art of writing
poetry," she murmured to herself.

She closed the newsprint. Oh, she hoped Agatha and
Mable didn't decide to show up at her door today! Maybe
she and Auntie would spend the entire day out, just so there
would be no possibility she'd have to see the two young
ladies.

Catalina opened another section of *The Daily Herald*,
and her breath caught in her throat. Her mind was screaming
"no," but no sound came from her open mouth. She blinked
several times, but her eyes were not deceiving her. The newsprint fluttered from her hands, fell to her lap, and then slid
silently to the floor.

She was too late.

She had waited too long.

The story had been printed.

Why hadn't she told Iverson last night? No, why hadn't
she told him that very first day he'd come to her house? She
could have accepted all his anger at one time and gotten

it over with. What had made her think she could find her father and get the story back before it was published? She knew time was fleeing, and still she waited. When her father hadn't come home after his usual week's stay, she should have told Iverson. But she had wanted to save Iverson the pain and save herself the admission.

This was her fault. Her fault.

She looked at the clock. It was half past nine. Perhaps she could get to Iverson's house before he read the newsprint. Maybe there was still time for her to tell him.

Catalina jumped from the chair and ran to the bottom of the stairs and called, "Auntie, I need you. Bring your bonnet and wrap and don't dawdle, please. Come quickly! We must go now."

With shaking hands and a dull ache in her chest, Catalina grabbed the bonnet her maid had laid out for her and quickly fitted it on her head. Her fingers trembled as she tied the ribbon under her chin. She then swung her lightweight cape over her shoulders and fashioned the satin strings into a bow.

"Auntie!" she called again.

She picked up her gloves and started to pull the first one on when she heard three loud raps against the door knocker.

Her hands stilled. Her breath lodged heavily, tightly in her throat. She was too late again. He was here.

Her first clear thought was to run and hide in her room so she wouldn't have to face him. But she quickly shook off that cowardly idea. There was nothing to do *but* face him. She had to. She wanted to.

"Catalina, what's wrong?" her aunt said, coming down the stairs dressed in her night robe but with a wrap and bonnet in her hand. "I've not finished dressing yet."

"It's all right, Auntie. Nothing's wrong. You go back to your room and finish dressing."

"Must I continue to hurry?" she asked in a concerned voice.

"No, take your time." She gave her aunt a shaky smile. "All is well."

"Good."

Her aunt headed back up the stairs, and Catalina saw Mrs. Wardyworth lumbering down the corridor.

"I'll take care of the door, Mrs. Wardyworth. Go back to whatever you were doing."

"Thank ye, missy."

The housekeeper turned away as the door knocker was rapped again. Catalina took in a deep, steadying breath and opened the door. She was fully prepared for Iverson to look even angrier than he'd been when he saw her last night at Madame Shipwith's. But it wasn't anger she saw in his handsome face. She saw calm disbelief, and suddenly her heart felt as if it were breaking.

They stood staring into each other's eyes. He seemed to be weighing what he wanted to say.

He took off his hat and asked, "Were you going somewhere?"

She remembered she had on her bonnet and cape, with her gloves still in her hands. "Yes," she admitted quietly. "I was, but I don't need to do that now. You're here." She laid her gloves on a table. "Would you rather talk in the drawing room, the garden, or perhaps you don't want to come into my house at all and will remain in the doorway?"

He stepped into the vestibule and closed the door behind him. "Here is fine. You know why I'm here."

She nodded, not trusting herself to speak for a moment. She had such strong feelings for him deep in her soul. Looking into his questioning gaze, she feared she'd lost any chance of his ever wanting to be a part of her life.

Keeping his distance, he said, "Why didn't you tell me?"

She sensed the pain inside him and winced, knowing she had caused it and not knowing how to make it go away. "Will any explanation I give satisfy you?"

"Probably not."

She devoured him with her eyes, knowing this would probably be the last time he would be this close to her. "Then why should I try?"

"Perhaps because I deserve some kind of answer, even if you can't come up with the truth."

His hurtful words and the disappointment she heard in his voice stung like a thousand needles. She took an imploring step toward him. "Of course you deserve the truth, but will you believe it when you hear it?"

"I can't promise that."

His voice was low and husky. Suddenly she felt as if she was suffocating, and her breathing became shallow. She untied the ribbon of her cape and calmly laid it on the table. She then took off her bonnet and placed it on top of the cape.

Her breaths were still rapid and shallow, but she set her gaze on Iverson's face and said, "I didn't tell you because I had hopes of sparing you the anguish of knowing there was more to come. I thought I could get the rest of the story back from Mr. Frederick before it was published. You made me realize how callous it was of my father to poke fun at your family. I went to *The Daily Herald* the day after you first came to my house. I insisted, and then I begged Mr. Frederick to return the story to me, but he wouldn't and demanded he talk to my father."

"So you didn't turn in the rest of it that day?"

She shook her head. "No. No, I never would have turned it in after I talked to you. It had been delivered earlier in the week. I didn't worry overly much at first, because it was time for my father to return. I knew I could convince him to get the story back from Mr. Frederick. But the days continued to pass and Papa didn't return. I knew time was running short, but then I had reason to believe he was at the Cooked Goose Inn, so I went there, hoping to find him and bring him back home." Catalina took another step toward him. "That's why I followed you to Madame Shipwith's. I knew if I could just find Papa, he could get the story back. Iverson, after last night, the way I was feeling when we—"

"Don't, Catalina," he whispered, with dark emotions clouding his eyes.

The earnestness she heard in his voice made tears form in her eyes. It hurt her deeply that he wanted no reminder of what they'd shared in her carriage. She swallowed the lump in her throat and took a step back. She couldn't blame him for not wanting her near him.

She cleared her throat, willing the tears that burned her eyes not to spill over. The hope that he could see sincere sorrow and regret in her eyes faded, yet she had to try again. "I want you to know that after last night I knew I couldn't wait any longer for Papa to return. I had to tell you today, no matter the damage. That's not an excuse for not telling you that first day you were here. It's the truth. And I'm sorry."

His gaze fluttered down her face for a moment, and she

wasn't sure he believed her. She wanted to say more, but she didn't think he wanted to hear more from her.

"Will there be a *Part IV*?" he asked, sounding more disillusioned than angry or frustrated.

"I promise there is no more, and there will be no more."

"So tomorrow will be the end? There is nothing else to tell?"

For a moment she had the urge to disclose she had written the last few pages of the story. She had Sir Mortimer die at the end of it, so the story would be complete and there would be no reason to continue the tale. Iverson probably deserved to know that, as well. But what would happen if he was so angry with her and her father he told others she had finished the story? If that became common knowledge, her father would never earn another penny as a poet or a writer.

She wanted to tell Iverson, but should she? Could she trust him not to make that information known to others?

She thought of her aunt and the staff. Who would take care of them if her father could no longer earn a living? Who would hire Briggs, Nancy, or Mrs. Wardyworth? Could she tell on her father and risk the livelihoods of so many for the sake of being totally truthful to the man she loved?

Her shoulders relaxed. "There is nothing else to tell. The story is complete and finished after tomorrow."

Iverson turned around, opened the door, and walked out.

Catalina winced and hugged her arms to her chest as she looked at the closed door, the symbol of Iverson gone forever from her life. Tears welled in her eyes again. Her throat ached from holding them at bay. She turned and slowly walked back into the drawing room and stood in front of the window. She closed her eyes and let the warmth of the sunshine fall on her face.

She had expected him to be implacable, half mad and demented with anger, with rage, but he was none of those things. She wished he had been. She could have borne his anger much easier than the cool, distant, wounded man who turned so effortlessly away from her and left. He would never know how deeply it hurt her to disappoint him so severely.

She should have known she and Iverson were doomed from the start. Just like Romeo and Juliet. A lifetime of love for them wasn't meant to be.

Oh, she had many regrets concerning Iverson. But she had wondrous, happy memories, and intensely sensual ones, too. And perhaps the one that would stay in her mind the longest was the few moments she spent with Iverson last night with his weight settled possessively upon her.

Eighteen

If you want happiness for an hour, take a nap. If you want happiness for a day, go fishing. If you want happiness for a year, inherit a fortune. If you want happiness for a lifetime, help somebody.
—Chinese proverb

HELLFIRE, HE WAS MISERABLE.

Iverson stepped onto the side portico for fresh air. The night wind was chilling considering it was a month into spring, but he didn't mind the discomfort. He wanted to be lost in the darkness for a while. He'd arrived at Mr. and Mrs. Peterson's house late. Very late. He had always been a nighthawk, and he was through making parties early just for a chance to see and speak to Catalina.

He was determined not to allow her treachery to get the best of him, though it was more of a struggle than he expected. She was not an easy lady to forget. When he'd first arrived, he'd seen Mrs. Gottfried sitting with her usual group of ladies surrounding the small dance floor, and his heart had started thumping like the hooves of a thoroughbred on hard-packed ground. He'd made three searches of the house before he convinced himself Catalina was not at the party. It surprised him that she had allowed Mrs. Gottfried to venture out without her.

Over the past couple of hours, he'd twirled several name-less young ladies around the dance floor, had three glasses of champagne, and been clapped on the back more times than he could remember by men who said, "Jolly good ending to the story printed in *The Daily Herald*, Brentwood."

Why was it so damn difficult for others to understand that the parody was not humorous to him and he'd never be a good sport about it?

Perhaps he would have done better to have stayed at home tonight, but somehow he'd felt the need to get out and prove to himself and to Catalina that he could have a per-fectly enjoyable time at a party without her being the center of it. Unfortunately, just the opposite was proving true. It had been two full days now since he'd walked out of her house, and he longed to see her. That was the true reason he was at this party.

Iverson leaned against a column and looked out over the small lighted garden. A couple sat on one of the benches, talking intimately. He watched them with a dull ache in his chest. And for the life of him, he couldn't keep from wish-ing he was on that seat with Catalina. He closed his eyes and brought to mind one more time the taste of her sweet lips on his, the feel of her soft skin against his palm, and the sound of her pleasured sighs wafting past his ears.

"Good evening, Mr. Brentwood."

Iverson opened his eyes and straightened as Lord Waldo walked up beside him. That man had a knack for showing up when Iverson would least like to see him. It was best to excuse himself quickly, because Iverson wasn't in the mood to trade words with him.

"Lord Waldo," he greeted tersely and turned to walk away.

"Mr. Brentwood, before you go, could you tell me if you've seen Miss Crisp?"

The mention of her name stopped Iverson. When he'd last seen Catalina wasn't something he wanted to share with the duke's brother, but something in Lord Waldo's tone of voice made Iverson turn around and ask, "When?"

"Oh, tonight, of course. I looked for her and couldn't find her. I thought perhaps she might want to check on her aunt."

Iverson tensed. "Mrs. Gottfried? Is something wrong with her?"

"I'm not sure anything is wrong, but I don't think Miss Crisp would be happy with what's happening at the moment."

"I'll tell Miss Crisp if I see her," Iverson said, already walking away from the blade. He had a feeling he knew Mrs. Gottfried's problem, and if Catalina wasn't around to help her, he would have to take care of her.

Iverson headed into the drawing room where he'd last seen Catalina's aunt, but neither she nor her usual group of friends were sitting around the dance floor. He then walked into the front parlor. The room wasn't crowded, but there were still several people standing around. He spotted Mrs. Gottfried with a group of four men. They were all laughing.

The hair on the back of Iverson's neck prickled, and anger flashed like lightning through him. He had no idea what she was saying, but it was clear to Iverson the men were having a big laugh at her expense.

He strode over to the cluster with single-minded purpose and said, "Good evening, Mrs. Gottfried, gentlemen."

The men stopped laughing, and a couple of them quickly cleared their throats uncomfortably.

Mrs. Gottfried's eyes widened with surprise, and she

hiccupped. "Oh, it's the charming Mr. Brentwood." She looked at the man to her left and grabbed hold of his arm to steady herself. "He reminds me of my dearest Mr. Gottfried. Have you gentlemen met this fine gentleman?"

Catalina's aunt's face was flushed a dull red. Her eyes were bright and glassy. She swayed on her feet and was slurring her words. She needed help, and she obviously wasn't going to get it from any of the ill-mannered louts crowded around her. He would have to remember to thank Lord Waldo for alerting him that something was wrong.

"I'm here to take you to your niece, Mrs. Gottfried," Iverson said.

Her eyes widened. "Oh, does Catalina need me?"

"Yes, madam." He extended his elbow for her to take.

She turned loose of the man standing beside her and swayed on her feet as she grabbed for Iverson's arm. He clamped his hand around her wrist for extra support.

"Well, then lead the way. Excuse me, gentlemen, I must go."

Iverson took two steps and then turned back and gave each of the men a cold stare. "Perhaps you bird-witted oafs can go somewhere else to find your amusement tonight and something more honorable to fill your time."

As soon as they were away from the group, Iverson asked, "Where is your niece, Mrs. Gottfried?"

She stopped walking and gave him a befuddled look. "I don't know. I thought you knew."

More than a little exasperated, Iverson said, "I've searched this house several times and I can't find her. Did she come with you tonight? I want to make sure you don't leave without her if she came to the party with you."

Mrs. Gottfried rolled her eyes from side to side as if she

hoped to find the answer to his question somewhere in the air. "No, she didn't come with me. I'm sure she said she had a headache and was going to bed."

That didn't sound like Catalina. She was too protective of her aunt to want her to go to a party by herself. "Does Catalina know you are here alone?"

Mrs. Gottfried laughed and put her finger to her lips as she swayed and said, "Shh. Of course not. And don't tell her. I had to slip out of the house. She wouldn't like it."

"That's what I was thinking," he muttered under his breath. "Come on, I'll see you home."

"Did you know you remind me of my Mr. Gottfried?"

"You may have mentioned it," he said.

Iverson stopped at the front door for their cloaks, and then holding tightly to Mrs. Gottfried, he asked, "Is Briggs waiting for you?"

She gave Iverson a blank stare. "I don't know."

Iverson frowned. "Didn't you tell him to wait for you?"

"No," she answered, shaking her head.

"Why not?" he asked and then thought better of it and added, "Never mind, it doesn't matter. He should know to wait for you without being told. If he's not out there, some-one needs to speak to the man about this."

"No use speaking to him. He can't hear."

"I know that, Mrs. Gottfried, but Catalina knows how to make him understand what she is saying."

A big smile broke out on Mrs. Gottfried's face. "She can talk to anyone, but Briggs would just tell her he didn't bring me here."

"He didn't?" That was surprising. "How did you get here? Adam?"

She shook her head and staggered. "I walked. It's not that far, you know, and I can walk."

All of a sudden, Mrs. Gottfried laughed again and stumbled over her feet. If he hadn't had a good hold on her, they both would have fallen to the ground. Iverson had to get her home and quickly.

"Well, you aren't going to walk home. I'm taking you."

It took great effort, but with his driver, Iverson managed to get Mrs. Gottfried into his carriage. Once inside, she had an attack of giggles, but thankfully they didn't last long. It was more of a struggle to get her out of the carriage at her house, because once she'd gotten still, she was ready to go to sleep.

He was certain if he hadn't kept talking to her, she would have passed out on him. And there was a moment or two he thought she might do just that before he got her to the front door. Doing his best to hold her up with one hand, Iverson struck the door knocker several times.

Finally the door opened, but hardly more than a crack. Iverson saw Mrs. Wardyworth on the other side, clothed in a night robe and something on her head that looked more like a stocking than a nightcap. She held the lamp under her chin and her pinched face looked more dour than usual.

She looked him up and down and then said, "He isn't here."

Iverson swore under his breath. The woman could try the patience of a saint. "I'm not here to see Sir Phillip."

"This isn't the proper hour to be calling on Miss Crisp, either."

"I'm doing neither, Mrs. Wardyworth," he said, frustrated, feeling Mrs. Gottfried slipping down his side and trying to pull her back up. "And I don't have time for this. Open the door. I have Mrs. Gottfried with me."

She opened the door a little wider. "What'd ye do to Mrs. Gottfried?"

"Nothing, you—" Iverson caught himself. "I did nothing but bring her home," he managed to say in a much calmer tone than he was feeling. "Now if you don't mind, open the blasted door so I can get her inside."

Mrs. Wardyworth stepped back and held the door wide while he walked Mrs. Gottfried into the vestibule.

"Auntie!" he heard Catalina exclaim.

He looked up to see her rushing down the stairs, her long, chestnut-colored hair billowing around her shoulders. He had an instant desire to lift the length of her shiny tresses in his hands and crush its lush softness between his fingers before letting it tumble to grace her shoulders again. She was dressed in a white, long-sleeved nightgown, and she looked more tempting than an angel.

Iverson's heart melted, and he knew he wasn't angry with her over the story anymore. Maybe he'd never been angry with her. He had been wounded by her silence, but there was no anger.

"Yes, it's me," Mrs. Gottfried said in a loud voice. "Eloisa Lucinda Gottfried."

Catalina threw Iverson a quick, worried glance as she made it to the bottom of the stairs. "Iverson, what are you doing here? Auntie, why are you hanging onto Mr. Brentwood?"

Her aunt swayed again. "We're trying to get in the door."

"How did you get out?" Catalina asked.

"I just opened the door and walked out."

Catalina's concerned eyes darted from Iverson to her aunt. "Why? Where have you been?"

"I've been to a party," she answered giddily.

"A party?" Catalina glanced at Iverson again and went to her aunt's other side to help him hold her steady on her feet. "You left the house without my knowing it? Auntie, why would you do that? You know better."

"Then you should come with me when I ask you to," her aunt said petulantly.

The pain of incredulity edged Catalina's features. "I would have if I had realized it was that important to you."

She looked up at Iverson with such painful emotion, his heart constricted. Tears were brimming in her eyes.

"You were at the party and brought her home?" she asked. He nodded.

"Did she—did many people see her this way?"

"No," he lied without regret or guilt. "It wasn't a well-attended party, and most everyone had gone home."

"Thank you," she whispered gratefully, lowering her lashes. "Thank you for taking care of her." She looked back to her aunt and said, "You've had too much to drink."

"I know I'm a wee bit tipsy," Mrs. Gottfried said on the tail end of a half laugh. "But I'll be just fine in the morning."

"Should I wake Nancy to make her a cup of tea, missy?"

"No," Catalina said, glancing toward her housekeeper. "She needs to go straight to bed."

"Should I wake Sylvia to tend to her?"

"There's no need to disturb anyone else at this hour, Mrs. Wardyworth. I will take care of Auntie tonight. You may go back to bed, too. We'll be fine." She looked at Iverson. "Do you mind helping me get her upstairs and into her room?"

Catalina looked so distraught, he wanted to drop his grip on Mrs. Gottfried and hold her instead. He'd seen her swallow hard before she'd asked him to help her. "You don't have to ask," he said, letting his eyes drink in the sight of her. "You know I will help you."

"Thank you," she whispered again, her voice as full of tears as her eyes.

It wasn't easy, but with Catalina on one side and Iverson on the other, they managed to get Mrs. Gottfried up the stairs. But before they made it to her room, Iverson had to pick her up and carry her because she'd passed out. Catalina opened the bedchamber door and threw back her covers so Iverson could lay her down. He then stepped out of the room and waited in the darkened hallway.

Iverson heard Catalina talking softly to her aunt, even though she must have known the woman couldn't hear a word she was saying. He'd seen enough people insensible from drink to know she wouldn't be awake for quite some time. Still, he knew it was in Catalina's nature to soothe her aunt, take off her shoes, stockings, and jewelry, and make her comfortable before leaving her.

Leaning against the wall, Iverson remembered the tears brimming in Catalina's eyes, the concern in her voice, and a knot twisted in his gut. He knew how much Mrs. Gottfried and her staff meant to Catalina. She, who was without a mother, mothered them all.

Something Iverson didn't recognize swelled in his chest. He remembered Catalina giving him her handkerchief to dry his face. She'd warmed his hands and lips at the risk of being caught by her aunt. She was a compassionate giver, yet he never heard her asking for anything in return—from anyone.

And for a woman like that, he could forgive anything. But what would she say to him? How did she feel about him? Would she ask him to leave?

Suddenly Iverson was desperate to hold her. And God help him, but he knew that before this night was over, he would have to comfort Catalina. He had to do it for Catalina and for himself.

Nineteen

Passion is the element in which we live;
without it, we hardly vegetate.
—Lord Byron

SHE WAS INCONSOLABLE.

Catalina had done all she could to make her aunt comfortable, but there was no relief for her own anguish. She didn't know if she would ever forgive herself for failing her aunt this evening. She brushed a lock of hair away from her aunt's forehead and reached down and pressed a kiss to her soft, flushed cheek. Her aunt's face was peaceful, though she breathed deeply and noisily.

Catalina had always tried so hard to hide her aunt's recurring condition so no one would ever see her the way she was tonight. But she had not been there this time to safeguard her aunt's state from the eyes and ears of others.

And merciful heaven! What rotten, punitive course of fate had chosen Iverson to be the one to bring her aunt home? After what she and her father had done to him and his brothers, Catalina was certain he was the last man who wanted to help her family.

Oh, but there was peaceful joy, too, joy that gladdened her heart and made it soar. The one man who claimed he wasn't a gentleman had done the gentlemanly thing and seen her aunt home.

That he would help her aunt after all she and her father had done proved Iverson was not the cold, hardhearted man he often claimed to be. She hadn't heard him leave but was certain he had rushed down the stairs and fled out the door as quickly as he could. She blew out a soft, rueful chuckle. He was probably halfway back to the party by now.

She couldn't blame him. What man wanted to be saddled with a female who'd had too much to drink? Especially a lady he didn't even know very well. But she was so thankful he had. Though he may not want or appreciate it, she would send him a note tomorrow telling him once again how grateful she was that he came to her aunt's rescue.

Catalina tiptoed out of her aunt's bedchamber and quietly shut the door. When she turned toward her room, she saw Iverson standing in the shadowy corridor a few feet away.

Her heartbeat faltered, and her chest tightened. He hadn't rushed out after all.

But why not?

Maybe he wanted to scold her for not going with her aunt tonight. Or perhaps he wanted to rant about her withholding the information about *A Tale of Three Gentlemen*. But no matter the reason he was still there, and while she welcomed the sight of him, she didn't think she could take his onslaught of anger or disappointment or whatever he was feeling. She was too close to tears from having let her aunt down. Catalina hadn't felt as fragile as she did right now since her mother died. She would give anything if she could run into his arms and be comforted. But Catalina knew she was the last person he wanted to hold.

She shored up her inner strength, and trying to sound in control of her emotions said, "She's asleep. I'm glad you're still here. It gives me the opportunity to tell you again how grateful I am you left the party and brought her home."

"You've thanked me enough, Catalina. I've become quite fond of your aunt. I wanted to help her."

Unexpectedly, she felt an overwhelming need to explain to him. "I don't know what got into her tonight. She hasn't gone to a party without me all year. She knows she's prone to drink too much, and I always leave parties early so I can get her home before she, before she—" Catalina bit down on her bottom lip. Suddenly, she just wanted him to go away so she could fall on her bed and cry. She tried to swallow the large lump in her throat, but it wouldn't go down. "I just wasn't up to going to a party tonight."

"A headache?" he asked.

"No," she admitted honestly. "I was fearful I would see you dancing with some beautiful young lady, and I couldn't—" She wanted to say she couldn't bear seeing him happy with other young ladies. "I'm sure you want to go. I'll show you to the door."

"I know where the door is, Catalina. If I wanted to leave, I would have been gone by the time you came out of your aunt's room."

She didn't know how to take what he said. The huge lump in her throat seemed to grow larger and constrict her breathing.

"I need no more thanks and no more apologies from you," he continued.

"Then why are you still here?"

"I need to be here with you." Iverson stretched out his arms toward her. "Come here."

Catalina knew there was no hope of ever winning Iverson's

love, but maybe he would consent to giving her one night of his loving. She then did what she had wanted to do several times in the past: She ran to Iverson. He caught her in his powerful arms and brought her up to his hard chest. Their lips met softly in a kiss so tender it was heavenly. It was as if he knew what a delicate hold she had on her emotions right now and was gently soothing her with kisses too sweet to describe with words.

Filled with love, Catalina threw her arms around him and hugged him tightly, hoping he would sense or know what she was feeling for him at that moment. She wanted to share with him all that bubbled inside her—disappointment in herself for not protecting her aunt, deep anguish because she had hurt him so greatly, anger because her father had not come home to help her—but she remained silent and kept all she was feeling to herself.

Catalina wanted to enjoy the pleasure of being in his arms once again. She sighed contentedly. This was where she wanted to be. This was what she wanted.

The longing and the passion between them was too intense for their embrace to stay tender for long. When their tongues touched, soft and sweet, the kiss deepened quickly. Iverson kissed her hungrily. Catalina accepted his eagerness.

Heated with the intensifying rush of desire, Catalina thrust her tongue into his mouth, impatient, desperate to taste him again. He moaned softly, deeply, in his throat, eager to yield to her demand to explore before taking his turn to kiss her in the same way. There was a desperate urgency in the way he held her tightly and plundered her mouth. His tongue swirled and skimmed along the lining of her lips. Heedless of the fact they stood in the middle of the corridor right outside her aunt's room, Catalina matched his fierceness with her own hunger.

He dragged his lips away from hers and whispered, "I couldn't get the thought of you out my mind, the taste of you from my lips, or the touch of you from my hands. You drive me to madness, Catalina."

"Then you know how I have been feeling these past three days," she answered.

He chuckled low in his throat. "You cannot possibly feel what I am feeling, for you are an innocent, and you have not yet experienced the full knowledge of lovemaking."

"But I want to, Iverson, and I want to experience it with you."

"You tempt me too much, Catalina. I am not used to denying myself whatever I want, but with you I always have to hold myself back."

"Then don't," she pleaded. "Don't tonight."

"I did not come here to seduce you. In my heart, I truly do not want to seduce you like this, but my body keeps overpowering my mind."

"I want to be with you. If you want to be with me, I am yours."

"If I want you?" he asked huskily. "You do not have to ask that. I have wanted no one else since the first day I saw you."

He brushed her moist lips with his, easing over them with the lightest contact. She opened her mouth, and his tongue thrust in quickly, deeply. His hand raked down her unbound breast to her waist, where he gently squeezed her before letting his hand graze the flare of her slim hip and back up to her breast again. Through the cotton of her night garment, his touch seared her to the bone, heightened her desire, and made her tremble. He fondled her breast with tenderness, yet he kissed her as if he couldn't get enough of her and demanded more.

When he raised his head and looked deeply into her eyes as if he were questioning her about a serious matter, she could see he was conflicted. She had no doubt he wanted to continue what they had started, but she also knew his sense of honor was playing havoc with his desire for her. She saw by the movement of his throat that he swallowed hard. He had told her he did not want to take her virtue from her.

His hand sailed down the column of her neck to the neckline of her white long-sleeved gown, and he played with the hollow of her throat for a moment before pulling on the ribbon that held the bodice together. He untied the bow. With gentleness that touched her soul, he brushed the front panel of her gown aside and slid it off her shoulder. He gently kissed the crook of her neck and shoulder and then slipped his hand inside and cupped her bare breast.

Her breaths became shallow. She could not help but wonder if he was testing her, making sure she knew what she was consenting to, giving her time to back away, time to say no.

Catalina knew what she wanted. She was ready and willing.

He studied her for so long Catalina thought he was going to deny her, so she said, "Will you walk away from me tonight, or will you stay?"

"You are certain of your feelings?"

She heard his increased breathing, and hope surged within her. "I am."

"Is your room the one with the light?"

"Yes," she answered with a raspy voice, remembering she had lit the candle by the bed when she heard the first knock on the door. "My aunt and I are the only ones who sleep on this floor. She will not awaken for some time."

"Not before dawn, for sure. I must be gone before the servants are up."

His gaze stayed on hers. His hand continued to cup, caress, and knead her breast, sending wave after wave of pleasure spiraling down to that womanly part between her legs.

She held her breath, and her stomach tightened, willing his words to mean what she hoped. "You'll stay?"

"You're asking me to?"

He still wasn't sure, and for some reason, that pleased her. He was leaving this decision totally in her hands. "Yes. Take me to my bed, and stay with me tonight."

The first hint of a smile played at the corners of his mouth. "The way I'm feeling right now, Catalina, nothing could make me leave you tonight until I have had you beneath me and had my fill of you."

He reached down and hooked his arm under her knees and lifted her off the floor. Catalina's heart soared. She curled her arms around his neck and breathed a shaky sigh of relief. When they stepped inside, he held her with one arm and quietly closed the door with the other.

"The key is in the lock," she whispered, and then a second or two later, she heard it click.

He walked over to the bed and laid her down. The lone candle didn't give off much light, but enough for her to see he kept his gaze on her as he shrugged out of his coat and dropped it to the floor. Catalina watched in awe as he untied his neckcloth, unwound it from his neck, and dropped it, too. His collar came next, and then he unbuttoned his waist-coat and rid himself of it. He stepped out of his wide-buckled shoes as he yanked his shirt from the waistband of his trousers. He pulled it over his head, letting it fall on top of the other clothing on the floor.

Catalina was mesmerized by Iverson's disrobing. She'd never seen a man's nude chest. She shivered with expectation as she looked at his gloriously masculine body with solid, well-defined muscles in his arms, chest, and down his torso. She couldn't help but think it was a shame to cover all that beauty with clothing.

He unbuttoned his trousers with one hand as he walked toward her, letting the front panel fall open. With one easy motion, he sank onto the bed beside her and took her into his arms. She arched her back and lifted her face to his.

Their lips met and moved sensuously together. He kissed her softly, tenderly, longingly, and lovingly. He kissed her as if he treasured her, and Catalina melted against him. Her hands slid around the smooth, firm skin of his powerful body, and she clasped him to her. Her hands rubbed up and down the contours of his shoulders, back, and waist. She relished the way his skin felt to her and the way touching him made curls of desire swirl, dip, swing, and explode inside her.

Iverson lifted his head so he could kiss the outside corner of her eye. His kisses made a warm, moist path down her cheek, over to the hairline near her ear, where he drew in a deep breath and whispered, "My lovely Catalina."

His lips then glided along the line of her jaw and over her chin. He tortured her with sweet little dewdrop kisses on her heated skin. With a confident hand, he pushed her night-gown off her shoulder and kissed his way down the crook of her neck and across the top of her shoulder, sending shivers of delight spinning rampantly all through her body.

He slipped the bodice of her night rail down her arm, exposing her breast. Her shallow breaths made her chest rise and fall rapidly. He cupped and kneaded the fullness of her breast with his strong, gentle hand. He found her puckered nipple and rolled it between his thumb and finger. She lifted her chest to him and his lips left her shoulder as his mouth covered the tight bud of her breast. The sensations made Catalina tremble and gasp with exquisite delight.

"I love the taste of your skin on my tongue." His warm breath floated across her skin with each word he spoke, heating her even more. "I love feeling the weight of your beautiful breast in my hand. Firm, round, and unbelievably soft."

She gasped with pleasure yet again as he pulled her nipple deeply into his mouth, sucking gently and making it feel full, tight, and deliciously achy.

"You please me with your soft sounds of enjoyment, Catalina."

She circled his head with her arms and gently held him to her bosom. "You please me, Iverson, to the point I can't be quiet, I can't be still, I can't—" She wanted to tell him she couldn't live without him, but she knew he didn't want to hear such endearing comments from her, so she finished by saying, "I can't wait to find out what comes next."

Iverson raised his head and looked into her eyes. "Your eagerness excites me. There is more. Much more."

"Show me."

He reached down and grabbed hold of the hem of her white gown and slowly pulled it up her legs, past her knees, her thighs. She swallowed hard when the most intimate part of her body was exposed to his gaze, but he didn't stop. He kept sliding the gown upward past her abdomen, past her waist, to tickle over the peaks of her breasts. He then lifted her back from the pillows, and in one fluid, easy action, pulled the garment over her head, off her arms, and dropped it to the floor.

With a quick look, his gaze traveled down the length of her body once, twice, three times before settling on her eyes again. He placed his fingertips on her forehead and watched every movement as he gently began to trace a slow path down the side of her face, over her jaw, along her neck, shoulder, and chest, across the tip of her breast, lingering there for a few moments. The trail resumed with his fingers skimming down her midriff to the indention of her waist, along the slender plane of her hip and across her abdomen, and then blazing a trail down her thigh, over her knee, along her leg to the end of her toes. With breathtaking slowness and feather-light caresses, he took the same sensuous path back up to her face. She remained quiet, wanting to be everything to him as he was to her.

When he was finished, he looked into her eyes and smiled. "It's official," he said.

Apprehension shot through her, her mouth went dry, and her body stiffened. "What?"

"You are the most beautiful woman I have ever seen. I've just checked every inch of you, and you have no equal."

Catalina relaxed and laughed softly. She lightly touched his cheek, letting her forefinger trace the outline of his lips. "I'm sure that is not true, Iverson, but I don't care. I loved hearing it anyway."

"I wouldn't have said it had it not been true."

Catalina reached up and hugged Iverson as tenderly as she knew how. She whispered into the crook of his neck, "I don't know why, but you have made me feel beautiful from the first moment our eyes met."

He gathered her up against his chest. "That's because you are."

Catalina leaned back and let her gaze caress his strong face. She wanted to tell him he was the man of her dreams, the faceless man she had always imagined when she read poetry and books about deep, soul-shattering love. Instead, she said, "You have teased me long enough with your kisses and caresses. My body aches for you. Show me what comes next."

Iverson slowly skimmed his trousers down his lean hips and legs, taking his stockings with them as he kicked them off his feet. For the first time, shyness overtook Catalina, and she averted her eyes while he straddled her thighs.

He held his weight off her legs and asked, "Will you not look at me?" in an amused tone.

Slowly, she lifted her lids and gazed on the man she had given her heart to, and her love for him overflowed inside her. "You are extraordinary, amazing."

He grinned. "I'm the only man you've ever seen, right?"

"Yes."

Iverson chuckled softly and then, as he stretched his legs down beside hers, he lowered his head and took an erect nipple into his mouth and tugged on it possessively.

Catalina wound her arms around his torso and let her hands rove freely over his back, shoulders, and down low over his hips. Iverson's open hand drifted down her ribs to her abdomen, and then to the downy thatch of hair between her legs. Catalina tensed from the intrusion. The muscles of her thighs clenched tightly, even as a feeling of exhilaration washed over her. His finger touched her with soft, circular movements, and her stomach quickened with surprise at the sensation.

"Relax," he whispered against her skin. "I'm not going to hurt you."

"I know," she answered, breathless. "It's just—"

"Your first time," he finished for her. "I will be gentle, I promise."

"I have no doubt about that, Iverson, but whatever you are doing is going to drive me mad with pleasure."

He chuckled. "I have to take it slow so I can please you."

"Then why is it I feel as if my body needs some kind of urgent release right now, this moment, no, this instant?"

"Because what you are feeling is what making love is all about. And I'm going to keep doing it a little longer, all right?"

"Yes, please," she managed to say between erratic, raspy breaths that seemed to be coming faster and faster.

"You need to be ready for me. There will be a little pain the first time."

"I've heard that, too, but I don't believe it. How can there be pain when I am drowning in immense pleasure?"

He chuckled lightly. "I'm told there is."

"You are too gentle to hurt me, Iverson."

"Your words please me, Catalina."

"And your touch pleases me."

Iverson placed his lips on hers and kissed her fiercely, passionately. Their breaths, sighs, and moans of gratification mingled softly. As Iverson continued to kiss her and touch her, Catalina felt her breasts and abdomen tighten with thrilling new sensations. With every second that passed, she felt she was getting closer and closer to the brink of something, but she didn't know what.

Iverson carefully positioned his body over hers and settled his weight upon her, fitting his lower body between her legs. His warmth was promising, his hardness evident, and Catalina's body unfurled and opened to him. With caution and gentleness, he positioned himself at her womanhood.

Catalina lovingly surrendered to Iverson. Her arms circled his strong back, and she pressed him to her. She basked in the enticing way Iverson's naked chest felt pressed against hers. She couldn't keep her hands still as she closed her eyes and sighed with pleasure.

She felt a thick, probing pressure, and an intense, constant pushing, but his fingers never stopped moving and working their magic of sensations. His touch was exquisite torture. He didn't stop kissing her or touching, and gradually she realized he had joined his body with hers.

"Are you all right?"

She felt an unusual, unfamiliar fullness that was uncomfortable but not painful. "Yes, yes," she whispered. "I am exhilarated."

"Ah, Catalina, my love," he whispered, "you are as passionate as I knew you would be."

He kissed her deeply as he moved in and out with long, sure strokes. Instinctively, her hips started moving with his rhythm, and soon she was thrusting her hips in perfect harmony with his. A tremor shook his body, and Catalina knew he was as affected by these strange new feelings as she was.

Catalina's breath trembled. Once again she felt on the

brink of something she couldn't control. There was demanding, mounting pressure in the meeting of their mouths and their bodies.

Her hands found the back of his head, and her fingers wove erratically through his hair. She felt the cord that held his queue, and without thinking, her fingers touched the ends, the tiny, short tassels. He still wore the silken cord she'd given him that day in the carriage. She smiled beneath his lips. He could have easily discarded it, thrown it away, but he had kept it. All her loving, passionate feelings for him bubbled over, and her body was suddenly racked with one amazing sensation after another. She jerked and trembled as if an explosion had taken place inside her. She pressed her lips into Iverson's shoulder so she would not cry out with overwhelming, rapturous, and wondrous joy.

Within moments, Iverson gasped and pushed hard toward her. He kissed her deeply. She lifted her legs around his hips and tightened them around him, and his body shuddered until he let out a long, shaky breath.

A wonderful feeling of immeasurable satisfaction flowed over Catalina, and she felt her body relax upon the bed. Iverson rested upon her, burying his face in the crook of her neck. He kissed her skin softly.

They lay there for several moments with neither of them moving, their arms and legs tangled together. Catalina couldn't bear the thought of disturbing her adoration for what happened between them. She wanted to enjoy the moment for as long as possible.

But far too soon, Iverson rolled over on his side, pulling Catalina with him.

In the dim candlelight, she looked into his blue eyes.

"Is it possible to experience that more than once?" she asked.

Iverson grinned. "There are no limits to the possibilities that stem from making love, Catalina."

"That is good to hear."

"I'm assuming that means you were quite pleased with your first experience."

She rose up on her elbow and whispered, "Oh, it was much more than merely pleasing. It was breathtaking, astounding, overwhelming, and amazing."

Iverson laughed softly, quietly. "I get the idea."

"Was it the same for you?"

His penetrating gaze answered *yes* before he spoke the words. "Exactly the same."

"In that case, may we do it again?" she whispered and then kissed him.

Twenty

The bosom can ache beneath diamond brooches;
and many a blithe heart dances under coarse wool.
—Edwin Hubbell Chapin

THE FIRST SHARDS OF DAWN BROKE THROUGH THE PARTED draperies, bathing the room in soft gray light. Catalina stirred beside Iverson. There was a chill to the early morning air, but his warmth drew her like a blazing fire on a freezing night. She snuggled deeper into his heat and felt his arms tighten around her. She smiled. Even after all her years of reading stirring, romantic love poetry and stories, she could never have imagined what actually happened between a man and a woman or how it truly felt to have one's body joined with another.

When it came right down to it, she thought, poetry and writings didn't do justice to the actual act of making love. After last night, she was convinced there were no words to describe all the sensations and the feelings of being transported to that ethereal state where nothing mattered but the essence of being loved.

She finally knew what Shakespeare meant when he wrote:

Shall I compare thee to a summer's day?
Thou art more lovely and more temperate:

Rough winds do shake the darling buds of May,
And summer's lease hath all too short a date:
Sometime too hot the eye of heaven shines,
And often is his gold complexion dimm'd;
And every fair from fair sometime declines,
By chance or nature's changing course untrimm'd;
But thy eternal summer shall not fade,
Nor lose possession of that fair thou ow'st;
Nor shall Death brag thou wander'st in his shade,
When in eternal lines to time thou grow'st:
  So long as men can breathe or eyes can see,
  So long lives this and this gives life to thee.

Catalina rose onto her elbow and looked down at Iverson. She loved him with all her heart. She thought about the possibility of telling him. How would he respond? What would he say? That he was not the kind to share just one woman's bed? That she knew he was a rake when she invited him to stay in her bed? That she must not ask of him things he cannot give?

No, she could not tell him, for she attached no strings or vows to her invitation last night, and she couldn't present any to him now.

The night had ended. It was wrenching to think about it, but the time had come for him to go. She didn't know if he would ever come back to her bed. There had been many touches and words spoken, but none concerning the future. Should she ask him if he would return to her, to settle her quandary and know for sure, or should she simply stay quiet and hope he might?

She studied Iverson at her leisure and liked what she

saw. Not just his strong, handsome face, but the man inside the body, too. She liked that he teased her about Lord Bighampton, that he'd hit the man who accosted her at Madame Shipwith's establishment, and that he was fiercely loyal to his family and his mother's memory.

His eyes were closed, though she didn't think he slept, and she couldn't let him. She touched his cheek with her palm and felt the scratchy stubble of beard. She ran her hand down his firm neck and across his strong shoulder. He opened his eyes, caught her fingers in his, and kissed her open palm.

"The servants will be up soon," she said. "You must go."

"I know, but I don't want to." He rose on his elbow and moved her long hair to the back of her shoulder, exposing her breast for his view. "You are beautiful."

She smiled. "Thank you, kind sir, but you still must go."

Iverson looked intently at her and said, "I have been in bed with many women in my life, Catalina, but your bed is the first one I've not wanted to leave."

His words made her heart beat faster, but not daring to hope, she said, "That would be dangerous."

"I know, yet I want to linger here until I've had my fill of you."

She gave him a teasing smile. "How long would that take?"

He grinned. "Much longer than we have right now."

"Does that mean you will come back?" she asked hopefully.

The loud slamming of a door startled Catalina and made her jerk. From below stairs, she heard her name called.

Her heart jumped into her throat. "That's my father!" she exclaimed. "He's home."

"Damnation! At daybreak!" Iverson threw off the covers and jumped off the bed.

"Yes." Catalina grabbed her nightgown from the floor and slid it over her head.

"I can't believe your father chose this moment to come home," Iverson complained, quickly stepping into his trousers.

"My father has no appreciation for time. He goes and comes, wakes and sleeps at his own pleasure."

"Bloody poet," Iverson murmured, snatching his waistcoat, neckcloth, and collar from the floor.

Catalina picked up Iverson's shoes and stockings and shoved them into his full hands. "I hear him coming up the stairs. There's no time to make the back staircase, you must hide in my wardrobe. Hurry!"

"Catalina, I will not hide among your clothing," he said. "I will go out the window like an honorable rake. It won't be the first time I've jumped to the ground from a lady's room."

"I have no doubt about that, but there is no time to do it, and you and I will get caught." She ran over to the wardrobe and with racing heart and trembling hands, opened it. "There is no time. Please, Iverson, hurry. He's coming down the corridor."

Reluctantly he climbed into the tall chest, and Catalina shut the door behind him. She rushed to her bedroom door and turned the key just as her father turned the knob. The door burst open. Sir Phillip Crisp picked up Catalina and swung her around several times while laughing heartily.

"I knew I could depend on you to rise and greet me. How has my fair daughter been?" He set her back on her feet.

"Well, Papa," she said, swallowing a dry lump of fear. "I've been well. I—" For an instant, she had a great desire to bury her head in his chest, weep, and say, "I've needed you. Where have you been?" But the moment passed quickly, and instead she whispered, "I missed you."

He reached down and hugged her again. "I missed you, too, my lovely Catalina." He stepped away and looked at her. "And you look even lovelier than the day I left. In fact, I see something different in your eyes."

Catalina tensed. Did he know a man had spent the night in her bed? Could he tell by looking at her that she was no longer a maid but now a woman who knew the thrilling joys of a man's gentle touch?

"What, Papa?" she asked breathlessly, thinking her heart might beat out of her chest.

"You don't look like a child anymore. You look like the beautiful young lady I know you are."

"Is that you, Phillip?"

He turned around and spoke toward the door. "Yes, Elle, it's me."

"It's about time you returned," Aunt Elle complained.

"I know. I know. I've been an unforgivable beast, but I had many places to go and many people to see, which I will tell you about later. Go back to sleep. It's too early to rise. Sorry to disturb you, dear Sister."

Catalina heard her aunt's bedroom door close again.

Suddenly Catalina was overcome by a wave of panic. She had to get her father downstairs so Iverson could slip out of the house.

"Papa, why don't we go below stairs? I'll get Nancy to make us some tea."

"This early? No, no, not for me. I have been traveling all

night and want to get some sleep. But first I must take the time to thank you for taking care of everything for me while I was away, just as you always do."

"I don't need thanks, Papa. Come, I'll walk you to your room. We will talk after you have rested."

"Ah, but first I must thank you for finishing *A Tale of Three Gentlemen* for me."

Catalina froze. "No, Papa, no!" she whispered almost soundlessly.

"You did an excellent job on the ending, my dear."

Catalina looked frantically at the wardrobe and then rushed to her father and placed her hand to his lips. "No, I beg you, do not say more."

"What's this?" he said, pulling her hand away from his mouth and holding her wrist. "Don't be shy about accepting my praise."

"No," she whispered earnestly again. "You don't know what you are saying. Papa, please don't say it."

Her father paid her no mind and continued to talk. Her body and mind grew cold. She felt so rigid she feared she might break if anyone touched her.

"Excellent idea on the ending, dear girl, excellent. I wouldn't have let Sir Mortimer die as you did. That was a stroke of brilliance, though you did get that from me." He stopped and laughed. "You are the one who deserves praise. All the praise I have been hearing in my travels. I've heard what a huge success the story has been. Everywhere I go, people are talking about it, and I owe it all to you. I had planned to finish it before I left, but when I realized I hadn't, I knew you would and turn it in for me."

He reached down and kissed her cheek, but Catalina

didn't feel it. She was frozen with disbelief, with fear. There was no doubt Iverson had heard her father implicate her. Iverson now knew she had finished the story. She felt as if her chest was caving in on her lungs. Her breathing became so shallow she felt light-headed.

He will never forgive me now.

"This reminds me, I have a special gift for you."

Catalina couldn't speak. She couldn't move.

"You look sad, my dear. Are those tears I see clouding your eyes? What's this? Tears? All right, all right, if you are that disappointed I don't have the gift in my hands, I will go below stairs, open my trunk, and get it for you now. I agree. I should have already gotten it out for you." With his thumb, he wiped a stray tear from her cheek. "Now, no more crying. I will get your gift and bring it upstairs to you."

Catalina's father walked out. She heard his footsteps on the stairs, but her gaze never left the wardrobe. She didn't want to face Iverson but knew she must. He might have forgiven her for withholding the truth about the continuing story, but he would never forgive her for helping her father write it.

Another fear gripped her heart like a cold fist. What would Iverson do about her father? Would he spread the news all over London that she helped her father write his poetry and stories? Iverson had no reason not to do it, and every reason to make the knowledge widely known. It would be a sweet revenge to get back at Sir Phillip by ruining his career.

The wardrobe door opened with a creak. Iverson stepped out. He had put on his shirt and stuffed it in his trousers. He held his shoes and the rest of his clothing in his hands.

Just as a few days before, she expected to see his face a mask of fury, but once again what she saw was disbelief. Catalina's heart broke all over again. She swallowed the sob that threatened to burst from her aching throat. She could see he didn't want to believe it was true, and she'd give anything if she could tell him it wasn't. She wished she could lie and tell him all her father said was wrong. But while she could withhold the truth from Iverson, she could never lie to him.

"You wrote part of *A Tale of Three Gentlemen*?"

The anguish in his voice cut her deeply. She nodded. "A few pages. I finished it and turned it in to Mr. Frederick."

"Why?"

"To get the money he owed Papa."

"*Money!*" The word spat from his mouth as if it was a filthy rag. "You did it for *money*?"

She was staggered by the pain and incredulity in his expression. Suddenly her stomach cramped so badly she almost doubled over from the pain.

"You don't understand," she rasped.

"Then make me understand, Catalina," he demanded.

The words were almost torn from his throat, and she shuddered at the emotion that stirred and echoed in his voice.

"I had no choice," she whispered, but even as she said the words, she knew how flimsy, how hollow, how inadequate they sounded. Yet her love for him forced her to continue. "There's never enough money for the mortgage, the staff, the food, Papa's traveling, his clothing, Auntie's tonics. You don't know how many times we've been one step away from the poorhouse, and Papa would just up and leave me to handle it all." She had to make him understand if not forgive. "I've been finishing his work for about three years. He just takes off and leaves us with nothing but words. The debts were mounting. Men arrived at our door to remove us from the house, but I begged for a few more days. That's when I finished Papa's work for the first time."

"Why didn't you tell me this when we spoke three days ago?" he asked in a gravelly voice.

"I wanted to, but I didn't trust you."

He pierced her with a look of agony and slowly repeated her words. "You didn't trust me?"

"I know how angry you've been at Papa for writing the story. I was afraid if you knew I helped him, you would tell someone, anyone, or everyone in order to get revenge. If it was ever made known in Society that I finished some of his works, it would ruin his reputation, and he could never sell anything again."

Iverson remained quiet, just looking at her. She inhaled deeply and choked back a heart-wrenching sob as tears blurred her vision.

"Iverson, do what you want to about me, but I ask you not to make it known that I have finished my father's work. Please don't take his reputation away from him."

"What reputation does he have, Catalina? A false one."

She gasped. "No."

"Yes. He is an imposter. You have been his co-author, and he has never acknowledged it."

"And shouldn't," she whispered loudly. "I don't finish all his work, and he was successful long before I starting aiding him. And he never asked me to. This is truly my fault, not his. Papa had left the story unfinished. I finished it, Iverson. I turned it in. So only I am to blame."

Catalina heard her father at the bottom of the stairs, and she frantically turned toward the door.

"I don't know what I will do about your father, Catalina, but I will not ruin your reputation."

He walked over to the window and brushed the draperies aside. He slid the window up and threw his shoes and clothing to the ground. He then sat on the windowsill, swung his legs around, and jumped without looking back. She heard him land with a thud.

Catalina stood in the chill of the room with tears flowing from her eyes, seeping down her cheeks, spilling over her jaw, and dropping onto her nightgown. What could she do? She'd lost Iverson forever, and she could no longer save her father from his wrath. If he wanted to tell the world she helped her father, he would. Catalina wanted to throw herself onto the bed and bury herself under the covers.

Then she heard her father stomping down the corridor. She slowly walked over to the window, closed it, and settled the draperies.

"Here you are, my darling. Wipe your tears away, and come see what I have for you." He opened a black velvet box, and on a bed of beige sarcenet rested a single string of exquisite pearls.

She looked up at him in astonishment and said, "Papa, we can't afford these."

"Nonsense. With the success of *A Tale of Three Gentlemen*, I could buy you a dozen strings of pearls."

"No, you've already been paid, and the money has been spent."

"Well, I'm sure more money will be coming in."

Catalina was not up to her father's carefree, happy, and everything-will-be-all-right disposition.

She turned away and said, "I don't want them, Papa. I will never wear them. You take them back."

"You don't like the pearls I've brought you? I will get you something else."

Catalina's shoulders drooped. Why couldn't her father understand? She shored up her courage again, and from somewhere found the strength to suck in another deep breath and not cry. Her father would never change. He didn't want to and wouldn't know how to if he tried. But she had to let him know how she felt.

Denying the ache in her heart, she faced him and said, "Papa, I could never wear those pearls. I could never accept anything you bought with money you made off *A Tale of Three Gentlemen*."

Her father looked bewildered. "Why? What does it matter where the money comes from?"

"It matters, Papa. I know you wrote the parody for entertainment, but the Brentwood twins didn't think it much of a laugh. They were offended by its implication that their mother had been unfaithful to their father."

"Oh, I see," he said, looking surprised. He closed the case of pearls and slid the jewelry case into his pocket. "The Brentwood twins, you say. You've met them, talked to them?"

"Yes, since you've been away."

For a moment, he seemed to ponder what she said. "And tell me, is there one twin you speak to more often than the other?"

Her throat ached with unshed tears, but feeling no desire to evade his question, she said, "Yes."

"Ah, now I understand."

"No, you don't," she whispered earnestly.

"Oh, but I do, my dear Catalina," he said, placing a firm grip on her shoulders. "I have been a lover and writer of love most of my life. I recognize the signs of love in a person's eyes and face when I see them. Who is this man who has stolen your heart from me?"

She turned her face away from him. "It doesn't matter."

He placed his hand under her chin and gently turned her back to him. "Of course it does. This man you love, it must be one of twins?"

"Iverson" reverently rolled off her tongue.

"I see," her father said solemnly and then broke out with a big smile and a hearty laugh. He picked her up and hugged her, swinging her around again before setting her down on her feet. "I knew there was something different about you, and it's that at long last you are in love."

Catalina swallowed another sob. "Oh, Papa, this is not something to be joyous about."

He kissed her on each cheek. "Why not? I am joyous every time I'm in love."

"He doesn't love me."

"What? How could he not? You are beautiful, intelligent, and a romantic. What man would not love you?"

Catalina shook her head in frustration. "Papa, you don't understand. You wrote about his family. He has been extremely upset about that."

"Oh, nonsense," he said, dismissing her words with a wave of his hand. "It was just a parody no one would take seriously. And I wrote it, not you. Besides, is he not going to love you because of me? I don't see that happening. Don't worry, Catalina. Now that the entire story has been published, he will forget about it. The Season starts next week. I'll have all new gowns made for you and see to it you look like a glorious angel. We'll attend every party every night. Mark my words. That gentleman will soon have eyes for no one but you."

He kissed her forehead. "Now go back to bed, because that is where I'm heading."

"Papa?" she called to him as he reached the door.

He turned back to her, smiling. "What, my darling?"

"I will never finish any of your work again."

"Catalina," he cooed.

"I'm serious, Papa. I will never do it again."

"We'll talk more on this later. I am weary, and so are you. Go back to sleep. Everything will be rosy."

Catalina was thankful when she heard her bedroom door shut. She was finally alone. Now she could collapse.

She crawled onto the bed where she had lain with Iverson only minutes ago. She pulled the pillow into her arms, and from the corner of her eye she caught sight of a piece of black cord. She pulled it from beneath the sheet. It was the drawstring from her reticule. She then recalled that Iverson's hair was down when he'd jumped from the bed.

She'd wanted to say more to him, to somehow make it right between them again. She'd wanted him to know she was as wounded by her actions as he was. But there was no placating him and no comforting her.

Some things simply could not be undone.

She gathered the string in her hand and pressed it against her heart.

Twenty-one

*There is only one way to happiness and
that is to cease worrying about things which
are beyond the power of our will.*
—Epictetus

HE NEEDED TO DO SOME THINKING.

And Iverson needed to be alone to do it. Home was the best place for that. After he shaved and dressed, he told Wallace he didn't want to be disturbed. He went into his book room to ponder all that had happened. Pouring himself a glass of port, he eased into his chair and propped his booted feet on his desk.

He smiled ruefully. How long had it been since he'd had to leave a lady's room by the window? Not since he was in his early twenties, when he'd made one hasty departure too many and managed to land wrong and twist his ankle. He couldn't walk for a week. That taught him it was best to stay away from a lady if he had to slip out of her house at daybreak. And until today, he had.

For a moment or two this morning, he'd considered staying in Catalina's bedroom and facing her father, but that thought seemed far from satisfying. He quickly realized it didn't matter that Catalina had withheld information from him again. He didn't want her father or anyone else to know they had been together last night. And the reason for that startled him. It wasn't because he was afraid of being caught in the parson's mousetrap. It was because his time with her had been too special. His time in her arms, in her bed, meant too much to him to share it with anyone.

Even now, knowing she helped her father finish that blasted story, he was still yearning to see her again. He was still thinking about her.

Now that he'd had time to think about it, he wasn't surprised she had to do her father's work for him. She'd told him once that she got up early to write, but it had never dawned on him she was helping her father. Catalina took care of everything else for the man: his house, his staff, his sister, his accounting. Why not his poetry and prose, too?

What bothered Iverson most of all was her saying she didn't trust him.

She didn't trust him not to tell others her secret.

That had been like a dagger thrown right into his heart. What kind of man did she think he was?

The kind of man who told her he would break her father's fingers if he wrote about Iverson's family again.

Iverson growled at himself, remembering the first day he went to Catalina's house. She should have thrown him out on his ear for that, even though with her engaging, capable way she had goaded him into saying it.

He had been a bit too forceful.

Maybe more than a bit.

And later, she'd seen him go after the Corinthian who couldn't handle his horse, and drag him off his curricle. She then witnessed him hitting the scoundrel at Madame Shipwith's when he made his ribald remark about Catalina.

No wonder she didn't trust him.

And he couldn't blame her. He hadn't given her much reason to.

Iverson brought his feet down from the desk with a stomp. He rose from his chair, and taking his port with him, walked over to the window that overlooked his small garden. The gardener was busy at work, digging in the soil. He watched the man for a time and continued to think about Catalina.

He'd seen her outraged, concerned, confused, and even devastated when he'd brought Mrs. Gottfried home drowning in her cups, but he'd never seen Catalina cower. Not even when the oaf at Madame Shipwith's had her in his clutches. She'd given him one mighty slap. And that had impressed Iverson.

From the beginning, he'd known she was a fierce protector of those she held dear. She had never deceived him about that. He just never knew why, and now he did. She was protecting their livelihood because her father wouldn't. And rather than that bothering Iverson, it made him love her all the more.

Love her?

"Did I just think that?" he whispered to himself.

Iverson remembered looking at every inch of her beautiful, naked body in the soft yellow glow of candlelight. He remembered the taste of her breasts and the feel of her smooth, supple skin beneath his hands. He remembered succulent kisses, sighs of wonderment, gasps of pleasure, and blissful contentment as he had settled upon her and joined his body to hers. He remembered sinking deeply, so deeply into her he never wanted to move. From the moment he'd met her, he'd known she was instinctively passionate and sensual, and she had not disappointed him.

"Hell, yes. I love Catalina!" he whispered to his reflection in the windowpane. Though he had never experienced love before, he knew what it was now that it had captured him. And he didn't mind acknowledging it.

It was pure love he felt for Catalina Crisp.

And she loved him. He was sure of it. She would never have asked him to stay last night if she didn't, but at the time, he'd been too caught up in his desire to make her his to ponder her reasons, or his. The only thing that was important was she wanted him and she surrendered herself to him. She'd shown she loved him in the way she had responded to him with such innocent giving of her body, the way she had looked at him and touched him.

They hadn't spoken about it, but there was love between them. Soul-deep love.

"I love her," he whispered again.

Why had it taken him so long to recognize it?

Iverson sucked in a deep breath. But a wife had to trust her husband. Without trust there could be no bond between them.

How could he gain her trust?

Would it be enough if he told her, no, *promised* her he would never tell her father's secret? Hell, he didn't want anyone to know she helped her father any more than she did. She would never have any peace if Society knew she could write poetry.

A knock at his door interrupted his thoughts. He started not to answer but knew it must be something important for Wallace to disturb him after he'd told him not to.

"Yes, Wallace," he called.

His servant slowly opened the door. "I'm sorry to bother

you, sir, but your brother said it's most urgent he speak with you."

"Of course, Wallace, send—"

Matson strode past Wallace and into Iverson's office before he had time to finish his sentence. "What's this, trying to keep your brother out?" Matson said. "Wallace was giving me such a hard time about seeing you, I was beginning to believe you had a woman in here with you."

Iverson grunted a laugh. "That would definitely be a reason to keep you out."

"But I see you have something almost as powerful."

Iverson frowned.

"Wine, when it's hardly half past nine. No wonder you wanted to keep me out."

"Oh," Iverson said and looked at the glass. He wasn't sure he'd even taken a sip of it. He walked over to his desk and put the glass down.

"What's the matter? Did you empty your pockets at the card table last night?"

"I came close," Iverson said, to put any further discussion of last night out of the way. "Now that you are here, make yourself comfortable and tell me what you've heard from our courier."

Matson took one of the upholstered armchairs in front of Iverson's desk, and Iverson returned to his chair.

"I can make that quick," he said. "The man couldn't find the duke. Apparently the duke is not at his estate, nor is he at any estate where the man was told he might be. It was as if the courier had been sent on one fool's errand after another."

"That's not good news, Brother."

"No, that's why he came back here for further instructions. He was told the duke would be in London in time for the first party of the Season, which is next week. The docking fees and all other monies are paid on the ships, so we have a little time to wait for him to return to London and hopefully get us out from under Sir Randolph."

"Then we're in good shape for now."

"Yes, on that count, but I have more news I'm guessing you haven't heard."

Iverson tensed, remembering the last time Matson told him there was more news and it wasn't good. "What?"

"Don't look so cheerless. This might not be bad news."

"In that case, I'm all ears. What is it?"

"Sir Randolph Gibson has just become a father again."

"What?" Iverson said for the third time and jumped from his chair, knocking it backward with a loud bang.

Matson rose, too. "Well, not a father in the true sense of the word."

"Spill it out, Matson. Tell me what you know about this."

"He arrived at a party last night with Miss Sophia Hart. She is the granddaughter of an old friend of his who died last year. Sir Randolph is now her legal guardian and charged with the task of seeing her properly wed."

Iverson relaxed a little, the fear that the man had more bastard sons who had come to town abating.

"You saw her?" Iverson asked.

"Yes," Matson said, averting his gaze from Iverson's.

"She's lovely?" Iverson asked.

"Mmm. She's fair," Matson answered, again not meeting his brother's eyes.

Iverson knew his brother's dismissal of her beauty meant

she was far lovelier than he was admitting. "Really? Just fair, you say?" he asked, prompting Matson to say more.

"Yes," Matson confirmed. "And the good news is her arrival now assures we are old gossip. London finally has someone new to talk about. I'm told everyone flocked around her last night as if she were a queen who had invited their full attention."

"And had she?"

"What?"

"Invited attention?"

"She's Sir Randolph's ward. How could she not? No doubt she will be all the rage now, and I for one am happy to turn that unappealing position over to her."

"So you were introduced to her?" Iverson asked, making himself comfortable in his chair again.

Matson remained standing. "Yes. Actually, I'd met her before, in passing, but didn't know who she was."

"Hmm, tell me exactly how one goes about meeting a young lady in passing?"

"It's a long story."

Iverson smiled. "I've got time."

Matson smiled too. "But I'm not talking."

That told Iverson more than Matson wanted him to know. "At least tell me what you thought about her."

"She has red hair."

That told Iverson even more. Matson had always been attracted to redheads. Iverson nodded and said, "Mmm. Red can be harsh. Tell me, is it golden, brassy, or that rusty shade of red?"

"Golden."

"And was her skin the color of warm alabaster?"

"Yes." Matson swore as he picked up a pillow from the chair and threw it at Iverson. "You blasted blackguard. Next time I'll leave it to you to find out all the latest news on your own."

Matson walked out the door, and Iverson laughed. And when he realized how good it felt to laugh, he laughed some more. He didn't know how long it had been since he'd teased his brother about a lady, but too long. But perhaps Sir Randolph's ward shouldn't have been the lady.

However, Matson's reticence to talk about her made Iverson a little uneasy, too. Usually if a man didn't want to talk about a lady, it was because there was interest. And Iverson sure as hell didn't want Matson interested in anyone connected to Sir Randolph. That would put them back on the gossip wheel faster than anything else. It was best Matson stay as far away from her as possible so their names would never be linked.

He would find his brother later and talk to him about her in a more serious tone, but right now there was another lady on his mind. He needed to see Catalina. They had much to discuss.

At the sound of a knock on the door frame, he looked up and saw Wallace again.

"I'm sorry to disturb you again, sir, but there is a Sir Phillip Crisp here to see you. I told him you couldn't be disturbed. He said he would wait until you were available to see him, and then he brushed right past me and entered the house without an invitation."

Sir Phillip was here to see him and using one of Iverson's tactics to gain entrance past unsuspecting servants? That didn't bode well.

"He's waiting in the vestibule. Should I ask him to leave?"

"No. Show him in."

There was only one reason Sir Phillip would come see Iverson. He must know Iverson had spent the night in his daughter's bed, and he'd come to force him to wed her. But what Sir Phillip didn't know was no force would be necessary.

Iverson rose from his chair and waited for Sir Phillip to walk in. The man came striding in with his hand held out as if he expected Iverson to shake it. "Mr. Brentwood," he said, smiling broadly.

That surprised the hell out of Iverson. It was not the usual way a father would approach the man he suspected of ruining his daughter. Obviously the man was not here because of Catalina.

When Iverson made no move to shake his hand, Sir Phillip lowered it and continued. "I understand you have been looking for me."

"Extensively."

"I've been here, there, and a little bit of everywhere, but here now. What can I do for you?"

Iverson had waited so long to come face to face with the man, he knew what he must do. He came from around his desk and stopped inches from the tall, slender man and settled a cold stare on the poet's green eyes. Keeping his voice low and tight, Iverson said, "You wrote about my family in an unflattering light."

"How could I not? It was such a good story."

"I didn't like it."

"Well, I mean, the best writer in all of England couldn't dream up a story that good. I kept hearing people talk about you, your brother, and Sir Randolph at parties. They were intrigued and fascinated by you. Society couldn't get enough of you. Even the common people started talking about you, too. Everyone had you on their guest list. You were all the rage, so I decided I should take advantage of your popularity and your story and write a parody. I assumed if they enjoyed talking about you so much, they would take pleasure in reading a story about the same situation, but with enough changes to make it deliciously interesting."

The man just kept talking and smiling, seemingly oblivious to the fact that Iverson's frown furrowed deeper.

"I wrote up the first part and sent it to Mr. Frederick, and he told me if the first sold well, he'd publish the rest. Naturally, it was a huge success."

This man was unbelievable.

Iverson bent his head so his nose almost touched the poet's. He reached down and took hold of Sir Phillip's fingers and squeezed with a little pressure. "If you ever write about my family again, I'll break your fingers one at a time, painfully slowly, and you won't be writing anything for a long, long time. Understand?"

Sir Phillip's facial expression and demeanor never changed. "The story's finished. Complete. How could I write more?"

"Good. Because I don't care if you are the king's personal poet, my wife's father, or my children's grandparent. Mention my family in any way in the future, and you will find it very difficult to ever write again."

The poet's eyes widened with surprise. "Ah, excuse me, but did I hear you say *my wife's father*?"

"Yes." Iverson let go of the man's hand and said, "I intend to ask Catalina to marry me, and I don't intend for you to have a problem with it."

A big smile spread across Sir Phillip's face. "No, no. None at all. Not from me. I'm actually quite pleased. Quite pleased indeed."

"Good. I'm glad we agree on that."

"Absolutely, we do. Catalina is a good judge of character. Takes after me that way." He laughed. "Though she gets her beauty from her mother. You know, you are quite strong, Mr. Iverson." Sir Phillip chuckled lightly. "It's a good thing I write with my left hand."

Iverson grunted a laugh. He couldn't rile the man or scare him, either. Catalina was clearly her father's daughter.

Twenty-two

In short, I will part with anything for you but you.
—Lady Mary Wortley Montagu

IVERSON WAS ON HER MIND.

The dreary, late-afternoon rain matched Catalina's somber mood. The dampness left the house with a cold chill, so she'd had a fire built in the drawing room in hopes of keeping warm, but today she was thinking she would never be warm again. How could she when her heart was broken in two and there was no hope to mend it?

She sat in a comfortable chair near the fire, listening to the rain patter against the windowpane. She lit a lamp and put it on a table beside her chair, hoping the cheerful glow would lift her spirits, but nothing seemed to be working today. She placed her needlework in her lap, and even though she'd sat in the room for over an hour, she hadn't picked up the embroidery to make a stitch. She was more interested in watching the flames. She kept wondering if there was anything she could have done differently that would have changed the outcome of her relationship with Iverson.

Somehow she had made him desire her, but she didn't know how to make him love her, and she certainly didn't know how to make him forgive her.

"May I come in?"

She looked up to see Aunt Elle standing in the doorway.

"Of course." She smiled at her aunt, whose hair and clothing were in perfect order and her cheeks naturally rosy once again. "What do you mean by asking if you can come in? Have you ever disturbed me?"

"Plenty of times. You've just always been too kind to admit it."

"Not true at all."

She walked over to Catalina, looked down at her with sad eyes, and said, "I made a fool of myself last night."

"What?" Catalina laughed lightly. "No, of course not. Don't be ridiculous."

"No, my dearest, your sweet words and kind expression cannot cover up my unforgivable behavior. I know better. I simply wasn't myself last night and took a spell of missing Mr. Gottfried and, well, I'm sorry. Will you forgive me?"

If her aunt hadn't slipped out of the house and had too much to drink, Iverson would not have spent the night in her bed. And she wouldn't have missed last night for anything in the world.

"Auntie, everything is forgivable," Catalina said, and as the words left her mouth, she doubted their truth. She didn't think Iverson would forgive her, and that made her heart ache all over again.

"Perhaps in time."

"Auntie, we have to believe the way Papa does. He's always said everything happens for a reason."

"I suppose that's true, too. I don't know what made me decide to go out after you went up to your bedchamber. I don't remember much of what happened, but I remember that handsome Mr. Brentwood had to bring me home in his carriage. Mr. Gottfried would have done something nice like that, too."

Catalina laid her embroidery aside, rose, and hugged her aunt. Aunt Elle's trembling arms slipped around Catalina's shoulders, and they held each other tightly for a few moments.

"Yes, he would have. And I've discovered something else, Auntie."

"What's that?"

"All of us do things we shouldn't from time to time."

"Not you, dearest. I've never known of your saying or doing the wrong thing."

Catalina smiled. "Oh, please, you know I have. And I'm not going to tell you what you don't know or remind you about the things you do know. But I do wish you would promise me never to go out on your own again. I can't protect you if I'm not with you."

"Never again." Aunt Elle smiled as she took her forefinger and drew an *X* over her heart. "I've learned my lesson. Now, would you like for me to have Nancy make you a cup of tea, or perhaps chocolate since it's so dreary?"

"Chocolate would be lovely."

"I'll speak to her right now."

Her aunt left the room, and Catalina returned to her chair and watching the fire. This time she didn't bother to pick up her sewing. There was no use pretending she was going to make a stitch. After a short time, she heard a knock on the front door. She cringed. If that was Mable and Agatha trying to see her again, she would tell Mrs. Wardyworth to say she wasn't accepting visitors. She simply couldn't face those two gabby girls or anyone else today.

She leaned her head against the soft cushion of the chair

and closed her eyes. Iverson immediately came to mind, and she smiled, even though thinking of him was sweet sadness. She could never have him for her own, but she would be for-ever grateful he gave her such pleasurable memories to relive time and time again.

"Catalina."

Yes, she could hear his voice so clearly, and it soothed her. Maybe the warmth of the fire was finally comforting her.

"Catalina."

When she heard her name again, her eyes popped open. She turned her head and saw Iverson standing in the center of the room. A quiver of longing surged through her. She jumped up. "Mr. Brentwood, you startled me."

"So I'm Mr. Brentwood now?" he said.

"Yes," she said, her stomach quaking because she couldn't tell him how happy she was to see him. "And you are supposed to be announced. I'll have to speak to Mrs. Wardyworth about that."

"When you do, be sure to remember a few kind words can lift a person's spirits."

Was that a teasing light she saw in his eyes as he reminded her of what she'd said to him the first time they met?

"I need no scolding from you concerning that."

"You know I wasn't reprimanding you." He walked closer to her. "I called your name twice. You must have been deep in thought. What were you thinking about?"

"Nothing," she said, moving away from him and closer to the fire. Didn't he know it broke her heart for him to be so casually in her home? "Not anything that would be of any concern to you, anyway. And it will probably please you to hear this, but I am feeling very defenseless right now and I'm not up to a verbal confrontation with you."

"No, it doesn't please me, Catalina, but perhaps this is my lucky day."

A bittersweet laugh passed her lips, and she gave him an incredulous look. "Well, I'm glad you are feeling lucky for I certainly am not."

"I meant only that you have always been so strong and capable. I thought if you were feeling vulnerable, I might have a chance of besting you."

She scoffed. "Always strong and capable? If you only knew how… I was anything but strong last night. And as far as besting me, did you not do that last night, Iverson? I asked you to stay, and I surrendered completely to you."

He moved closer to her again. His eyes softened. "You might have surrendered to me, but you never came close to losing your strength."

She whirled from him and walked over to the window, keeping her back to him. Didn't he know if he got too close to her she might rush into his arms and bury her face in his strong chest?

"I wasn't myself. I was upset for letting Auntie down… No." She stopped and blew out a breathy sigh. She folded her arms across her chest and rubbed her upper arms to keep from shivering. "There's no need to go through all that again. Just go, Iverson. You told me you don't want more apologies from me, and that is all I have to give you."

"No, there's something else. I'm not leaving until I get what I came for. I left something here last night."

She turned and looked back at him. He appeared so much

calmer than she felt. "What? The only thing I found was the cord from my reticule. Surely you don't want that?"

"Oh, but I do."

That surprised her. It was worthless. "Very well, it's in my room. I'll get it."

"Wait, not now," he said and moved in front of her so she couldn't pass. "There's no hurry for you to get it for me. I left something else."

She didn't search the wardrobe, but she hoped nothing was left on the floor for her maid to find. "I found nothing else, but I will look. Did you drop a stocking or your collar?"

"Neither, but there's no hurry about that, either. I have some news I thought might be of interest to you."

Her stomach lurched. "Please don't tell me one of the scandalmongers has written about Auntie."

He shook his head. "Not that I've read or know about. I talked with your father earlier today. Did he mention it?"

Catalina tensed again. "No, I've not seen him since he left my room this morning. Mrs. Wardyworth told me he went out, but he didn't say where he was going. Where did you find him?"

"He found me. He came to my house."

Catalina stiffened.

"Why?"

"He heard I was looking for him."

She felt as if a heavy weight pressed against her, affecting her breathing. "You didn't…?"

"Hurt him? No."

"Thank you," she said quietly, though the pounding of her heart didn't settle down.

"But I did threaten him, just as I told you I would. It was a matter of honor, Catalina."

"I understand. Did you tell him you know I have finished his work on occasion?" she asked, knowing she wasn't sure she wanted to hear the answer.

"No."

"Thank you," she whispered. "Do you plan to tell anyone?"

"No."

She let out a shaky breath of relief. "I'm grateful, though I certainly couldn't blame you if you had decided you had to."

"I never considered doing it, Catalina."

His softly spoken words made her eyes water. She blinked, trying to block off the tears of gratitude. "But it would be the perfect revenge for you."

"The act of revenge is never as sweet as the anticipation of it. Besides, I never wanted revenge for his writing *A Tale of Three Gentlemen*. I wanted only to ensure he never wrote about my family again."

"Did he give his word?"

He nodded. "I want to keep the fact that you helped your father a secret as much as you and your father do."

Her eyes rounded, and she saw the teasing light had left his eyes. There was a gentle softness to his expression. She moistened her lips and said, "You do?"

"Yes." He stepped close enough to touch her, and she didn't move away. "Do you trust me to keep that information secret, Catalina?"

"I... I... Of course," she said earnestly. "If you tell me you won't, I believe you. I know you are a man of honor, and you're bound by your word."

"Would you trust me with your life?"

"Yes," she whispered, feeling confused by his questions. "Of course."

"And what about your heart, Catalina? Will you trust me with your heart?"

An unexpected shiver shuddered through her. She had withheld information from him before, but she wouldn't this time. She looked deeply into his blue eyes. "I already have, Iverson."

He smiled and caressed her cheek with the backs of his fingers in that tender way she loved so much. His touch burned into her soul, and she had to resist the temptation to grab his hand and hold it to her chest.

"That's what I thought. And that's what I came for today, Catalina. You are the other thing I left here this morning. You belong to me, and I came to ask you to marry me."

A roar filled her ears, and she realized the sound was her heart beating so fast. "Marry you?" she whispered almost silently.

"Yes, Catalina. I not only threatened your father, I told him I intend to make you my wife."

"Do not play me for a fool, Iverson," she said desperately.

"I would never do that."

Suddenly fearful, she turned away from him again. "No, we could never be happy. My father has been a barrier between us since the day we met. I fear he always will be. I cannot keep him from writing about you or anyone else."

"Catalina, I'm not asking you to control your father or his writing. Your father and I understand each other."

She whirled to face him, feeling frantic, wanting to believe they could be together but afraid to hope. "But I deceived you, too."

Iverson gently took hold of her upper arms. "You kept information from me," he said, rewording her admission.

"Twice."

He smiled. "I've never met a lady so willing to point out her own faults to me."

"Iverson, don't make light of this. What I did was serious. How can you forgive me?"

He caught her up in his big, strong arms and gathered her close to his chest. "Look into my eyes, Catalina, and see the soul of the man who loves you deeply. We both are passionate about protecting those we love. I understand that. I accept it, and that's the way I want it. Just tell me you love me, that you will marry me and put me out of my misery."

Excitement danced through her senses so quickly she felt light-headed. "Yes, I love you, and yes, yes, a thousand times yes, I'll marry you." Her arms slid around his waist and squeezed him tightly, hoping he wouldn't let her go. She laid her cheek on his chest. "I've been so miserable today, thinking I would never be this close to you again."

He kissed the top of her head as his arms held her close. "I knew from the moment I met you there was something special about you. It just took me a long time to admit it to myself because I wasn't looking to fall in love with anyone."

"I wasn't looking for love, either, but I am so in love with you and so thrilled to hear you love me, too, that my legs are weak and shaky."

He laughed softly. She lifted her face to him and whispered, "I need your kiss."

A shudder of excitement rushed through her when she heard his intake of breath. "That's exactly what I wanted to hear."

His moist lips covered hers with exquisite softness. Catalina moaned and leaned into the kiss as desire for

Iverson exploded inside her. A few hours ago she thought she'd lost him forever, and now she was once again basking in the pleasure of his touch.

Catalina raised her head a little and said, "What did my father say when you told him you want to marry me?"

"He said: 'She's been a whole lot of trouble to me. How soon can you take her off my hands?'"

Catalina gasped in surprise. "He did not."

"Of course he didn't." Iverson laughed. "He actually seemed quite pleased. You didn't tell him we had—?"

"No," she said quickly. "And I don't think anyone needs to be privy to that."

"I couldn't agree more." He smiled as he looked into her eyes. "I love you, Catalina."

Catalina smiled, too, and then whispered, "And I love you," just before she captured his lips once again.

Epilogue

Whatever our souls are made of,
his and mine are the same.
—Emily Brontë, *Wuthering Heights*

IT WAS HER HOME NOW.

Catalina stood in the back garden of Iverson's small, leased town house and smiled. It was only her second full day of marriage, but already she was making changes in his household to better fit with the way she wanted things accomplished. The rain had kept her inside yesterday, which she didn't mind at all because Iverson was home, too. She kept finding reasons to go into his book room so they could spend a few private moments teasing each other with kisses and caresses.

But today the sun was out, Iverson was gone, so she intended to look over the grounds and make suggestions to the gardener.

When she heard the back door open, she looked up to see Iverson walking down the steps, holding something behind his back. She greeted him with a smile and a wave.

Iverson stopped in front of her and bent down and kissed her lips. "Good morning, my beautiful wife."

"I do believe it is afternoon, sir."

"Oh, afternoon already? I hadn't noticed."

"Yes, but it is a good day, is it not? The sunshine is warm, and I am a very happy lady." She reached up and kissed him again.

"I am delighted, too, my love."

She wound her arms around his neck and said, "Then why don't you embrace me and show me how happy you are?"

"Because I am bearing gifts in my hands and must give them to you before I can."

"Oh," she said and stepped away from him.

Iverson pulled his arms from behind his back and presented to her a bouquet of red roses in one hand and a cluster of violets in the other as he said:

> Roses are red,
> Violets are blue,
> The Baltimore Rake
> Says "I do."

Catalina laughed and took the flowers from him. "They are beautiful, husband, and how clever of you to bring me both roses and violets, but perhaps we should work on your poetry. Maybe you'd like to join the Royal Poet Society with my father and Lord Snellingly. I'm sure they would love to have you as a member."

"My dear Catalina, that will never happen. And it's not my poetry," he said, pulling a sheet of newsprint from his coat pocket. "We are once again the cast for Lord Truefitt's gossip column today. The roses and violets for you are in honor of what I hope, now we've married, will be our last appearance in his column."

She gave him a pretend look of disappointment as she smelled the lush fragrance of the deep-red roses. "That would be such a shame, but if he is going to continue with his poetry theme much longer, we must find out who this man is so Papa can give him poetry lessons."

Iverson wadded the paper. "I'm afraid he is like Lord Snellingly, a man who merely fancies himself a poet but who has no skill or talent." He gently took her arm and said, "Come, I have more to tell you." He led her to an iron bench under the arbor, and they sat down. "I talked with your father today."

Catalina tensed and laid the roses and violets on the seat beside her. "I fear it will always worry me to hear you have talked to my father."

"You must believe me when I tell you there is no ill will between your father and me. Maybe what I have to tell you now will convince you. I had to talk to him in order to get your wedding gifts."

"Gifts? You have given me a gift. I have your love and your name. What more could I possibly want?"

He shrugged. "I had several things in mind I thought you might want."

She wrinkled her brow. "Several? I can't imagine what they must be, but no matter, I have nothing for you. You must wait until I can—"

He placed a finger against her lips and said, "No, no, my love. I cannot wait to give you these gifts. May I proceed?"

She nodded.

"First, I asked your father if I could buy his house."

Her eyes widened, and her mouth dropped open. "You didn't! Why? What did he say to you?"

"He said yes, of course."

Catalina gasped.

Iverson continued. "I remember your saying it was very expensive to keep up, not to mention the mortgage, staff, and the grounds. Anyway, he seemed quite happy to sell it to me."

"But where will he live?"

"With us, of course. And your aunt, too, as long as it's all right with you."

It was almost too much to believe. "Aunt Elle, too? I don't know what to say, but, Iverson, you would let my father live with us?"

"Why not? Your father is off on his idle wanderings most of the time anyway. And I know how much you love your aunt. I'm quite fond of her, too."

Catalina's chest felt heavy with love, and tears of happiness stung her eyes. "I'm so astonished. I would never have thought that would even be a possibility. I don't know what to say, but thank you."

He reached over and kissed her. "Your happiness is all the thanks I need. However, you might not be as happy when you hear I also told your father you would never again finish any of his poetry or stories."

Catalina smiled, deciding not to tell him she had already assured her father she would not be doing that again. She was content to let Iverson take the credit for that. Instead, she said, "It is your wish, and I will honor it for the rest of my life. Iverson, these are truly wonderful gifts, and I don't know how to thank you."

He laughed. "Then I will show you later. But there is more."

"More?"

"Yes, I've already spoken with your father's servants, and all of them have agreed to stay and work for us, including Mrs. Wardyworth, Briggs, and Nancy."

Tears filled her eyes, and her throat tightened so she couldn't speak.

"What's this?" He wiped the corner of her eye with his thumb.

"I'm so happy. What a lovely, lovely wedding gift. I don't know what to say."

"I know what you can say."

"What?"

"I love you."

With more joy than she had ever felt swelling in her breast, she whispered, "You know I do. I love you with all my heart, and if you will allow it, I will take you to our bedchamber right now and lock the door and show you just how much I love you."

Iverson grinned. "If I will allow you? I will insist upon it, but first I have one more gift."

"No, you have given me all I could possibly want."

"I think you will want this, too." He pulled a piece of paper from his coat pocket. "This has the name and address of a young apothecary on it. He's just finished his training and opened a shop. I talked with him and explained Mrs. Gottfried's tendencies. He has assured me he can give her new tonics, elixirs, medication, or whatever she calls them that are not filled with brandy, port, or wine. He will do this gradually, so she won't even know it's happening. He believes if she's not drinking alcohol-based medicines during the day, she should tolerate a glass or two of wine in the afternoon and evenings."

Love for Iverson overflowed inside Catalina. She threw

her arms around his neck and buried her face in his neck-cloth. "Oh, Iverson, these are wonderful, wonderful gifts." She raised her head and looked into his eyes. "You know, the first time I saw you, I thought you looked like the hero in all my dreams. And you really *are* my hero."

He stopped her words with a kiss. "I want only to be the love of your life."

She smiled. "Consider it done."

Catalina pulled the tasseled silken cord from her pocket and handed it to him. "This is the only thing I have for you, and it is a gift that has already been given."

He took it and squeezed it in his palm. "You don't know how much this meant the day you gave it to me, and I will always treasure it. But more important, you gave me your heart, your trust, and your love. There are no greater gifts that can be given, Catalina. And I'm one lucky man that you saw beyond my rough edges and decided there was something in me worth loving."

She circled his neck with her arms, and he pulled her up close. "And I do love you, Iverson, with all my heart."

Their lips met, and Catalina kissed him with all the love she was feeling, letting her hands roam over his broad shoulders and strong back. With her heartbeat fluttering excitedly, their mouths brushed, nipped, and nibbled until Iverson pulled away and said, "I think it's time we went to our bedchamber, don't you?"

"I believe I do."

Iverson stood up and reached his hand down for Catalina to take. She picked up the roses and violets from the bench, placed her hand in Iverson's, and thrilled to her husband's touch.

About the Author

Amelia Grey grew up in a small town in the Florida Panhandle. She has been happily married to her high school sweetheart for more than thirty years. Amelia has won the Booksellers Best Award and Aspen Gold Award for writing as Amelia Grey. Writing as Gloria Dale Skinner, she has won the Romantic Times Award for Love and Laughter, the Maggie Award, and the Affaire de Coeur Award. Her books have been sold in many countries in Europe, in Russia, and in China, and they have also been featured in Doubleday and Rhapsody Book Clubs.

Amelia loves flowers, candlelight, sweet smiles, gentle laughter, and sunshine.